"This is an above-average thriller that never ceases to surprise readers . . . [T]he experience that Andrew Mayne has created for us [is] one to truly savor."

—Bookreporter

THE FINAL EQUINOX

"Science fiction fans will want to check this one out."

—*Publishers Weekly*

"A lively genre-hopping thriller written with panache."

—*Kirkus Reviews*

"This mix of science, thrills, and intrigue calls to mind the work of James Rollins and Michael Crichton. *The Final Equinox* has it all and shows why Mayne is one of the brightest talents working in the thriller field today."

—Bookreporter

MASTERMIND

"A passionate and thorough storyteller . . . Thriller fans will be well rewarded."

—*Publishers Weekly*

SEA STORM

"The fast-paced plot is filled to the brim with fascinating characters, and the locale is exceptional—both above and below the waterline. One doesn't have to be a nautical adventure fan to enjoy this nail-biter."

—*Publishers Weekly* (starred review)

"Andrew Mayne has dazzled readers across the globe with his thrillers featuring lead characters with fascinating backgrounds in crime forensics. The plots are complex, with meticulous attention to scientific and investigative detail—a tribute to the level of research and study Mayne puts into every novel. A world-renowned illusionist with thousands of passionate fans (who call themselves 'Mayniacs'), Mayne applies his skill with sleight of hand and visual distraction to his storytelling, thereby creating shocking twists and stunning denouements."

—Authorlink

"As I said before, a solid follow-up with thrilling action, especially the undersea scenes and the threat of Big Bill. Here's to more underwater adventures with the UIU."

—Red Carpet Crash

"As with the series debut, this book moved along well and never lost its momentum. With a great plot and strong narrative, Mayne pulls the reader in from the opening pages and never lets up. He develops the plot well with his strong dialogue and uses shorter chapters to keep the flow throughout. While I know little about diving, Mayne bridged that gap effectively for me and kept things easy to comprehend for the layperson. I am eager to see what is to come, as the third novel in the series was just announced. It's sure to be just as captivating as this one!"

—*Mystery & Suspense Magazine*

"Mayne creates a thrilling plot with likable yet flawed characters . . . Fans of detective series will enjoy seeing where the next episodes take us."

—Bookreporter

"Former illusionist and now bestselling author Andrew Mayne used to have a cable series entitled *Don't Trust Andrew Mayne*. If you take that same recommendation and apply it to his writing, you will have some idea of the games you are in for with his latest novel, titled *Black Coral*. Just when you think you might have things figured out, Andrew Mayne pulls the rug out from under you and leaves you reeling in fits of delight."

—Criminal Element

"The pages are packed with colorful characters . . . its shenanigans, dark humor, and low view of human foibles should appeal to fans of Carl Hiaasen and John D. MacDonald."

—*Star News*

THE GIRL BENEATH THE SEA

"Distinctive characters and a genuinely thrilling finale . . . Readers will look forward to Sloan's further adventures."

—*Publishers Weekly*

"Mayne writes with a clipped narrative style that gives the story rapid-fire propulsion, and he populates the narrative with a rogue's gallery of engaging characters . . . [A] winning new series with a complicated female protagonist that combines police procedural with adventure story and mixes the styles of Lee Child and Clive Cussler."

—*Library Journal*

"Sloan McPherson is a great, gutsy, and resourceful character."

—Authorlink

"Sloan McPherson is one heck of a woman . . . *The Girl Beneath the Sea* is an action-packed mystery that takes you all over Florida in search of answers."

—Long and Short Reviews

"The female lead is a resourceful, powerful woman, and we're already looking forward to hearing more about her in the future Underwater Investigation Unit novels."

—Yahoo!

"*The Girl Beneath the Sea* continuously dives deeper and deeper until you no longer know whom Sloan can trust. This is a terrific entry in a new and unique series."

—Criminal Element

THE NATURALIST

"[A] smoothly written suspense novel from Thriller Award finalist Mayne . . . The action builds to [an] . . . exciting confrontation between Cray and his foe, and scientific detail lends verisimilitude."

—*Publishers Weekly*

"With a strong sense of place and palpable suspense that builds to a violent confrontation and resolution, Mayne's (*Angel Killer*) series debut will satisfy devotees of outdoors mysteries and intriguing characters."

—*Library Journal*

"*The Naturalist* is a suspenseful, tense, and wholly entertaining story . . . Compliments to Andrew Mayne for the brilliant first entry in a fascinating new series."

—*New York Journal of Books*

"An engrossing mix of science, speculation, and suspense, *The Naturalist* will suck you in."

—*Omnivoracious*

"A tour de force of a thriller."

—Gumshoe Review

"Mayne is a natural storyteller, and once you start this one, you may find yourself staying up late to finish it . . . It employs everything that makes good thrillers really good . . . The creep factor is high, and the killer, once revealed, will make your skin crawl."

—Criminal Element

"If you enjoy the TV channel *Investigation Discovery* or shows like *Forensic Files*, then Andrew Mayne's *The Naturalist* is the perfect read for you!"

—*The Suspense Is Thrilling Me*

DEATH STAKE

Other Titles by Andrew Mayne

Trasker Series

Night Owl

Underwater Investigation Unit Series

Dark Dive
Sea Castle
Sea Storm
Black Coral
The Girl Beneath the Sea

Theo Cray and Jessica Blackwood Series

Final Equinox
Mastermind

Theo Cray Series

Dark Pattern
Murder Theory
Looking Glass
The Naturalist

Jessica Blackwood Series

Black Fall
Name of the Devil
Angel Killer

The Chronological Man Series

The Monster in the Mist
The Martian Emperor

The Station Breaker Series

Station Breaker
Orbital

Other Fiction Titles

Public Enemy Zero
Hollywood Pharaohs
Knight School
The Grendel's Shadow

Nonfiction

The Cure for Writer's Block
How to Write a Novella in 24 Hours

DEATH STAKE

A TRASKER THRILLER

ANDREW MAYNE

THOMAS & MERCER

Text copyright © 2024 by Andrew Mayne Harter
All rights reserved.

Published by Thomas & Mercer, Seattle

www.apub.com

Amazon, the Amazon logo, and Thomas & Mercer are trademarks of Amazon.com, Inc., or its affiliates.

ISBN-13: 9781662522222 (paperback)
ISBN-13: 9781662522215 (digital)

Cover design by Shasti O'Leary Soudant
Cover image: © Sam Edwards / Getty; © eFesenko / Alamy

Printed in the United States of America

DEATH STAKE

TELEPHOTO

Three hours ago, an air force colonel I've never met before, probably sitting in a soul-sucking beige office in the Pentagon, called my private line and started screaming at me in a tone that has resulted in other men getting thrown out of windows above the first floor.

"You tofu-eating, dipshit, granola-enema, clueless Silicon Valley dimwits!"

"Mom, is that you?" I asked.

"Goddamn unpatriotic, quisling, Mao-loving, clueless sons of bitches . . . !" he continued, not letting my quip interrupt his rant.

"You said 'clueless' twice," I replied.

"I'll fucking say it three times, you clueless bastard!"

I checked the caller ID again. This was definitely a call from the Pentagon.

"Marine?" I asked.

"Do I sound like I was dropped on my head? I'm a goddamn air force colonel, and *God* to you, you carpetbagging asshole," he snarled.

"I mean, you talk like a fellow marine. How did the Corps miss you?"

"Because I took an IQ test and goddamn passed it, you jarhead numbskull!" he snapped back.

I looked up to make sure the door to my office was closed. "Listen, I'm not going to lie and say I'm not a little bit aroused by this conversation, but I'm on the company clock here and can't talk to every air force officer who's feeling lonely. Is there something I can help you with?"

"Maybe you could start by not walking our national secrets straight into Beijing and asking the CCP to take turns having their way with you."

"Let me make a note of that . . . How many *c*'s in CCP?"

"Smart-ass . . . I'll pull your goddamn contract! I told them it was a bad idea to fund your horseshit. This is exactly why."

Contract? Now it was starting to make sense.

"Is this about Blue Beyond?" I asked, using the name Pentagon public relations had given a joint project between the air force and Wind Aerospace, the company I worked for.

"How did someone this stupid get to be head of security for a billion-dollar company?" asked the colonel.

Well, it started with a chance encounter with the CEO after my son died, and then I ended up saving the CEO's life on multiple occasions . . .

"Colonel, clearly there's a problem here. And by your tone, someone just dumped it on your lap and now you're dumping it on me. If you need to get a few more insults out of the way, go for it, but the sooner we get to what's going on, the sooner we can fix it."

"You can't unscrew what's already been screwed," he replied.

As much as I wanted to explore the semantics of that expression, I just took a long pause and waited for him to catch his breath—not sure if I'd get another tirade or something more productive when he did.

"Trasker, you're the wrong man for this job. I know all about you. Aside from the IQ deficit, you're a triggerman. I know the type. You go in and break things or burn them down. You're an arsonist, not a fireman."

Aside from the way the message was delivered, he wasn't completely wrong. "Sure. Fine. But I'm the guy you have to deal with right now. What do I need to do?"

"Build a time machine and go back seventy-two hours and stop whoever took the photo from taking it and giving our enemies our secrets."

I didn't say anything. I just took a long pause and let him complete his thoughts.

"This photo is a problem, Trasker, but that cat's out of the bag. I need to know there won't be others."

"Let's start with the photo. What are we talking about?" I asked.

"Check your messages."

I looked at my phone and saw that he'd sent me a text. When I opened it, I was greeted by an image that made the pit of my stomach fall through the floor.

"Can I call you back on a secure number?"

I had to make sure this wasn't some elaborate prank or fishing expedition.

I typed the number from caller ID into our internal database, and the name "Melchor" popped up in a list of Defense Department officials involved with a variety of our industry contracts. He was one of a dozen people doing God knows what, but he was legit.

Two minutes later we were connected again after I called back on the number in the resource directory.

"Colonel Melchor, this is Brad Trasker," I announced after he picked up with a growl.

"You get a good look at the photo?"

"I did. I'm not happy about it either."

The photo was a long-distance shot from the hillside overlooking the Wind Aerospace facility.

It wasn't the location where the photo had been taken that mattered, it was the direction. The photographer had managed to get a shot of a partially open hangar door showing our top-secret hydrogen engine complete with AI-designed cooling system.

"We have procedures to prevent this. Normally there are supposed to be screens put in front of the engines when the doors are open," I explained.

"So much for your procedures, don't you think?"

I could have pointed out that Communist Chinese pilots were currently patrolling off the coast of Taiwan in fighter jets that were copied from designs stolen from US manufacturers but decided not to complicate the matter. Melchor was rightfully pissed.

This blunder had happened under my watch. We do regular patrols of the land around the base, and we bought up as much land as we could, but it's a lot to cover. I even have two sharpshooters on staff who take down drones flying over. We've caught four so far—two in the last week.

The last were launched from buried positions and had been sitting out here for weeks waiting to be activated. Afterward, I sent teams with metal detectors out there to comb all the ground we could, but it's an impossible task.

Kylie, the CEO of Wind and my boss, is working on a laser system that should make disabling drones easier, but that won't stop all the other forms of intrusion.

"Where did the image come from?" I asked.

"I'll send you a URL. It's an aerospace forum," said Melchor.

"So, not a spy?"

"You tell me. Somebody launches a fan site to cover aerospace technology, and they start getting anonymous donations every time they post photos like this. What do you call that?"

"Spying by proxy."

"There are plenty of useful idiots out there. Some are more useful and idiotic than the others," he huffed.

"I'll make sure this doesn't happen again."

"That's not enough. I need you to come down hard on whoever did this. I need you to find the person who posted it. Who knows what else they have? It couldn't have been luck that they just happened to get the perfect shot at the right time. They knew when and where. Either they figured it out or someone told them."

"What about the FBI? I can talk to my contacts there. We have a pretty tight relationship," I offered.

"Fuck no. This is a closed loop. We handle this. I'm talking to you, Trasker. You may be shit at preventing this from happening, but you might be slightly useful at finding who did this and extracting what they know and then cleaning it up. I don't want to see more photos posted while we're waiting for the FBI to decide this is worth their attention. If you know what I mean," he added. "Man to man, you and I know what your real job is. Your boss may not understand it. That's fine as long as you understand it. You don't protect a castle by standing on the drawbridge. Find out who did it. Make sure it doesn't happen again."

The message was loud and clear. While Melchor wanted to keep things between us, I might have to bring in the FBI at some point, but right now I needed to clean up the mess. As much as I'd like to think I'm a different man doing a different job than when I left the intelligence world, that's a delusion. Same job. Different employer.

❧

"What I would have given to hear him talk to you like that," says Brenda Antolí, my assistant chief of security, after we park our electric motorcycles at the top of a bluff.

A cool early-afternoon breeze blows in from the west, but Melchor's rant still rings in my ears. "His language was certainly colorful," I tell her.

Brenda takes off her helmet, pulls her black hair back into a short ponytail, and starts digging into her backpack.

After ending the call with Melchor, I called Brenda into my office so we could do a quick postmortem on what happened. Whip-smart and able to get things done fast, Brenda has become my right hand. She took a literal bullet for the company and fought fiercely when her colleagues were being gunned down. Since then, her resolve has only increased.

While I did everything in my power to make sure nothing like that ever happens again, I can't change the fact that it did.

After figuring out how this latest breach happened, Brenda and I realized that our policy for making sure the engines and other equipment were behind screens when the hangar doors were open only worked when the hangar manager was actually in the hangar.

When the illicit photo was taken, the hangar manager was at the other end of the facility, and the safety manager had decided to open the doors when the smoke from a laser-sintering robot arm was more than they deemed safe. They didn't make the wrong call—but someone should have thought ahead. In this case, that someone was me.

Next Monday we are going to have a staff meeting about proactive security protocols.

Brenda kneels and takes a photo of the hangar using a camera with a huge telephoto lens—the closest match we have on the base to the device that captured the photo and caused all this fuss.

She shows me the display. I take out my phone and compare it to the one Melchor sent me. The angle is an exact match.

We found this spot by setting up a laser in the hangar and aiming it back along the path that photo was taken from. The green laser dot still gleams on the rock near where we parked our bikes.

I squat on the overlook to see things from the photographer's point of view. This part of the Mojave is a mixture of flatlands and hills with winding arroyos creating thousands of places to hide.

Someone could be hunkered here with a desert-camo blanket, and you could walk by two feet away and never see them.

We found this out the hard way. Last year, a sniper parked in front of the runway took out one of our experimental craft with a portable rail gun. He'd been hiding there for several days like a burrowing rat, and we'd driven right over him dozens of times.

We do have dogs and other countermeasures, but these hills are an ongoing issue. On the other side is land owned by a trust that refuses to sell. A ten-mile road runs from the highway to another unmarked road out of our control that hikers and dirt bikers use.

If I had my way, my security perimeter would extend from Hawaii to New Jersey. But I have to make do with foot patrols around the immediate vicinity, off-road trucks and motorcycles beyond that, and our own surveillance drones patrolling the outer edges—and maybe a bit beyond when the FAA isn't paying attention.

"Anything?" I ask Brenda.

She's been searching the dirt in one-meter grid sections, looking for any kind of clue.

"Nada. I can send a team up here later to do a closer inspection. Get them to sift through the dirt," she says.

"All right. I think this person cleaned up after themselves, though."

She nods. "I'll check the cameras for anyone sketchy."

I turn around and point to the road behind the hills. "Sometimes get a dozen people a day up this road."

"We need to put some cameras facing out this way," she notes.

"I've made the request. I'm still waiting," I reply.

"You should just go to Kylie."

"I try not to bother her with the little stuff."

"This doesn't feel like a little thing anymore," she replies.

"Fair."

One of the reasons I like Brenda is she's not afraid to point out the obvious to her boss. She picked up early that information needs to flow fast and freely on the company's defensive front. We can't afford to get mired in politics.

If I suggested something that was stupid, come to my office and tell me.

Brenda has suggestions on an almost daily basis.

"Now what?" she asks.

"Since I couldn't get cameras in the last budget request, I had to improvise. Follow me."

I walk and skid down the hill to the dirt road below. Brenda follows a bit more gracefully—a gazelle to my rodeo bull.

I start walking up the road toward the junction. "Just ahead."

"You put up your own camera?" she asks.

"Nope."

"All right, now I'm really curious. Just when I thought I'd seen all the Trasker tricks."

As part of our weekly planning sessions, I try to teach the security team a new technique I picked up while working in counterintelligence. Since I have to skip over the ones like which bone to break first in an interrogation or how long to wait before following a diplomat into a brothel, I've been demonstrating my corporate-safe tricks. Which lately have included some of the memory methods I've acquired since my mother first taught me how to construct and use memory palaces.

I try to drill into the team they need to photograph and document everything but also must be able to memorize things quickly. You might not have the chance to get your camera out quick enough to get a license plate or use your Notes app to write down a name.

I start meetings by grilling the newest hires about the names of other people in the company.

"I've never met them. This is my first day," they'll often say.

"You sat next to them in the lobby for ten minutes," I'll point out.

I make it clear to them they always have to be alert. The next day I'll ask them if they realize that they were followed home by someone else in security. When a photo of them walking out of a restaurant with their significant other appears on the meeting room display, they get the message real quick. I can also spot the cheaters and other security risks depending on how they handle that revelation.

I come to a stop at a round trash can mounted on a post standing alone on the dusty terrain. Its receptacle is brown like the surrounding desert, with a black bag folded around the rim.

Brenda steps over and looks down at the can. "You got a monkey with binoculars in there?"

"Not quite." I put on a pair of rubber gloves and reach down inside the bag and pull out a sixty-four-ounce soda cup with a straw sticking out of the top. "From the look of it, I'd say this has been here about three days."

Brenda points to the logo for Gas-N-Go on the cup. "We can get their security camera footage and match cars to the ones the camera on the southeast road captured. That might narrow things down."

"Yep," I reply, then stick my hand into the bag again.

Brenda kneels down and sees the wad of trash at the bottom. "All of this from him? I don't get it."

I pull out a McDonald's bag. "Have you ever been on a stakeout? Your car gets filled with trash. This person was sleeping in their car waiting for the right moment to go get the photograph. They decided to tidy up."

"Doesn't sound like a pro," says Brenda.

"Maybe not at this. But that doesn't mean they didn't know they were up to no good."

I sort through the trash and pull out a wad of yellow paper and unfold it.

"Bingo." I hold it up for Brenda to read.

"You're kidding me? A car rental receipt?"

"They didn't send their brightest."

"No. Josiah Levenstein does not seem like the sharpest tack. Now what? We tell Broadhurst at FBI?"

Agent Shirley Broadhurst is our contact at the Bureau and our go-to for security situations.

"I've been told to handle this first ourselves. I'm going to pay a visit to Mr. Levenstein," I reply.

"When do we leave?" asks Brenda.

"*We* don't. This is the kind of thing I do off the clock. Neither Kylie nor anyone else needs to know. Understand?"

"I do. But I'm willing to do what it takes. You know that," she says.

"I know. But I don't want you dragged into anything you don't need to be dragged into."

"Got it, but just know: I'm all in. Even if that means bringing a shovel and no questions asked," she tells me.

I am both flattered and chilled by the ease with which she said that, but I don't think dealing with Josiah Levenstein will require anything that extreme.

I hope not, anyway.

THE VICE

It's a quiet evening by North Hollywood standards. I can barely hear the sound of the police helicopter in the distance over the sound of the wind rustling through the palm trees that line the side of the Canyon Cove apartment complex.

I've been waiting here for Josiah to get home after his shift at Panda Express. Though I couldn't connect him directly to the specific website where the photograph was posted, I have no doubt he's my man.

A quick search found his name as the registrant of two other websites. One dedicated to Japanese manga fandom, the other an aviation site featuring discussions of military aircraft, including flight-route information for test craft. The second site featured a "Donate with bitcoin" button.

Now, the million-dollar question—and what Melchor wants me to find out—is if Josiah is just a dimwit who stumbled onto this grift by himself or if someone suggested to him that if he took up the hobby of photographing experimental aircraft and then posting them online, he could make some money.

I've seen this approach used more in recent years, now that almost everyone has a side hustle. To me, taking anonymous money to publicly post military secrets isn't any different from taking photographs of the inside of submarines and passing them on to your Russian handler for cash. Josiah may not consciously think he's a spy for the Chinese because he never met someone in a parking garage and got handed an envelope full of bills—but it's the same job.

While I've been waiting for him to come home, I've been trying to devise the right approach. I contemplated waiting in the back of his 2010 Scion tC and scaring the hell out of him when he climbed inside but decided that if he bolted and ran, I'd look pretty suspicious on the security cameras that ring the parking lot. The last thing I need is to be a person of interest to the LAPD.

I have different methods for different people. If he were an innocent bank teller working in Juarez and I needed to get the secret account number for a cartel front company in a hurry, I'd break into his house while his wife was at the store and call the bank and tell them to have him call home.

When he called to find out what's wrong, I'd answer and tell him I had a gun to his wife's head and he had to look up the information on his computer or I'd blow her brains onto their bed.

Once he complied, I'd remind him that it was best not to go to the police and tell them he just handed over the financial details of their main provider of bribes. And just to smooth things over, I'd let him know there was an envelope with a thousand dollars sitting in his nightstand.

The money wouldn't be to alleviate my conscience. It would ensure he'd take my call the next time and we wouldn't have to go through the make-believe that his family was in danger.

I can be a brutal man, but I'm nothing compared to the people on the other side.

By the time I hear the courtyard gate opening, I've decided on my approach.

Josiah is about five foot seven and thin as a rail. The Panda Express uniform hangs off him. His dark-blond hair looks like he cut it himself. In one hand he carries a bag with takeout, in the other a comically large soft drink cup like the one I found back at the base.

He glances at me but then avoids eye contact once I look back. The moment he's closest to the table I'm sitting at, I kick out the chair across from me.

"Josiah, why don't you have a seat," I say calmly.

His knees buckle.

To understand why, you have to understand me. I'm what you call unassuming. It's why I'm good at my job. I'm not tall. I'm not short. I have a face that could be your plumber's or your banker's. Most of all I'm forgettable—until I don't want to be.

My mother, the first person to teach me espionage tradecraft, taught me that the second most important weapon besides your mind was your voice. She was also the only mother I knew who made her kid take target shooting and theater classes.

She wasn't trying to teach me to be a spy. It was just the kind of thing she was interested in. Maybe she thought it would help me be a politician or a newscaster. When I ask her nowadays, she simply tells me that it was "fun."

From the tone of my voice, I wasn't asking Josiah to take a seat. I was telling him.

Mom would play me VHS tapes of clips of Anthony Hopkins, Christopher Lee, Jack Nicholson, and other actors who could make you shudder by uttering a single syllable.

The voice he heard was deep and knowing. It's the one he's been dreading. Not the friendly FBI agent asking questions he can innocently explain his way out of. It's the devil coming to claim what's his.

Josiah turns but hesitates to make eye contact.

My fingers are interlocked and my elbows rest on the arms of the patio chair. There's a folder in front of me to engage his curiosity. To really mess with him, I'm wearing dark coveralls because last Halloween, Josiah dressed up as Michael Myers. Next to my feet lies a tool chest.

"I . . . have to go inside," he stammers.

"We can talk in there if you like," I reply. "Just let me get my tools."

His face goes pale at the thought of being trapped inside his apartment with me. The word "tools" is better than "gun." "Tools" implies torture and dismemberment.

If I'd said I had a gun, he might yell or run. I'm playing the same game I do with everyone else—the one where I don't tell you the rules.

My mother explained it to me using *Jaws* as a reference: the shark you imagined was always scarier than the one you finally saw on the screen.

Josiah sits down in the chair, still holding his takeout and cup.

"Why don't you set that down and have a look in the envelope," I tell him.

Josiah almost knocks the cup over as his shaking hands place it on the edge of the table.

He reaches out for the envelope and slowly pulls it over. I have to patiently wait for his trembling fingers to undo the flap and pull out the photograph inside.

It's the one he took of the engine.

He trembles even more as his eyes focus and he registers the image. Hesitantly, he glances up at me. He's speechless.

"Who told you to take that photograph?" I ask.

"I . . ." he stammers.

I hold up a finger to shush him. "You have two choices. Tell me the truth or stay silent. No lies."

Josiah looks around the complex hoping for someone to come to his rescue. Other than the flicker of a television behind the blinds of an apartment across from me, there's no activity.

"I think I should go . . ." he finally manages to say.

I nod to my tool chest. "I think you'd prefer we do this out here. Who told you to take this photograph?"

"Austin99," says Josiah.

"And who is that?"

"He's a forum member. He told me when and where."

"In exchange for what?"

14

"N-nothing."

"Nothing? The rental car was expensive. That camera wasn't cheap. Remember what I said about lying. That includes lying by omission," I explain.

"I'm telling you the truth," he says with fake resolve.

I use my foot to kick my tool chest, rattling the wrenches inside. "Lie."

"I'm not—"

I kick it again. "Lie."

"I . . ." he begins.

I glare at him and grip the edge of the chair. "Go ahead. Tell me. One. More. Lie."

"I got a deposit in my crypto wallet for about five hundred dollars of bitcoin right before he emailed me. He called it a thank-you ahead of time. He said there'd be an even bigger one if I took the photo."

What he's not telling me is even more interesting. Clearly Austin99 knew Josiah was the right person for the job because Josiah had done this kind of thing before. The two might even have history. The flight-tracking forum was probably where Josiah realized there was money in this. The anonymous forum he created was his attempt to build a business—a business built on preexisting work.

"Does anyone else run the forum with you?" I ask.

"No," replies Josiah. "Just me."

"Did you code it yourself?"

"It's a template a friend gave me. He doesn't know anything about this. He had some kids make it," Josiah explains.

"What's your friend's name?"

"Kevin? He doesn't know about this. He's just a guy I know online," Josiah replies.

"I'll want his contact information."

"I think I need a lawyer," says Josiah.

I reach down and pick up my tool chest. I set it on the table and flip open the latches.

Josiah's eyes widen. "I . . . I . . . I'll pay you. Whatever they're paying you, I'll pay you more. I can get it. You know where I live."

I smell fear and urine.

"You'll pay me to do what?" I expect him to say let him off the hook.

Instead, he says, "To not kill me."

"I have an alternative offer." I remove an envelope from the chest along with a printout and a pen.

I take the photograph from his hand and push them in front of him.

He's too nervous to read. It must feel like a nightmare in which your brain can't process sentences.

"Just sign it," I explain.

"What is this?"

"It's a bill of sale. You're going to sell me your phone, laptop, and any other computer equipment you have. There's ten thousand dollars in the envelope. That's fair, right?"

"I . . . I'm confused," he says.

"Along with your passwords and anything else I need to access what's in there."

"You're not going to kill me?"

I don't tell him I won't kill him. Instead, I say, "I can be gone in ten minutes, and you'll never see me again."

"My life is on my laptop," he says.

As is everything I need to find out what he was up to and whom he was talking to.

"Nothing you really need to live. It's gotten you into a lot of trouble, hasn't it?"

"Yes," he says meekly.

"We'll need to go to your apartment, but we can keep the door open, okay?"

Josiah is so scared it takes him twenty minutes to write down the passwords to all his accounts, including his crypto wallets. As he sits on his secondhand IKEA couch in his piss-stained pants and stares into space, I search his apartment for any other hard drives or computers.

Now done, I stand at the door with his computer and peripherals in an Amazon box. Josiah's still in shock—still too afraid to look at me. He clearly thinks I might kill him.

I wouldn't call what I'm feeling guilt . . . but I'm reminded of . . .

It doesn't matter.

I take one look back and realize that Josiah is crying. He's crying like you do in a police interrogation room when you realize your life is over as you know it.

Suddenly it hits me. "Josiah? What else am I going to find on this computer?"

Finally, he looks up at me. Some other voice, maybe an inner one he's been trying to suppress, speaks up. "Bad things."

My sense of guilt is replaced with another sensation as I glance down at the laptop: dread of what I'm about to learn.

DARK DRIVE

I'm sitting in my office waiting for Colonel Melchor to call me while I look through new-hire applications, only half paying attention—and probably giving a thumbs-up to several Iranian and Chinese spies.

I flew back last night in a company jet and drove Josiah's laptop and phone straight to the Kern County Sheriff's Office—after making encrypted copies of both that neither the sheriff nor the FBI needs to know about.

Because this was a criminal matter, I couldn't hold on to the devices without notifying the authorities. As much as I'd like to dive into the contents, it's a legal hot potato.

I could have taken the devices to Agent Broadhurst, but it might be weeks before the technicians at the FBI's LA office take a look, whereas the sheriff's department can do it right away because their deputized computer forensics expert, Elena Myros, is also an employee of Wind Aerospace—thanks to one of the law-enforcement grants we provide via a nonprofit we fund.

My phone rings and I answer. "Trasker."

"Is this your secure line?" asks Melchor.

"Yes."

"Jesus Christ, man. Maybe you read a little bit too much into what I told you. But you're on your own with this. We're not offering any cover."

"The laptop and phone? I have a receipt. If he was recording me, I said nothing that's a clear threat. Give me some credit."

"No, you dumbass. This isn't some banana republic where you can pull shit like this. We have laws. Even for a piece of shit like him. If anyone connects you to him, the contract is fucked. You're fucked. And I'm not letting you drag me down."

"Wait. Did Josiah talk to someone? I'm not sure I understand the problem."

I hear Melchor take a deep breath. "Are you trying to play me right now? I don't go for that bullshit."

"You wanted me to handle it. I did. I got him to hand me his laptop, phone, and passwords, along with a legally binding document. I didn't hang him over a railing and force him to sign. I did it all out in the open. If anyone overheard us, all the better. That was the plan," I explain.

"Yeah. Sure. Great plan. What if what we need isn't on the laptop? What if we want to try to entrap his handler?"

"Then we have the FBI pick up Levenstein and take that route."

"Trasker, if you're fucking with me, just hang up. If you're worried I'm trying to entrap you, end the call. Understand?"

"I'm not."

"We can't have the FBI pick him up," Melchor tells me. "His brains are splashed all over the interior of his car."

"What?" My fingers start furiously typing on my computer to pull up any news reports.

"Josiah Levenstein killed himself last night."

Damn it.

I do a news search. A small item on the *LA Register* website is the top search result. It shows Josiah's photo. The report says a patrol car found him with his brains blown out parked behind a store five blocks from where I'd met him. The fact that the article lists Josiah's name implies they've already notified his family.

Damn. How did I miss the gun?

"Jesus," I tell Melchor. "This wasn't me."

"I want to believe you," he says.

"Let me put it to you this way. If it was me, you wouldn't be reading about it right now."

"Maybe so. But this looks bad. I'm afraid to ask you to clean it up, given what happened last time. But I need you to fix this."

"I understand. I'll talk to our attorney, then we'll reach out to our connections at the FBI and the LAPD."

"I'm not telling you what to do. But maybe let sleeping dogs lie. If you're telling the truth, don't invite any problems you don't want. For your sake, this conversation never happened. For your employer's sake, I'd let things end here."

❦

Morena Jennings, head legal counsel for Wind Aerospace, looks up as I enter the office and shut the door behind me and close the blinds.

"Something tells me we're not going to have a quickie," she says, reading me accurately.

Morena and I have a complicated professional and personal relationship.

I sit down and let out a sigh I almost never allow in front of other people. Maybe Melchor was right and I should just carry on like I never spoke to a living Josiah Levenstein last night, but if LAPD calls and asks why I was in the neighborhood, I can't have Morena caught off guard.

"Live boy or dead girl?" she asks, referencing an old joke about political scandals.

"Dead man," I reply.

The smile vanishes from her face. "Shit. What is it? Or do you want to give me a hypothetical?"

We use coded language at times, in case we're ever called to testify about certain sensitive matters.

"I'll give it to you straight. I went to speak to the person who took the photograph I mentioned in my email yesterday. I bought their laptop and phone from them and turned the devices over to the sheriff's department to do a forensics exam before I turn them over to Broadhurst," I begin.

"Okay. That sounds fine. Get to the dead-man part."

"After I left, apparently the person I spoke to pulled into a parking lot and blew his brains out."

"How long after you left?" Morena asks.

"I don't know. Maybe an hour or two," I reply. "I checked his apartment for weapons and other electronics, but I forgot to check his car."

"Did you park near any security cameras?"

"I try to avoid them."

"That may work against us here shortly after. But we can manage this. Where was it?"

"North Hollywood."

"That's Broadhurst's jurisdiction. I'll call her. She'll know who to call at LAPD."

"And say what?"

"Did you go inside the apartment?"

I nod. "I wanted to make sure he didn't have any other devices. I left the front door open the whole time, if that helps."

"What about where he was found? Were you ever near there?"

"I was already at the Burbank airport by then. I think," I tell her.

"What did you do when you got back?"

"I took the laptop and phone to Myros at the sheriff's department."

"Okay. That helps us." Morena thinks for a moment. "I'm going to call over and have them gunpowder-swab the laptop. Someone we trust, just in case. Assuming it's negative."

"It'll be negative. I didn't kill the kid."

"I wasn't asking. Anyway, we'll have Kern offer that to the LAPD. Even if the timeline's murky, we should be fine. Assuming . . ."

"Assuming?" I ask.

"Could anyone have heard you threatening him?"

"Not directly. I kept my voice low." I don't mention that I was dressed in horror-movie-villain coveralls.

"We'll be fine. With Broadhurst calling and the likelihood of there being an FBI investigation into his selling secrets, I doubt the LAPD will pursue it. They'll see this as a suicide."

"Sorry for putting this on you," I tell her.

She smiles. "Cleaning up messes is my job."

And I have a habit of leaving some pretty big ones.

"Just an FYI, Colonel Melchor advised me to keep this under wraps and not tell anyone," I explain.

"Goddamn military jackasses. I think he's watched too many movies." She sighs. "Are you okay?"

"Yeah. I'm fine. Josiah Levenstein seemed sure I was going to kill him. When I was leaving, he said there was really bad stuff on the laptop. God knows what else he was up to." I shake my head.

"Well, I don't think it was you that triggered him into killing himself. Just the realization that he'd been caught," Morena offers.

"Maybe. I don't get it. I pushed him, but not that hard. At least I didn't think so."

"Any chance someone else did it?" asks Morena.

"Huh? I didn't think about that. Who? Why?"

"The photos? Was he working for somebody?" Morena replies.

"Maybe. At worst some low-level Chinese operative paying him for tips. Nobody that was going to come kill him, as far as I know. The cops seemed confident it was a suicide," I conclude.

"How hard would it be to fake a suicide like that?" she asks.

"For a normal person? Hard. For someone that knows the twenty different forensic markers to account for, not too hard. Blood spatter is the trickiest part. But there are ways to handle that."

This has me thinking. "Let's get a copy of the forensic report."

Would it make me feel better if he was murdered?

"Okay. He was probably just a bit off-balance," says Morena, picking up on what has me worried.

"I'm sorry, Morena," I tell her.

"Stop it. Before you doubt yourself too much, remember: you've done way more good than harm for this company. I haven't had a problem with how you've handled things so far. Kylie's *alive* right now because of you. Me too. You're a great wartime security chief. But we won't always be at war. Not everyone who undermines us is a Russian hit man. Sometimes they're just doofuses who don't know any better. This world isn't as black and white as the one you're used to."

"Trust me, it wasn't that black and white," I tell her.

"Yeah, I'm sure. But the lines were drawn for you—imaginary or not. There's no such thing as acceptable collateral damage in our world. If you get what I mean."

"I do."

Did I come down too hard on Josiah? I had once pulled the same stunt on an accountant who worked for an arms dealer—but he at least was directly connected to weapons used to target civilians.

Josiah worked at Panda Express.

What if all Josiah had on his laptop was some revenge porn? I mean, that's awful . . . but did I push him hard enough to kill himself?

Morena snaps me out of it. "Brad, don't dwell. We've got a meeting in ten minutes."

"Yeah. Sure."

"One other thing."

I raise my eyebrows, waiting.

"Let's not mention this."

"Even to Kylie?" I ask.

"I'll give her the sanitized version."

"We need to be honest with her."

"Actually, we need to keep her from being indictable." Morena rises and puts on her jacket.

"She just needs to know what kind of person I am. What she hired."

"We all know and we have no regrets. As far as this situation goes, I promise I'll tell her what she needs to know," Morena pledges.

"But you're biased."

She lets out a laugh. "Listen, you're good in bed, but not that good. I'm not going to let you tank my career or hers for it."

"Um, thanks."

I follow her down the brightly lit hallway, trying to simply admire the sway of her walk while I mask my emotions.

She turns back to me. "Don't worry. There'll be plenty of new bullshit to deal with."

SELFIE SHTICK

I'm sitting in the conference room with Brenda, Morena, and the other department heads as we conduct our latest security review. Brenda stands next to the display screen at the far end, playing a TikTok video of one of the cafeteria workers doing a dance.

My mind has been wandering until now. The question I wish I'd asked Josiah has finally come to me: How did he know *when* to be on that ridge to capture the shot through our open hangar door? Was it luck?

Lord knows it's not hard to find us screwing something up. The TikTok video Brenda is presenting is our latest fuckup.

She's pointing to the view counts. "So this little gem got 120 likes before we realized it was up and had her take it down. We're reasonably sure that the Chinese already got the file and time stamp."

Alyssa Albridge, a recent hire in human resources, raises her hand. "I'm confused. It's not like she's filming our airplanes or anything secret. We should encourage our employees to have fun."

Brenda looks at me. I give her a small nod, basically telling her to go all out.

My generation might have overly romanticized spy tradecraft, but this one thinks it's merely a plot point in a Netflix series, and the only difference between us and the people throwing gay men from the tops of buildings in the Middle East or putting millions of Muslims into Chinese reeducation camps is bad PR.

"Well, Alyssa," she says, "let's analyze what's in this video. First there's the time stamp. She was working a midnight shift, which tells anyone watching that we have cafeteria workers at that hour, which means we have employees working at that hour. Which means extra shifts. Which means we're on a deadline. Which could mean a crucial piece of technology is on the way."

"Not to be overly simplistic, but you could tell that by watching the parking lot," says Alyssa.

A vein in Brenda's neck just twitched. Oh dear.

"So are you saying that we should make it easier for people to spy on us? You know, make them not have to do any work?"

"This isn't my area of expertise. I'm just trying to apply some common sense here. Help me understand it," Alyssa says in the most passive-aggressive way possible.

Morena catches my glance at her. She can probably tell what I'm thinking: *Why the hell did we hire her?*

"We had to bury some of our friends because someone leaked a schedule," says Brenda. "But let's talk about the other part of the video."

She advances a few frames and points to a blurry person in the background. "See that?"

"The blur?" asks Alyssa, unwisely trying to defend her position.

"Yes, the blur. Let's use a simple off-the-shelf algorithm to make it clearer."

The image comes into focus, and the face of a middle-aged man with a crew cut resolves into view.

"That would be a military officer I won't name that we have to drive in and out of here in a tinted vehicle so our enemies don't know his identity and make a connection to what we're working on. But months of secrecy are pointless now, because we can be pretty sure Russia, China, Iran, North Korea, and everyone else who cares now knows," Brenda concludes.

If our enemies are really paying attention, they'll know that the officer shows up on test days for the engine . . .

Alyssa's cheeks are red. "How could the cafeteria worker know all of that?"

"She doesn't need to. She just needs to know that no cell phones are allowed in the red and blue sections. That's what the signs are for."

Alyssa points to the phone in my hands I'm using to look up her profile. "Like that?"

Knowing this is going down a path she'll regret, Martin, head of propulsion systems, pulls the top of his hoodie over his head like an ostrich avoiding conflict.

"That's a company phone. There's no TikTok app or anything else on it."

I look over at Morena. She nods, giving me approval for what I'm about to do.

"Ms. Antolí, why don't you take Ms. Albridge aside and go over the security protocols. I think it would be beneficial for her before attending any further briefings."

"Now?" asks Alyssa.

"Yes. I think that would be a good idea," I reply.

"Let me help you with your stuff," says Brenda.

Alyssa grabs her laptop and looks confused. She can't tell if she's going to be chastised or fired.

I don't know either. We'll see how her session with Brenda goes.

We've fired more than a handful of people on their first day. The problem is, a lot of them come from other tech companies where security isn't taken as seriously, and they expect the workplace to be a democracy. They've been conditioned to act on emotions, not according to logic.

Kylie encourages debate and free discussion. You can flat-out tell her that something is stupid, and she'll hear you out. She's compassionate to a fault. But there's another side to our CEO. I once heard her tell someone who was ironically complaining about not feeling safe around all the security personnel, "Why do you choose to be so vulnerable?"

I feel bad for the ones like Alyssa. She sees herself standing up to authority—but she has no idea why it exists in the first place. There's a right place and wrong place to do that. Here, she might as well be arguing with the firearms instructor at the gun range about why we all have to point our weapons in the same direction.

I know I'm getting old, but it's not just that. I look around at the young faces and feel like they weren't just born in a different time, they were born in a different world.

I think between cataclysmic events like 9/11 and COVID, life just happened to them. The only sense of control you have is what streaming service you're going to watch.

As far as Alyssa is concerned, Brenda is the Starbucks barista that displeased her. One star. Dislike.

I worried about my son becoming that way. A term he used was "NPC"—a nonplayer character. Those are the fictional characters in video games that exist only as background to the human player.

I'm fairly certain, having participated in more than one overthrow of a government, I'm not an NPC. I feel like a relevant player. But maybe that's the problem.

Maybe the world would be better for NPCs like Alyssa and Josiah if there weren't as many players like me fucking it up for them.

I mean, Kylie is definitely not an NPC, but she's an agent for good. Me? I cause chaos. Mostly against the people trying to cause chaos for us, but that still produces additional chaos in the world.

Post-interruption, Morena resumes the presentation and starts flipping through slides. "We're in the process of leasing more tracts around the area and the old Arrow Rockets facility. Also we're about to close a deal on a small company with a new laser-welding robot. Kylie's very excited by that. The only other minor news is our start-up portfolio looks like it has to take a small loss because the founders of one of the companies we invested in appear to have absconded with the funds. Thankfully it's only about $500,000."

A mere half a million . . .

"What did they do?" I ask.

"Crypto. Blockchain technology," says Morena.

"Really. That's not the kind of thing Kylie normally has us chase after," I note.

"No. This one's different. It was focused on contracts and micro-transactions in the developing world." Morena sees my expression. "You want to chase this one down?"

To be honest, it sounds a lot more straightforward than an employee taking a selfie in a restricted zone or a dimwit accepting bribes to take photos from private property.

There's also the fact that less than twenty-four hours ago I was dealing with a gig-worker spy who was getting paid in crypto. I don't see any connection, but I don't want to have one materialize out of the blue without warning.

"Actually, yes," I reply. "This seems clear-cut. Someone stole from us. I don't like that. Let's not let it slide."

Martin drags a finger across his neck. "That'll be the costliest and last mistake they ever make."

He has no filter, and I kind of respect that about him. He doesn't blindly challenge things or double down on his bad calls like Alyssa did. He just tells you what he thinks.

I'm now realizing that his slit-throat gesture reveals what Martin really thinks about me.

I don't want to acknowledge it, but I feel I must in order to not make it seem so serious.

"I'm just a guy asking questions," I remind him.

"That's how it always starts," says Martin without making eye contact.

Hmm. That's more passive-aggressive than typical for him.

I decide to drop it and let Morena continue.

While she speaks, I wish I could make Martin and the others realize what real bad guys are like. Not face-to-face. But enough to understand that we can't all be NPCs, even if we'd like to be.

❦

"What else do we know about xQuadrant?" I ask Kylie.

I'm sitting in Morena's office with her and Brenda, learning for the first time about our absconded-funds situation.

"I just remember speaking to Vik at a start-up event. Real sharp kid. He led xQuadrant. They'd found some useful applications for crypto that I thought could actually help people," she explains.

"And the missing 500K?" I ask.

"Weird. I didn't get to know his colleagues. He might have been played by them, though I think they were all friends. I got a good read on Vik. It's not like it was all that much money, at least in the start-up world."

"D-bags on TikTok can raise twice that much with an ICO rug pull," says Brenda.

"I understood three words in that sentence," Morena responds.

"I'm sorry. I mean some social-media influencers can earn more than that with crypto investment schemes," Brenda explains.

"But these guys weren't into social media?" I ask.

"Not that I'm aware of," says Kylie.

"Yeah, but for every jerk that pulls one of these, there's some nerd pressing the buttons," says Brenda.

"But we have no idea they were up to anything like that," Morena replies.

"I think that's the point. They could have made money like this, so stealing doesn't make sense. As far as we know," I add.

"So we have the Josiah Levenstein case where he's getting paid in crypto, and we have a group of developers we funded who went missing with our investment. Is there a connection?" asks Morena.

"Not an obvious one. Crypto is everywhere," I reply, then turn to Kylie. "Was there any connection between the start-up and us besides the funding?"

"No. I'll send you my emails with Vik."

"Thanks."

Kylie is smart and not the type to fall for a phishing scam and end up with a keyboard logger on her computer sending secrets to enemy agents.

But we're all human and make mistakes. She's been scammed before—by her mom's longtime boyfriend, who used a laptop she'd left open on a kitchen table to steal files.

It's the kind of thing anyone could fall for. Having been burned by that, Kylie now second-guesses herself more often. I don't know if this is a good trait or not.

"Okay, Brad, what do you want to do next?" asks Morena.

"I'd like to dig a little bit more."

"Hello World started today," says Kylie. "Someone there might know something."

"Hello World?"

"Same conference where I spoke to Vik last year," she explains.

"And it's this week?"

"Yeah. They probably would have been there," Kylie replies.

Maybe I want additional closure on the Josiah case, or maybe I'm just eager to get off the base and chase something. Either way, I'm not in a sitting-still mood.

"I'll check it out."

"Want me to come?" asks Brenda.

"No. I want you to look into how Levenstein knew when to photograph our hangar," I tell her.

Brenda nods, mentally already on it.

"Keep me in the loop, Brad," says Morena.

"Don't I always?"

"No. No, you don't."

That's because some things I need to do are better off being done and then reported on afterward—or not at all.

As an attorney, Morena understands that, but as a friend, not so much.

Kylie squeezes the trigger of her Glock 19 and fires off three rounds, creating a tight grouping in the head of the paper target at the other end of the quarry. She lowers the pistol like she was taught, barrel to the ground and away from her feet. She looks over to me.

"Good job," I say loud enough to be heard through our earplugs.

I'm not surprised. Brenda told me that Kylie had become quite the expert shot after practicing under her supervision.

They come out to the gun range several times a week at lunchtime to practice. Ever since the shoot-out at the airport last year, Kylie has taken an interest in various forms of self-defense.

I'm no expert, but the best way I can think of to deal with a sense of helplessness is to not feel so helpless. A psychologist might have other ideas about how to handle that kind of trauma. Either way, for someone in Kylie's position, knowing how to use a gun is a good skill to have and hopefully never need.

In addition to target practice, we're also creating a training facility for our security team here. I don't just want Kylie prepared for anything; I want our team to operate at a higher level.

A lot of people get into corporate security expecting a cushy gig. Some of us found out the hard way that's not always the case. I might be overcompensating, but you never know by how much until it's too late.

Kylie clears her weapon, then puts it into her holster, signaling that practice is over.

I suspected she didn't want to come out here to punch holes in targets. Something else is on her mind.

"What's up?" I ask.

"I appreciate you taking the initiative on the xQuadrant situation. You're very proactive. It's one of the things I like about you," she replies.

"Thanks. We'll find out what's going on."

"I'm really worried about the leak, to be honest," says Kylie.

"Yeah. Me too. I thought we had things locked down. I'll look into other ways to make sure that doesn't happen again," I explain.

"Brad, I'm not upset with you. I'm just . . . I don't know."

"Worried about another leak?" I ask.

"Yeah. People don't get it. Even some of the smartest ones I know. I think it started with my generation. Corporate secrets and patriotism are just concepts to them. I don't mean to moan," she tells me.

"It started way before then, I think."

"It's not just that. I'm having trust issues in general. I like Agent Broadhurst and some of our other contacts at the FBI, but I wish I felt the same about everyone else.

"Half the military guys that come to the base to oversee projects ask about jobs with us. Which is great, but the ones in procurement are the pushiest, and I get a sense that there's some kind of unstated quid pro quo going on. Like we'd get more contracts if we start hiring their friends," explains Kylie.

"You're just discovering the military-industrial complex *now?*" I ask.

Kylie gives me a rare smile, then shakes her head. "Laugh it up. I guess I just didn't expect people to be so obvious about it. It makes me nervous."

"How so?" I reply.

"I always wondered how some of the people I've met kept their companies afloat when their tech is shoddy and unimaginative. Now I'm starting to realize it's not all about the engineering," she explains.

I get the sense there's something deeper she wants to talk about out here away from prying eyes and possibly even Morena.

"Give it to me simple," I ask her.

"Let me put on my tinfoil hat. I don't trust anyone. We're too big now for me to have a read on the people that work for us—not that I was ever good at that. And I don't trust the government—I mean politicians and certain bureaucrats. I worry that someone in the National

Security Council might slip the plans for our engine to the Chinese to get them to back off on Taiwan or something," says Kylie.

"That's very specific," I reply.

"I didn't mean for it to sound that way. I'm just saying that you're the only person I trust."

"Morena has your back," I respond.

"She has the company's back—and that's the way it should be. That also means doing things by the book. And that's where I'm a little unsure about her," says Kylie.

"She's smart enough to know when to look the other way. She knows why I'm here."

I mostly think this is true. But I understand where Kylie is coming from.

A year ago, I wouldn't have been comfortable with her knowing the kinds of things I'm willing to do to keep her safe for fear that she wouldn't understand. Now I don't want her to know for legal reasons and because I don't want that dark side to be at the back of her mind.

Kylie gestures to the concrete training buildings under construction. "Is that going to be enough?"

"We can train a first-rate tactical team. There are a couple of instructors I'm trying to recruit. I think we'll be in good shape if that happens," I reply.

"Okay. But what about being more proactive in general?" asks Kylie.

"How do you mean?"

"I don't want us to get another call from a guy like Melchor. Besides making sure *we* don't leak, what else can we do?"

"Short of creating our own counterintelligence unit? Tell people to stop making TikToks on the base," I respond.

"What about a unit like that? How much? What would it involve?"

"You mean a team that's actively looking for threats? Don't you think we should leave that to the government?"

"How did that work for us the last time? You told them point-blank what was going on. They ignored us. You took the laptop from that guy Josiah over to the Kern County Sheriff's Office because you knew the FBI would sit on it forever," Kylie points out.

"It would be a big undertaking. Not cheap," I reply.

"We've got the money. There are things in the works here I'm worried about," she says, cryptically.

While I know the personnel and the physical layout of the base, I don't know everything that goes on in every building or what the people wearing the name badges walking in and out of them are doing on their computers or in their labs.

Kylie would probably tell me if I asked, but I don't want to know unless it's a security threat. Maybe I need to ask more questions.

"Anything that might go 'boom'?" I say, trying to make a joke.

"Hopefully not. You know how AI is kind of the endgame for computer science? Mechanical engineering has its own endgame too. I have a team working on that. Things are promising." Kylie stares off into the distance. "We can get into it some other time."

"Let me track down your runaway start-up and then we can circle back on this," I agree.

"Yeah. I'm going to do a bit of a deep dive into our records. I'm still bothered by how that guy knew when and where to aim the camera. Things were too convenient," she explains.

"Don't go insane looking too deep. It could have just been bad luck on our part," I reply.

"Yeah. The thing about bad luck is it tends to happen less when you pay attention to the details."

We get into Kylie's truck and drive back to the base. She falls silent as the wheels spin in her head.

I've learned how to just give her room to think. However, I'm a little concerned that her current thinking is a bit paranoid.

Of course, people have thought the same about me. But there's a difference between a paranoid head of security and a paranoid billionaire with an IQ to match. I'm trying to decide what color to paint the walls of the new security team break room. Kylie is trying to figure out how to deconstruct matter while also creating her own spy agency.

INCUBATOR

Hello World is an online media and technology expo in Las Vegas that stretches from one end of the MGM Grand Conference Center to the other. Giant, bright banners displaying the faces of influencers loom overhead like dictators in a totalitarian regime taken over by musical-theater kids. Their names are alien to me and could easily be randomly generated, their pictures computer-created DALL-E images, for all I know.

There's feeling old and then there's feeling old and in the wrong dimension. Two young men who look like they could be linebackers on a high school football team walk past me in unicorn pajamas.

Start-up expos like Hello World are where founders of technology companies meet, compete for funding grants, and network for future work. Last year, the founders of xQuadrant, the start-up Wind Aerospace gave half a million to, were one of the show's pitch-contest winners.

They proposed a platform to make it easier for people in developing countries to create binding legal contracts using third-party enforcement. It sounds like a hundred other blockchain ideas I've heard of, but their angle was trying to simplify it and make it explainable to people who don't have access to traditional banking institutions. Although they'd positioned it as a crypto platform, their white paper and pitch deck described it as a platform to make contracts universal and understandable.

Kylie liked the idea because the youthful founders seemed more focused on helping people than making a quick buck and partying. Now that they've apparently absconded with the grant and other investor funds, it looks like it was a long con.

I make my way through the maze of booths and pop-ups the size of convenience stores to the Launch exhibit in the back of the hall. All cynicism aside, I can't help but marvel at the effort that went into all of this—even if the architecture is more Nintendo than 1893 Chicago World's Fair.

I spot the roped-off area in the back, full of beanbag chairs and long conference tables with young people either stooped over them or slumping. In the corner, a ruddy-faced young man wearing a T-shirt two sizes too small is presenting on a video wall to a dozen people all staring down at their laptops.

I think I'd feel more at home in the 1893 Columbian Expo, serial killers and all, than I do here.

The one person in the scattered crowd with perfect upright posture I recognize as Crystal Harrell, the director of Launch. Under her guidance, what started as a South Philadelphia after-school project for inner-city nerds to bond has turned into a launching pad for some of the most buzzworthy new tech companies.

I couldn't tell you what most of them are doing. I had to read through xQuadrant's white paper twice, then ask ChatGPT to explain it to me in caveman terms before I understood, but I do know that they're all building things. Despite appearances, these folks are not NPCs.

"Ms. Harrell?" I say as I walk over to the table where she's tapping away on her computer.

She looks up at me through orange-colored frames. "Mr. Trasker?"

"Brad. I work with Kylie Connor," I explain, introducing myself. "Mind if I sit down?"

"Sure. I only have a few minutes." She nods over her shoulder. "I have to wrangle up some judges for an event. Do you know anything about Rust, by chance?"

"Like how do I get it off my barbecue grill?"

"Uh, never mind," she replies in that way some of the staff at Wind Aerospace do when they realize that trying to explain something to me in clicks and grunts would be too exhausting.

"I wanted to hear what you know about the founders of xQuadrant."

"I only met two of them. Vik and Sonny. They were here last year and got invited back to give us an update. Then . . . you know. Nothing."

"Did they confirm they'd come back?"

"Vik said they were planning on it. That was about two weeks ago." She taps her keyboard. "Eight days ago."

"What can you tell me about either of them? Where are they located?"

To create the xQuadrant corporate entity, they filed in Delaware but used a registered agent in the US. My emails to him haven't been returned. Morena is in the process of writing a more formal request.

"They were kind of cagey about that. Sonny sounded Indonesian. Vik's accent was harder to place. A lot of these younger kids grow up watching anime and US television. There's a guy over there from Slovenia that sounds like he grew up in East LA," she says.

Back when I first went through training, they taught us how to identify an accent by looking for clues, like a mineralogist examining soil.

A dropped *r* or calling a Diet Coke a "Pepsi" or "pop" could be a giveaway that the person came from along the Mason-Dixon Line. Our language instructor would play a metronome along with audio of different speakers, and you could see the patterns form before your eyes. How you spoke was a cultural fingerprint.

Not so much anymore. Thanks to satellite television and YouTube, your culture is dependent on your newsfeed. The trade-off is that everything I need to know about you is voluntarily plastered all over LinkedIn, Instagram, and Facebook. Even the stickers on Harrell's laptop tell me more than I'll learn studying which syllables she lingers on.

"I'm just trying to track down their current whereabouts. Any suggestions? Did either of them ever mention anything?"

"No. Their email messages were pretty short. They used a proxy server, so there's nothing useful to be found there."

"Social media?" All I found was a website and a LinkedIn account that hadn't seen a post in months.

"Just the GitHub repo. They've been pretty active contributing to their open-source project. That's one of the reasons they got the grant. It wasn't the pitch deck. It was the code," she tells me.

GitHub is an online repository where software developers store and share code. You might never have heard of it, but almost all the software you use has some connection to it.

"So these guys are basically ghosts?"

"They're just private. I think they had at least one other person in their hacker collective, but I'm not sure," she says, glancing back at her monitor. "I gotta be going."

"Okay. One last question. Did anyone else here talk to them?"

"Yeah. Phaedra and Vik hung out a bit last year. They went off and did some K-pop karaoke thing over at the other end of the hall. You could try talking to her."

"Where could I find her?"

"She's dressed like Kofuku."

"Um . . . what?"

"Over there on the beanbag." Holly indicates a young woman wearing a pink Japanese schoolgirl outfit with a pink wig, typing on a laptop from a beanbag chair.

"Thanks. Please let me know if they surface, okay?"

"Real talk: Are they in trouble?"

"I don't know. Money went missing. It doesn't look good," I explain.

"That doesn't make sense. They're really smart. They seemed real," she muses.

"Smart people do dumb things all the time. Drugs, gambling, bad investments."

❧

I walk over to the section where Phaedra is sitting and realize that trying to initiate a conversation with a twentysomething young woman wearing headphones sitting in a beanbag dressed like a schoolgirl may be one of the more awkward introductions I've made in a long time—and I've met some strange informants in exotic places.

I grab a beanbag and drag it in front of hers, not too close, but clearly to talk to her. It's a psychological move. If I ask her for permission to sit down next to her and get denied, the whole conversation will be derailed.

I'm dressed in a dark suit with no tie. Thanks to Kylie, I have a VIP badge and don't look like some random who walked in off the street.

"Phaedra," I say as I hold up my hand to catch her eye.

She looks up from her screen and takes off her headphones. Her eyes immediately go to my badge as she tries to register who I am and if she should be annoyed that I'm in her space. Gen Zers can be more territorial than my Appalachian hillbilly ancestors.

"My name is Brad Trasker. I work for Kylie Connor, one of the sponsors for Launch," I explain, trying to make myself sound like I have an official capacity here.

"Hey, Brad. What's up?" asks Phaedra. "Did you have questions about my pitch deck?"

I guess I do. "I haven't had a chance to look at everything in detail yet. Can you explain it to me?"

I get ready to make polite nods and smiles of encouragement as she explains some harebrained scheme to make mutant-poodle NFTs or create makeup from organically sourced, fair-labor, ethically harvested materials.

"Sure. It's called EdCred. It's the one where we help teachers improve their social media. Make it easier for them to connect more with their students online via their curriculum. Mainly it's for college

41

profs, but also I have some high school teachers using it now." She flips her laptop around and shows me a screen with an Instagram feed.

"This is a math teacher at a community college in Kansas. We help him create math puzzles with AI that appear on blackboards in his Insta feed. He gives his students credit if they can come into the classroom with the right answer." She looks at me for a reaction. "I know. Pushing students into social may not seem like a good idea, but they're already there. I wrote my thesis on how nudging into positive trends can actually make young people engage in more prosocial behavior, like self-directed learning."

Okay, so I'm the idiot. This actually sounds clever and useful. The part about the thesis threw me off as well. I need to get calibrated for this.

"Very interesting. I think Kylie will like to hear more about it." I do plan to follow up with her, so I don't feel too guilty saying this.

"Thank you. I have about six thousand teachers on the platform right now. We're still thinking about monetization strategies, and we have a few we don't feel too icky about," she explains.

"That's good. So, I have a question about another start-up that didn't make it here: xQuadrant."

"Oh, Sonny and Vik. Yeah, that's too bad. I heard they just up and vanished. I hope they're okay."

"Me too. I'm trying to track them down. Do you know anything else about them? Crystal mentioned that you knew Vik."

"We hung out last year. We talk a bit in Discord. Mostly code and anime. I haven't heard from him in a week or so. That's not too unusual," she says with a shrug.

"Do you know where they're located? All we have is a Delaware PO box for incorporation."

"Ha. No. Those two were super mysterious. They wouldn't even say how many others were in xQuadrant. I thought they were trying to make themselves sound bigger. But Vik wouldn't say where he's from. He could speak French, English, and whatever his native language is.

I heard him whispering something to Sonny in it, but not enough to catch the language."

"Anything else?"

"Um . . . Vik likes to read. He'd share his favorite passages of books. He could recite them word for word. I think he has a photographic memory," she adds.

There's really no such thing, only techniques to get you close, but I don't tell her that. "He never shared anything that might tell you where he's based?"

"No. They were very private about that."

"Why do you think that is?"

"I don't know. I thought maybe one of them was a diplomat's son or maybe related to someone famous from where they're from, and they wanted to keep it on the down-low. At Caltech, I was in a class with some big sultan's kid from the UAE. He used another name to hide the fact.

"Another thought I had," she says, "was that they weren't really trying to keep anyone here from knowing about them but keeping it quiet so people from where they're from didn't know." She looks at me. "You know?"

Interesting. "What do you mean?"

"I know Chinese students working on things they don't want their government to know about. Privacy apps, that kind of thing. I also know some programmers who live in very poor countries who are just saving money and not spending it because it makes them a target. Vik and Sonny raised a small fortune. Who knows? Maybe they didn't want their government trying to take it in taxes."

Or they didn't want the people they took the money from to be able to track them.

"Anything else?" I ask.

Phaedra lowers her voice. "Well . . . I don't know how much I should tell you. You're not a fed, are you?"

"No. I work for Kylie," I assure her.

"All right. I shouldn't be saying this . . . but Vik called me up one night. He sounded a bit buzzed. He was kind of flirting. Which was cute, I guess. He asked if I really knew what he and the others were up to. In the background I heard Sonny or someone else yelling, 'We fucked them big-time!' Then Vik hung up. When I asked him about it later, he said they were just drunk and talking about a video game."

"But you don't think so."

"No. They sounded like they were celebrating."

"And drunk and high off of whatever they were celebrating, Vik decided to call and brag to the girl he has a crush on," I fill in.

"Yeah. Something like that. It must have been big for him to get wasted and let down his guard like that."

"Crypto related?"

"Maybe. I try not to think about it. They're super-nice guys. I'd hate to find out they were doing ransomware attacks or some dumb crap like that," she tells me.

"Thanks. Hopefully not. Anything else? Anything at all? I can't even find a photo of them."

Phaedra is quiet for a moment, then nods. "Yeah. I have a photo of Vik. He bought some custom Nikes and wanted to show me."

She taps on her phone and pulls up an image of a Southeast Asian–looking young man holding a white-and-yellow sneaker he seems inordinately proud of. In the background there's an apartment building and a utility pole covered in cables.

"Could I get a copy of that?" I ask.

"You want to see when the company did the shoe drop and try to trace it by that? It came out two years ago. This is aftermarket. And also ten times more expensive," she adds.

"It still might be helpful."

While the image might not reveal much at first glance, it could contain everything I need to learn about where Vik took the photo—*if* I have the right pair of eyes to look at it.

If I hurry back to the jet center, I can get this photo in front of those eyes before he goes to bed for the evening.

I manage to get up out of the beanbag chair and make my way toward the exit for the Launch area and notice that Crystal is pointing me out to a woman with auburn hair who appears to be in her early thirties. The woman waves me over.

"Hello, I'm Rebecca Gostler," she says as she reaches out and gives me a firm handshake—revealing that she probably has worked in a high-testosterone environment. "Crystal was just telling me that you've been looking into xQuadrant. So have I. Have a minute to chat?"

I decide I can always wake up the person I want to take a look at the photo later if I have to. He'll be equally cranky either way. "Sure thing."

We walk over to another table . . . with normal chairs, thankfully.

"Crystal said you work for Kylie Connor," says Rebecca. "I'm a big fan of hers. I think I've heard of you. That whole dustup at the airport? That was you?"

"Unfortunately," I reply. "What's your connection to all of this?"

"I work for a consulting group, Theocrates. We advise venture capitalists on risk."

"Like what not to invest in?" I ask.

"Basically. VC firms are usually pretty stretched as far as time when it comes to doing due diligence—despite being so well capitalized. We do background checks and that kind of thing."

"Is a grown man in unicorn pajamas a high risk?" I ask.

"Maybe. But if he's creating a new video-game company or social-media platform, I'd be even more concerned if he was dressed like you. No offense," she says with a disarming smile.

"Definitely none taken," I respond. "What do you know about xQuadrant?"

"I was going to ask you the same thing. One of my clients invested in them and is now wondering where their money went. And you?"

"Same thing. One of our funds invested and I was just following up."

"Find out anything?" Rebecca replies.

"Not much. You?"

"Not much? I'd think a guy like you would have their entire history down to their dental records by now."

I shrug. "Wait until you get to know me and I'll disappoint you even more. I'm just trying to get up to speed. What can you tell me?"

She lowers her voice. "Do you want the facts or the rumors?"

"Let's start with the dirt."

"My client never should have invested in them. Everything smelled funny from the moment they asked me to check them out—which is after they invested. These guys come out of nowhere using fake names and holding agents, which is much more sophisticated than I'd expect from a couple of twenty-year-olds."

"What are you saying?"

"Are we talking as friends here, Brad?"

"Sure. Best friends."

"It smells like some organized-crime scam. Probably an Asian gang that does ransomware and that kind of thing. Which would fit," she says.

"Fit what?"

"A source tells me that at least one of the members in xQuadrant was involved in a stolen-credit-card scheme. He got caught, but family connections were able to get it expunged. The others have sketchy backgrounds too."

"That just seems odd. If they were capable of rolling in here and able to raise close to a million dollars on the strength of their charming personalities, why bother stealing the money?" I ask.

"That's the point. This whole start-up could have been a con from the beginning. Maybe it was never their idea to begin with. Somebody back wherever they came from picked them, created the company, and sent them over here," she explains.

"And then empties the accounts and makes them disappear," I conclude.

"That's one possibility," she says, dragging it out like there's another.

"Or?"

"Maybe *they* wanted to keep it. The long con could have been to raise even more, but what if xQuadrant decided to quit while they were ahead?"

This sounds a bit complicated to me. "Seems like a lot of work."

"Local governments have been cracking down on call centers and other reliable forms of scamming. Some have started doing stock-market manipulation, propping up SPACs and outright lying on securities forms. The advantage of ripping off a bunch of Silicon Valley VCs is that nobody will feel bad for the VCs, and they'll just write it off. I'm not saying it's a perfect crime, but to the victims it's just a nuisance until it keeps happening."

"What firm did you say you were advising?"

"I didn't. I'm actually looking in on behalf of the partner that made the deal. He wants to keep this low-key. He's a bit embarrassed," Rebecca tells me.

I can think of a number of mistakes I've made that were far worse than trusting a bunch of likable kids with too much money.

"What's next for you?" she asks.

"This may be it. I told Kylie I'd come here and ask around and see what we could find out. So far, you've told me more than anything I've learned here."

"Which isn't much," she says.

"It's something. At this point all I can do is tell Kylie to pay more attention next time."

"I'll give you my card," Rebecca says. "She can call me direct."

ENHANCE

The second-best system for image analysis is a supercomputer sitting in a basement below a nondescript office park in Maryland that is covertly owned by the National Reconnaissance Office. Every image that's ever been posted online has been downloaded to their servers, along with all the metadata and everything else that describes it.

That pic you took of a moose standing alongside the highway at Yellowstone? It's there, along with the location data. But they don't care about that as much as all the images posted by stringer photographers covering the Gaza Strip or uploads from kids in Yemen showing the faces of their dads, who are also Houthi militants.

One image taken seven years ago of a Mercedes next to a rock with a single painted number on it near a bare tree might be all it takes to know exactly where to order a precision drone strike.

The amount of the US intelligence budget devoted to image processing isn't knowable because it's largely black budget.

However, the very best image-recognition system in the world lives inside a house built in the 1960s in the Berkeley Hills, now surrounded by redwoods and an overgrown lawn.

Usually, he's in bed by 9:00 p.m. I made it here with ten minutes to spare.

I knock so hard on the door that dark-green paint chips fall off.

"Don! Open up! It's me!" I shout.

I can hear the sound of creaking floorboards inside and a loud, pained sigh.

"'Open up it's me' is an insufficient way to identify one's self," says Don Larian's eternally exasperated voice from the other side.

"It's important," I tell him.

"That's a subjective term," he says as he opens the door and greets me in his night robe.

He has unkempt dark-gray hair above gold-rimmed glasses and a face that suggests he lost his razor among the many, many stacks of books and magazines that fill his home.

"Hello, Brad," says Don. "Still under the delusion that you're a positive force in the world?"

"I'm not in that game anymore. I work for the private sector."

"Oh goody. Now you're just in the industrial part of the military-industrial complex. I'm sure my former colleagues at Raytheon and General Dynamics are thrilled to call you one of their own."

"Save some of your cynicism for your students. Don't waste it all on me," I advise him.

"Oh, don't worry. I have an inexhaustible supply. Although my final lecture is now about how, in this era, they have many more choices to ruin the world, whether through destabilizing drone strikes or mind-controlling algorithms."

"Cheerful stuff."

Don teaches a class on digital image-processing at Stanford. A long time ago he was the go-to person in US intelligence for creating programs to analyze photographic data. Don has an encyclopedic understanding of light transmission, mineralogy, botany, highway markers, bricks, and a million other things I can't even fathom.

I was in a meeting once when some smart-ass handed him a Polaroid of a blank wall and asked Don to tell him where it was taken.

He looked at it for a moment, then replied, "US embassy in Paris. The signal room. You can tell by the hue of the lighting. They have to use standard fluorescent bulbs, but they're plugged into the Paris grid with a transformer that isn't tuned right. The paint is a matte-gloss but has lost some of its sheen, which means it's about seven years since this was taken. And from the discoloration of the photo, it was printed about eight months ago."

Everyone in the room was dumbfounded. Especially me. I was the one who'd handed him the Polaroid . . . as a gag.

"From the position of the flash, I'd say the photographer was about five foot six. Possibly a woman, given the average height for that office. If she has access to the signal room, that would mean she worked for the CIA station manager—who was Oswald Vargo then. I don't recall her name, but I think she's a brunette. Since you weren't there then, Mr. Trasker, that suggests that you had some kind of relationship that extended past your service there."

Then he *smelled* the photograph. "This was kept in a purse. That suggests it was handed to you personally and not mailed. Maybe some kind of rendezvous?"

"Okay . . . okay!" I'd pleaded, cutting him off before he revealed even more of my idiocy.

Don was a prodigy at MIT and made a name for himself publishing papers on image identification until the CIA came along and offered him an unlimited budget and the opportunity to pursue whatever he wanted.

It was a great relationship until he realized what was being done with the information he was producing. For Don, it was more complex than Military = Bad. It was more that Bureaucracies = Collectively Dumb. And that a room full of well-intentioned people with their fingers on kill buttons being yelled at by other people to use them will do so.

One day, Don simply didn't show up for work. He's not the kind of person you could threaten or replace—at least not with another human. When his former employers realized their wunderkind analyst wasn't going to be working for them anymore, they had to act fast.

That secret imaging facility in Maryland? It's basically a billion-dollar effort to re-create what went on in Don Larian's brain.

Don points out the one spot on the couch not covered in *National Geographic* magazines and landscape-photography books for me to sit down. He takes a well-worn easy chair covered in blankets across from me.

"How are things?" I ask.

"Is this sincere small talk, or is there something you're here to ask me?"

I look around the crowded shelves sloppily filled with books, magazines, and file folders. "Don't get many visitors, do you?"

"I have my liaisons," he replies with a sniff.

"I don't even want to unpack that. But it looks like you're still keeping busy."

"My classroom is filled with intellectually hollow zombies. But I have a few mentees that keep me challenged," says Don.

"'Mentees'? Isn't that the same thing as a student?"

"Are you still in the service?" he asks.

"No. I'm out. Completely out."

He leans forward in his chair, eager to talk. "I used to think I was the only one."

"The only hoarder? No, you're not. There are entire television shows dedicated to hoarders. There are also professionals who can help you."

"I still can't tell if the attempts at humor are part of who you are or a character you're trying to play. I've noticed that this . . . negging . . . as my students call it, comes out whenever you're around people with expertise. It's a kind of compensation, I suspect," he concludes.

"I thought I was being disarming."

"No. Just annoying. As I was saying, I'd never met anyone else like me with my level of interest in imagery—but now I've discovered two. A young man and a young woman who are excellent geo-guessers. Both self-taught. We have fun challenging each other. It's like knowing chess inside and out but not having anyone to play with," he explains excitedly.

"How did you find them?"

"One of my students showed me the YouTube channel for the woman. The young man emailed me directly. We've been communicating for months," Don replies.

"That's great."

"He's as secretive as I am. That's part of the fun."

"Cool. And he's not some Russian covert operator playing you, or a supercomputer in Langley the CIA is using to figure out edge cases?" I add. "Right?"

Don's face freezes. "The foreign operative I considered. Not the other one. How exactly do you tell when you're having a conversation with a self-teaching AI algorithm?"

"I don't have a clue."

"Hmm. I might have to try to spoil the data test with some false positives or test them—or *it*—with some steganographically encoded images," he thinks out loud.

"That sounds like a plan. Could I get you to look at an image in the meantime?" I take my phone from my pocket.

Don recoils like Dracula at the sign of a crucifix. "You're not freelancing for the government?"

"No, Don. I'm trying to find some people who have gone missing."

"If I tell you where the photo was taken, I better not read about a drone strike in that spot later," he warns me.

"I promise."

"That's the problem with men like you. You casually make promises that you don't really have the power to keep," he mutters.

"Listen. I can ask you or go to one of your geo-guessing play pals—one of which, I bet, is an undercover operative put in place to trick you. Either way, I'll get an answer." I shrug. "Maybe an even better one."

"You're a horrible person." Don slips on his reading glasses and takes my phone.

He pinches and zooms the photo while a smirk forms on his face. Finally, he looks up at me with what I think is condescension.

"I'd have thought with all of your parlor memory tricks that something I've taught you would have stuck."

"First, I have to make an effort—you know, decide if the thing someone is telling me is worth remembering. Second, I was never your student. Just let me have it," I tell him.

"Bangkok. I can tell you the neighborhood in a moment." Don proceeds to open up Google Maps and start zooming around on my phone. "Here you go."

He holds the screen in front of me. It's a street-level view of the building behind Vik.

"How?" I ask.

"You see a telephone pole with some wires. I see a square reinforced concrete utility pole with fiber optic, telephone, power, and couplings that tell me the provider, grid, and when it was installed. The number of fiber connections and the amount of power tells me how many air conditioners and internet connections are in this area—which gives you a pretty good idea of what neighborhood. There are other details, but I don't think you care about them." He hands me back my phone with Google Street View showing the address.

From the look of it, Vik took the photo from the second or third floor of a three-story building. The first floor has a scooter repair shop and a row of tables selling juices.

I look up at Don. "Who do you know in Bangkok?"

THIEVERY

I'm standing in the sterile white development hangar at Wind Aerospace, staring at Kylie's boots, the only part of her visible from outside the fuselage of the sleek jet she's working on. "Hands-on" barely describes a young woman whose eighth-grade science fair project about creating a more fuel-efficient lawn mower led to three patents and a Westinghouse prize.

"You ever worry that someone might seal you inside of there?" I ask.

"Worry? That's kind of my secret fantasy," she says from somewhere inside the wiring harnesses and cryogenic pipework.

Morena, standing to my right and leaning on a tool cabinet, shakes her head. "Kids these days, amiright?"

Nearly thirty, Kylie isn't exactly a kid, but Morena feels the same generational divide that I do in a workplace where "casual Fridays" now means wearing pajamas.

"One second," says Kylie, followed by a hiss and a cloud of white steam that billows from the interior.

The other engineers in the bay toiling over (and under) elaborate pieces of machinery don't seem alarmed. I still twitch. I've already seen Kylie get blown over by an exploding aircraft once, and that was enough.

I'm about to reach for her feet and pull her out when she calls, "Almost there. Just venting a nitrogen line."

Morena rolls her eyes. She's much more used to this than I am. I doubt I'll ever feel her sense of ease during moments like this.

Kylie slides out of the fuselage and hops to the ground before I can push a ladder over for her.

"So what's this about Thailand?" she asks.

"Brad was able to locate the last place one of the xQuadrant members was seen," Morena tells her.

"I *think* I did. We have a photo of Vik taken a few months ago in Bangkok. We were able to identify the location, but getting anyone to talk there is difficult," I explain.

"Difficult? How?" asks Kylie.

"When I called the scooter shop on the street level and mentioned the people living upstairs, they hung up. Same with the store across the street. I tried the landlord, and nobody answered the phone. I even had Thomas, who was born in Thailand, call and see if speaking the language helped. Nobody wants to talk."

"That's not encouraging. Why do you think that is?"

"I can only speculate. In Vegas, I met a consultant who says she's working for an investor also trying to track them down. She speculated, and I emphasize *speculated*, there could be some organized-crime element. That this could have been a scam to fleece a bunch of VCs. Which sounds implausible, because you guys put in a bunch of safeguards for funding, right?" I ask.

"Well . . ." Kylie's voice fades.

"Venture capital is more reputation-based than people realize," Morena jumps in. "You send a check, maybe you talk to their banker and look at their books if you're suspicious. But for amounts this small, it's typically not worth the effort."

"That seems dumb," I reply.

"Well," Morena says, "it's kinda like, be careful what you look for. If you check the books of most early-stage start-ups, you'll find lots of suspicious expenditures: parties, travel, nightclub rentals, luxury-vehicle leases. You just assume a certain amount of the money's gonna go towards that.

It's not until they raise real money that it's worth looking closer—but most firms don't. For a hot start-up, why bother dealing with that static when another investor's willing to hand over the money, no questions asked? At the end of the day, what matters isn't how much money was spent renting Amazon cloud services or partying at Burning Man; it's the value of the company when it's sold. VCs care about return on capital. If part of that return was because of weeklong cocaine benders that got the product out the door, then all the better."

I sigh. "Now I'm seriously reconsidering the years I spent on a government salary dodging bullets and having to write expense reports to get reimbursed for two-dollar long-distance calls."

"It's never too late. You're in your prime entrepreneur years," Kylie says, punching me in the shoulder.

"I'll take that into consideration. Anyway, back to Vik and the others at xQuadrant: I have more questions than answers. We've located where they lived at one point, but that's it. Everything else is speculation."

"I don't buy it," says Kylie.

When it comes to character judgment, I'd like to remind my boss that her mom's boyfriend was the reason she had hit men trying to kill her. Although in Kylie's defense, she never got a good vibe from him in the first place.

"There could be other factors. Maybe it wasn't a choice. Maybe they were coerced," I suggest.

Kylie wipes her hands off on a rag. "I understand all that. But you get a sense for people. Vik was brilliant. He'd ace any kind of entrance interview you could give him. He was rare. Also, an idealist. I never got the sense that he was in it for the money. The spec he wrote on decentralized microtransactions for the developing world? That was the real him," she says.

"Well, in the photo he was holding up a pair of thousand-dollar sneakers he was proud of."

"So what? He's a kid. He's trying to impress a girl. I've got a half-million-dollar McLaren sitting in my garage just so I have something to talk about other than my planes."

It's easy to forget the talented young woman in front of me with disheveled hair and wearing Dickies coveralls is worth billions.

"I get that. But there's still the missing money. Maybe there was some other pressure."

"How much was it total, again?" she asks.

I look at Morena, who keeps track of these things.

"There's the half million from you. I don't know what other investors put in. The number is close to a million, I think," she tells us.

"Where did we deposit the money?" Kylie asks.

"I believe it was Saturn Financial. They were doing a lot of banking for start-ups in that fund," says Morena.

"Call Terry and ask him what the balance is on their account."

Morena pulls out her phone and dials.

"Terry?" I ask.

"He's the head of the bank. In our paperwork, we have a clause that lets us check fund balances. I've never used it. Mainly because I know what it's like to have people breathing down your neck. Also because of what Morena said. I kind of don't want to know," she confides.

"You don't want to know how much they're embezzling from you?"

"No. It's not that. I get the pressure start-ups are under. They—"

"Well, that's interesting," Morena announces, ending the call.

"How much is gone?" I ask.

"None," she replies.

"None?" Kylie responds.

"Their account has a balance of $827,843. Terry says they never took a dime from it. The angel money went in and nothing came out.

By the way, he says they can add alerts for when large amounts are being withdrawn."

"Wait. Nothing is gone?" Kylie asks again.

"Correct. We could even recover our money. I'd say that's good news."

"No. It's not." Kylie sounds more distressed than ever. "This has never been about the money. It's about Vik and the others. If the money's there, where the hell are *they*?"

"Flaking off?" Morena suggests hesitantly.

Kylie turns to me. "Brad?"

"Hard to say," I reply.

"Bullshit. Tell me what you're really thinking."

"I think they may be involved in more than we realize," I admit.

"Organized crime? You think that's real?" asks Morena.

"I don't know. They could have fallen off a cliff." I look at them watching me. "I really don't know!"

"I don't like the organized-crime aspect," says Morena. "If we were indirectly funneling money to a group that was actually doing ransomware attacks, that would be bad. Especially *because* we weren't ripped off."

"I don't care about that. If they're in some kind of trouble, we need to help them," says Kylie.

Morena cocks her head. "Even if they're the cause of it?"

"They're good kids. We should help them, even if they screwed up. Who do we have in Bangkok? Can we send a private detective?" Kylie asks me.

"We could. But since we have no idea what's going on, we should keep this close and quiet. And we definitely can't send someone private into a situation that might have an organized-crime element."

"Local police there? FBI? We could talk to Broadhurst," offers Kylie.

Morena has said nothing, but she's looking at me. She doesn't want to suggest it.

"It has to be me," I tell Kylie. "We don't know what's going on. If Vik and his team did something stupid and need help getting out, then the local police or even our friends at the FBI won't be of much use."

I leave it at that and don't go into the other possibilities, because if Kylie understood the potential stakes, she wouldn't let me go at all.

HQ

293 Lat Phrao 65, the Bangkok address Don Larian located from Vik's selfie, looks remarkably like it does on Google Maps and how I recall it from memory—or rather my imagined memory of the location.

In my line of work, it's a good idea to study maps of where you're going before you pack your bags to leave. The importance of maps is often overlooked and ignored at the peril of whoever doesn't think they're essential tools. Empires have been built on better maps.

When you ask someone in the US intelligence community what's the most important agency, you'll get a wide variety of opinions. While there are arguments for the CIA, one might also argue that the Agency creates the majority of problems they're supposed to solve. The eavesdropping prowess of the NSA is both incredible and terrifying, yet finding a useful signal in all the noise remains a challenge. My money is on the NGA, the National Geospatial-Intelligence Agency, with a close second to the NRO, the National Reconnaissance Office.

The reason is simple. When you want to put troops into the battlefield, decide where to build your support command, know what roads to use and what buildings to bomb . . . without the NGA, you'd be lost.

The NSA provides constant satellite surveillance, and the NGA helps the people on the front lines know where they're going and how to get there.

My interest in maps started with an innocent question posed to my mother while watching a James Bond movie on a VCR she'd brought back from Japan. I'd remarked that Bond had no trouble finding his way around Las Vegas. I asked if he'd already been there in another movie.

Mother replied, "He reads maps, dear. That's what all good spies do. They learn to memorize where they're going."

My mother, also a professional, realized there was a lesson to be taught here. She reached into a cupboard filled with maps, pulled one out, and set it on the table.

"This is Budapest. I'm going to quiz you later. Do well and there might be ice cream," she added.

"What are the red Xs?" I asked.

"Those aren't important," she replied.

Years later I found a map with similar markings in the CIA map room in the American embassy in Berlin.

My mother, posing as a Pan Am flight attendant, had been sent to Hungary to mark all the KGB listening posts they used to spy on American diplomats.

She had trained on memory techniques that she tried to teach me, to some effect. The key to remembering maps of places you've never been to, she explained, was to exaggerate the details.

"You see this building? What does the top look like?" she asked.

"Like a blimp," I replied.

"Yes. That's their parliament building. Imagine a blimp filled with hydrogen, exploding like the *Hindenburg* and all that hot air. And when you think of hot air, you think of politicians, right?"

I nodded.

"Now I want you to imagine that in that explosion, it blew their constitution out the front door and straight down the street. Can you imagine that?" she asked.

I closed my eyes and watched the pages fly down the street and flutter to the ground.

"That street is called 'Alkotmány,' which is what they call their constitution. Understand? 'Alkot' means 'create.' You don't need to worry about it. Just imagine at the end of the street, where it intersects with another road, a man is standing in the middle with his arms out trying to block Nazis from trampling on the papers and reaching the capital. You got that?"

I was eager to learn any lesson that involved fighting Nazis. "Yes."

"That man's name was Bajcsy-Zsilinszky. He fought the Germans in World War II and is a hero in Hungary. They named the street for him," she explained.

And so it went. An hour later I knew more about the layout of Budapest and history of Hungary than any red-blooded American kid had any business knowing.

History class was a breeze. As Mother explained, all you had to do was study the maps. The past was inscribed into cities like the furnishings in her memory palace.

I remember making a smart-ass comment about how well her tricks would work with ancient civilizations. The next morning, I awoke to a dusty collection of Georg Braun maps from the sixteenth and seventeenth centuries on my nightstand.

In this district of Bangkok, the street names aren't loaded historically like European ones. 293 is the building address and "Lat Phrao 65" literally means "Road Number 65 in the Lat Phrao district."

While memorizing all of Bangkok wasn't practical over the last two days, I was able to make note of the features around xQuadrant's location: the nearest police stations, hospitals, internet cafés, red-light districts, and scooter-rental companies. I knew I could fill out the rest as I went along.

As I get out of the taxi, a man in a Jeep jersey selling boxes of honey from a table under an awning looks up at me and then back down to the package he's taping up.

I have to suppress a smirk, because I recognize him from the Google Maps photo. It was taken four months ago and his face was blurred out, yet here he is, an image come to life.

I step onto the sidewalk and take in the apartment building. There are three floors. The first one, across from the honey salesman, has a scooter-repair shop and a tiny grocery store. A narrow passage in the middle leads to a staircase that goes to the upper apartments.

Thailand is filled with tourists and Western businesspeople, so I don't even qualify as a curiosity to locals here.

I walk past the scooter shop, which is filled with muffler dust and reeks of motor oil, bad cigarettes, and some kind of incense that smells like burning dog hair, and head up the stairs. An old man sits in the corner tapping away on his phone while a boy, who looks to be about thirteen, cleans a gear shaft in a plastic bucket filled with soapy water. He looks up from his work for a moment to see who is walking by, then returns to it.

There are two apartments on the first landing. One on the left and one on the right. Straight ahead is a view of a narrow alley and houses beyond. I get to the second landing and come to the floor where Vik took the photo.

To my right is the apartment next to theirs. To my left is what I presume to be, or to have been, the door to the headquarters of xQuadrant.

The first detail that catches my eye is that the doorjamb is splintered from being kicked in at some point.

The second is the thick padlock securing a hastily attached hasp on the door.

The third is the sign taped above the padlock with the national police logo.

I take a photo and ask ChatGPT to explain the rest:

Sealed by order of RTP. Contact Inspector S. Srisutham.

I look up S. Srisutham online and find a reference to a Royal Thai Police homicide investigator with that name.

This isn't good.

NEIGHBORHOOD WATCH

"Do you know what happened to the people that lived on the third floor?" I ask the old man sitting on a stool surrounded by moped parts.

He looks over at the young boy with the pail of soapy water.

"Grandpa doesn't speak American," says the boy as he gets up and wipes his hands on his shorts. He looks me up and down. "Who are you?"

"My boss may have done business with the people that worked up there. Do you know what happened?"

The old man is listening carefully to our exchange. When he sees me point in the direction of the stairs, his eyes follow the movement, then return directly to my face.

"Ḥubpāk," he says to his grandson.

My Thai is a bit limited, but that meant "shut up." The older man didn't say it angrily, but with fear.

In the reflection of a small glass-door refrigerator, I can see behind the counter in back of him. There's a plastic bin with what look like vehicle serial-number plates. If I had to guess, a lot of the scooters he works on here weren't brought in by the original owners.

So I'm not sure if he's hesitant to let his grandson talk to me because of what he's doing here or what happened on the third floor. I know I wouldn't trust some random tourist who walked in and started asking questions.

"Grandpa says we didn't know the guys that lived on the third floor," replies the boy.

I look at the old man. "Do you know anybody who does?"

He glances at the boy, who then translates for me.

The man replies and the boy answers in English. "No. He says I have to get back to work."

"Tell him thank you. One other question: Do you know where I can buy some manga for my nephew? He'd love it if I brought back some. Maybe someplace where they can help me pick out good ones?"

"The 7-Eleven at the end of the street has a lot of them. That's where I go. But Mr. Sal doesn't know anything about the guys who lived there."

"Okay. I'll figure it out."

I'm eating one of the two toasted ham-and-cheese sandwiches I bought from the man behind the counter as I look at the spines of the different Japanese comic books on a rack at the front of the 7-Eleven. My son, Jason, used to read these. I'd bring them back from trips to Asia. He actually learned enough *kanji*, *hiragana*, and *katakana* to read them.

After he died, I saved a box of them from his room and kept them in a corner of my office. I've been meaning to sit down and try to read through them to get a sense of what Jason's chosen fictional world was like.

I spent time with my son, even after the divorce, and never got the sense that he felt he didn't see enough of me, but I was always a bit of a stranger in his life. Even when we were on camping trips and long car rides having deep discussions, he remained very much his mother's child.

I asked my own mother if she felt that way about me. She said that Jason was an introspective person. He didn't really know himself.

This made me profoundly sad, because I trust her insights into people. Her skills would put most shrinks and profilers to shame.

I'm looking at the cover art for *Hunter x Hunter* when I hear the bell above the door ring, and the kid from the moped repair shop walks in. He spots me by the manga.

"My brother likes that one," he says.

"What about you? I'm Brad. What's your name?"

"Tommy," he says as he stares at the covers. "*Death Note*'s great. You ever heard of it?"

Jason owned a copy. "The one about the book that kills people?"

"Yeah. I like that. But I like comics more. Not the new stuff. Classic ones. Like from the 1990s." He picks up a manga and starts thumbing through it.

The store manager shouts something too quickly for me to understand.

Tommy holds up a hand and says, "Yeah, yeah. I cleaned them this time."

"Anything here you want?" I ask, making an attempt at a subtle bribe.

"Nah. I'm good," Tommy replies.

I take out my phone and show him Vik's photo. "Was he one of the people upstairs?"

Tommy barely glances at it. "Yep. I saw him. He always had a different pair of sneakers."

"What did they do?"

"I thought they went to the university or fixed computers. They were always bringing computers back and forth," says Tommy.

"And what happened to them?"

"I don't know. I came to Grandpa's shop and the police were here and they were gone."

"Did your grandfather tell you anything?" I ask.

"No. He said they were bad men. I asked Mr. Chantapong what happened. He said that a black car pulled up, and some men in masks ran inside. A while later he heard a 'pop pop pop pop,' and they came running out and left. Then the police came."

"Any idea who the men in the car might have been?"

"Gangsters," Tommy says with confidence. "One time Grandpa put the wrong serial number on a motorbike, and some gangster pulled up in a black car like that one and told him he was in a lot of trouble. Grandpa started handing him money and apologizing. The man kicked over my cleaning bucket, then left.

"Grandpa didn't want to talk about it. I asked him why he didn't go to the police. He said that man's brother was a police captain." Tommy looks at me and shrugs.

I'm not sure if the kid understands the full scope of what was going on above his shop.

"You go to school?" I ask.

"Duh. Mom only lets me work in the shop to make extra money and help Grandpa out."

"Did the police talk to your grandfather about what happened with the men upstairs?"

"No. He said they showed up and asked him to close the shop. Everyone else too."

"Did he see any bodies?" I ask.

"Grandpa says he didn't see anything. Mr. Chantapong says they told him to leave too."

"Did the police talk to him?"

"I don't know." He puts a manga back and picks up another one.

"You see anything?"

"I wasn't there. But there have been more people around. Strangers. I've seen a couple Chinese men in a car sometimes at the end of the street."

"Doing what?"

"Just sitting there smoking cigarettes."

"Watching the building?" I ask.

"Maybe. I've seen others too. White guys. They come driving by looking into the shop. I asked Grandpa. He told me to mind my own business. Which I thought I was." He looks up at me. "It seemed like they were minding *our* business."

I hand him the extra sandwich I've been holding. "You can have this."

"I already ate."

"Take it anyway."

I leave Tommy inside the 7-Eleven along with a stack of small bills and a number to text if he sees anything else.

I don't know how accurate his retelling of secondhand events is, but sometimes the details are in the blank spaces. If the police didn't go around questioning people, that implies they already knew what happened.

If it was gang related, that would explain why they shut the street down. It would help prevent reprisals against witnesses they talked to.

This part of Bangkok is relatively safe. It's working-class—which means the gangs are also blue-collar. Their businesses include gambling and fencing stolen goods. Most stores and shops are legitimate, but some, like Tommy's grandfather's, work with organized crime.

The gangster that came into the shop was probably upset because the old man accidentally used a serial-number plate from a stolen vehicle on a motorcycle that was supposed to be clean.

I need to find out more about who's running things around here. But more urgently, I need to know what happened upstairs.

While I plan to ask Inspector Srisutham directly, I need to gather some intel firsthand so I know whether he's being truthful with me.

That means paying a visit to the upstairs apartment later tonight.

NIGHT OPS

Tommy's mention of other people watching the apartments made me realize that maybe Brad Trasker shouldn't have been the one to show up and start asking questions.

In addition to using a different identity, I should have considered a disguise.

My mother had bookcases filled with books on espionage. Some of the books she'd collected as a child. I loved those older tomes. They told stories of crazy spy contraptions using perfume bottles, hairpins, and elaborate disguises. Some of them had great ideas for Halloween costumes, while others described borderline racist caricatures.

At Summer School, my education continued in a formal setting, and I learned many new techniques. Summer School, an off-the-books training facility, had a different curriculum from CIA training—where I'm told there are now courses on whether tanning or using bronzers is a culturally inappropriate way to spy.

One of my instructors at Summer School went undercover inside the Russian Mafia for three years—in Russia. He was born Scott Stein in Glendale, Arizona, and played in his high school marching band and drama club. To this day, he still has the mob tattoos.

For my return trip to the xQuadrant apartment, I've put a little more effort into concealing my identity—but nothing too extreme.

If you close your eyes and try to think about what people on the streets in Bangkok, Shanghai, Tokyo, Caracas, or Cairo look like and how you could blend in with those crowds, most people would struggle.

However, if you look at photos or videos of people moving through these cities and really pay attention, it becomes quite obvious.

You get a moped.

Riding a moped comes with permission to conceal your face with a motorcycle helmet. Throw on a fluorescent green or orange jacket so oncoming traffic can see you, and you'll be so conspicuously inconspicuous you'll start to wonder if the streets of these cities are actually filled with Caucasian spies whizzing by on mopeds disguised as couriers and food-delivery drivers.

To cover my tracks, I rented a moped four blocks from my hotel using a credit card with a name different from my own. I also kept my helmet and vest in a bag until I was a kilometer away and could switch while nobody was watching.

This was to make it difficult for anyone following me from the hotel to track me. I wasn't worried about that before, but after listening to Tommy's innocent observations, extra precautions made sense.

On my way to 293 Lat Phrao 65, I pick up an order of noodles I can carry to look like a delivery person when I'm on foot.

I park the moped two buildings south of the apartment complex, casually send a text message on my phone like I've observed other local drivers do, then get off the bike and walk to the entrance to the apartment.

Tommy's grandfather's moped-fencing shop is closed behind a metal roll-up door. The other shops are closed as well, except for the 7-Eleven at the end of the block and another closet-size shop at the other end, where a middle-aged woman is selling tobacco products.

I don't see anyone on the street watching the apartment, but it would be stupid for me to assume it's not being watched—especially in an age where you can stick a tiny ten-dollar camera with a transmitter on a telephone pole across the street.

I walk with purpose through the faded blue entrance, past the locked mailboxes, and up the stairs. The twinkling lights of the city are visible through the opening on the opposite of the landing. The alley below is a dark pit.

I can see light through a barred window to my right on the second floor and hear the clanging of pots and pans.

On the third floor, the door to xQuadrant's HQ remains padlocked with a police seal. There's no overhead light, so I'm concealed at least partially in darkness while I pick the padlock.

It's an older barrel lock that only requires a plastic pen casing with a couple of strategic ridges. I prepared the one I'm using in the hotel.

A missing lock is less suspicious than an open lock, so I place the open lock in my pocket. It also rules out somebody trapping me inside—although it's hard to get trapped in a third-story apartment with a balcony and several windows.

I enter and shut the door behind me. Light from the street illuminates the thin window shades covering the balcony to my left, casting a soft glow in the apartment.

From studying aerial photos and looking at listings for similar apartments, I had some idea of the internal layout. The main area, often the living and sleeping space in Asian homes, is where I'm standing now. The room is sparse.

There are sleeping mats on the floor, a small futon, several plastic laundry baskets with clothes, and stacks of magazines with motorcycles and anime characters on them. A faded rug with a traditional pattern covers the floor, looking a little out of place.

Against the wall to my left, there's a large-screen television on the floor connected to a PlayStation with a pile of games in the corner.

Cans of tea and energy drinks are scattered around along with take-out bags. To my right is a small kitchen with a table and four chairs.

A trash can in the corner overflows with garbage. I smelled it when I entered.

My body feels it first. I wouldn't call it nostalgia—but it's still a kind of memory that overwhelms you. This space reminds me of Jason's dorm room. I remember the night I had to go gather his belongings after the accident. He and his roommates didn't live that differently from this. Neither did Josiah Levenstein, for that matter. Everything important to them was laid out on the bare floor: eating, sleeping, working, gaming. And for Jason, Vik, and his crew—but not Josiah—hanging out with friends. The ability of a group of unrelated but well-adjusted young men to bond like brothers over a weekend is a pattern that's obvious when you look for it.

I take careful steps, watching where I place my feet so I don't step on anything that might be evidence in an investigation—although I don't see much sign of police work.

There's a small bookshelf behind the table. I use the light from my phone to read the titles. It's a mixture of books: coding, manga, science fiction, and a few nonfiction books on memory that I recognize, including Harry Lorayne's *Super Memory - Super Student*. My mom had already taught me most of these methods before I'd ever laid eyes on Lorayne's books. I gifted them to Jason, but they were never more than a curiosity for him. I probably should have taught him like Mom taught me. I probably should have done a lot of things differently.

I take the book from the shelf and flip it open. Inside the pages are slips of paper with grids of letters and numbers written in a precise script that makes me a bit envious.

I can mimic handwriting pretty well. My mother made me fill out all my own permission slips in her handwriting. But without anything to copy, my own penmanship looks irregular—a mix of print and cursive.

The slips of paper indicate the writer was creating their own peg method with the English alphabet. A peg method involves assigning each letter some physical item, person, or animal. I personally find people easiest to remember: biblical Adam for *A*, Batman for *B*, and so on. The technique was first described in the sixteenth century but is likely millennia older than that.

If I had to memorize the bookshelf, I'd start with the title on the upper right, *The Three-Body Problem*, and imagine one Adam fighting against two other Adams. For the book next to it, *Programming WebAssembly with Rust*, I'd visualize Batman covered in rust trying to make a webpage on the Batcomputer in the Batcave. And so on.

Three Adams in a fistfight and a rust-covered Batman are easier to visualize than the titles themselves—especially when you have lots of them to memorize. While the exact wording might not come to you, you usually have enough information to retrieve it later on.

On one of the slips of paper, the book's owner made a list of letters, numbers, and symbols. Next to them they wrote down words in Thai. I take a photo so I can look at it later.

Through a doorway in the kitchen there's a hallway. On one side there's a bathroom with a shower and a traditional Thai toilet that you squat over. On the other side is a closet.

Inside the closet, I find cables hanging from the ceiling and coming in from the walls. It looks like something was yanked out of here, possibly a computer server, or maybe a crypto-mining rig. I can feel a draft coming from a vent above me.

In the other room are two more mats and some piles of clothes. A portable clothes rack is pushed against the wall with several ironed shirts and slacks.

I'm not judging their lifestyle, but I've seen Balkan-conflict foxholes with more flair.

Although I see no apparent sign of conflict, it's hard to know whether this place has been ransacked or if this was just how they lived.

I make a recording of the apartment so I can examine things more closely later. Walking back into the main living area, where the streetlights hit the carpet, it strikes me again how out of place the rug looks.

I put my phone aside for a moment, kneel down, grab an edge, and roll the rug to the side.

The first thing I notice is a quarter-size chip in the concrete flooring. The shape and dark-red flecks tell an entire story.

Someone was shot point-blank with their head down on this spot, and the bullet went through their brain, ricocheted off the floor, and went back into their skull.

I aim my light at the other parts of the floor and see another indentation and a spot where the concrete is cracked.

Three bullets spaced a meter apart.

This wasn't a gunfight. This was an execution.

I've seen death up close. Sometimes even been the cause of it. But the thought of a helpless person with their head to the floor in a position of submission being killed like this sends a chill to my core.

Which one of these was Vik's final resting spot?

Were they killed one by one, in a line?

I search the floor for more clues, then freeze when I hear the sound of footsteps coming up the stairs.

Quickly, I throw the rug back into place and make a dash for the hallway beyond the kitchen. I make it into the utility closet by the time the door opens.

As heavy footsteps enter, I pull myself into the back of the closet to be as invisible as possible if someone opens the door.

Plan A is to wait them out and hope they don't check the closet. Plan B is to make one hell of a distraction and run for it.

Both depend on what happens next.

The sound of heavy boots makes me think this is a police officer checking on the premises. Maybe someone saw me go up and got suspicious when I didn't come down?

But the way the boots are moving around the room sounds erratic. It's similar to the pattern I made: someone looking for something.

There's a muffled chirp, a voice—the sound of a Royal Thai Police walkie-talkie dispatcher making an announcement.

I hear the mattresses being tossed over and what I think is a clothes basket hitting the floor. The footsteps then go into the kitchen, and books are pulled from the floor and tossed.

I get ready to make my move as the footsteps enter the hallway.

The bathroom door creaks open. A light is flipped on, then off. The person then enters the rear room. Wheels squeak as they start going through the clothes on the portable rack.

I slowly open the door to the closet and get a glimpse of a uniformed police officer tossing the shirts and pants to the ground, then kneeling to search another laundry basket.

As he reaches down to flip a mattress with his back to me, I move from the closet to the bathroom.

There's no sound of silence like he's pausing to listen. He keeps rooting through the room like a pig after a truffle.

And I realize that's exactly what this man is. He's looking for something to steal.

I don't know what would happen in an encounter between us. I still have the helmet on, so my face is masked. I can probably get the drop on him and make a run for it—but there are two flights of stairs. If I run into a lookout, I could get shot. If he decides to wait for me to run from the building and watches from the third-floor balcony, he could shoot me from that vantage point.

Whatever I do has to be decisive. I press a button on a device in my pocket that I keep ready for situations like this.

The sound of his boots comes closer as he exits the room and enters the hallway. The closet door creaks open as he takes a look where I'd been hiding.

His walkie-talkie chirps and he stops moving. I can hear heavy breathing and the barely audible sound of the dispatcher—as if he's holding it close to his ear.

A fraction of a second later, he bursts down the hallway, into the living room, out the door, and down the stairs. His boots make loud slapping sounds as they descend the steps.

Well, that clears one thing up. He wasn't supposed to be here either.

The radio dispatch he heard was a call for police to investigate a potential break-in at this address. The origin of the call was a radio transmitter in my pocket. It's not some fancy piece of spyware. It's a $200 programmable device that broadcasts radio signals from 300 to 900 MHz—the upper wavelengths the Thai police use.

Before tonight's excursion, I made a recording of an artificial voice calling for police to this address, along with several other messages. The one I was about to use was a call for backup for a shooting at a nearby convenience store—but that would have been useful only if the police officer was supposed to be here.

I wait a few minutes to make sure the coast is really clear, then exit the bathroom and make my way back out.

After double-checking that I'm not being observed, I place the lock back on the door and casually walk down the stairs like a guy who has nothing to hide.

On the second floor I contemplate lowering myself down over the edge into the backyard in case someone is watching the front, but I decide not to take the chance of a tetanus infection from whatever might be back there.

I reach the first floor, stroll past the closed moped repair shop, and head for my own vehicle.

That's when I spot them.

Two men who appear Han Chinese, both smoking, sit in a black Mercedes, watching me from the other side of the intersection.

I don't change my pace, even when they flick on their headlights. I just get on my moped as if I'm not being watched.

I start the motor, and their car pulls into the street.

The front of my bike is pointed in the same direction they're headed.

I keep up my act, then rev the engine, put my heel hard onto the ground, twist the handlebars, spin the bike in a 180-degree turn, and gun it.

DERISK

In my rearview mirror, I see the black sedan driving up over the curb to turn around. A streetlight catches the expression of the man in the passenger seat, and he seems not too happy with my maneuver.

I take a sharp left turn and almost run into a truck parked in the shadows. My knee comes within inches of the bumper, making me wince at the thought of the last time I shattered it.

I get my balance back and speed down the street, then make another turn into a side alley filled with covered cars, parked fruit carts, and potted plants.

The wheels of the Mercedes squelch in the distance as my pursuers make a hairpin turn. There isn't a lot of room for them to follow me down this alley, but something tells me they're not going to let logic and reason dictate their next moves.

I make another left turn, backtracking the way I came. My plan is to keep making random turns until they can't follow me anymore. This is generally a good method when you're being chased by a low-level thug who's not thinking a step ahead.

I pass an open construction site where a two-story building is being made out of concrete and steel. For a moment I contemplate taking the moped up the stairs and waiting it out inside but decide not to on the off chance that I get trapped inside.

My plan to keep making detours is derailed as I realize that I made my turn one street too soon; now I'm in an alley that doesn't have any side streets for half a kilometer.

The headlights from the Mercedes glimmer off reflectors in the road, and I hear the booming sound of a large plastic barrel filled with water getting smashed by their bumper a hundred meters behind me.

These guys are pissed.

So far, I haven't heard gunfire. But that's not a great indicator of what they'll do to me if they catch me—it's more a sign that they don't want to get the Thai police involved.

The road is coming to a junction ahead as it intersects with Chathima Alley. Straight ahead of me is a concrete wall with a banner for Domino's Pizza. To my left is a row of parked mopeds and bicycles. To my right, a 7-Eleven. Man, do they like their 7-Elevens here.

The problem with Chathima Alley is that it's a wide road; the much-faster Mercedes will catch up with me quickly. My moped may be nimble, but it's not fast.

I'd considered switching to a motorcycle . . . but I thought I should stay as low profile as possible.

When I had to escort a member of the scientific establishment out of a country that's known for its nuclear ambitions, I was given a special motorcycle that looked like a dilapidated 1960s Soviet postal-worker motorbike but actually had an electric motor and massive battery pack. That thing could shoot down the Sheik Something-Something Expressway like a supersonic missile flying into a uranium-processing site.

I wish I had it now.

I make a hard turn into the intersection, bringing my knee closer to the ground than you should, and feel my rear tire skid a tiny bit.

Not good, Brad.

Crash.

I catch a glimpse over my shoulder and see the Mercedes decided to take the shortest route toward me by driving right through the row of mopeds and bicycles.

As hilarious as that is, it's clear they're in take-no-prisoners mode—or at least, no unharmed prisoners.

Their engine screams as they prepare to ram me from behind.

I've got one more trick up my sleeve, and it's the dumbest one of all. So dumb, it's actually a two-parter.

Chathima Alley ends in another junction, this one connecting to Lat Phrao Road—*the* Lat Phrao Road, the main roadway in this precinct. For more than a kilometer in either direction, there's no intersection, only feeder roads from the direction I'm coming.

Lat Phrao is divided by a massive elevated-train construction project—at least it was when I looked at Google Maps.

Turning around isn't possible because it's a one-way road. But if you go the other way . . . well, that would be really dumb for a guy on a moped.

And especially dumb for two gangsters in a Mercedes that won't be able to weave through oncoming traffic—assuming there's oncoming traffic.

I see the shadow of their car overtaking my moped as they pass under a streetlight. Damn, they're even closer than I thought.

I veer to the right and take the sidewalk—a split second before their bumper occupies the space my bike was in.

I glance to the side and see a furious man screaming at me through the rolled-down window of the Mercedes and holding a 9mm pistol.

I make the wrong-way turn onto Lat Phrao, and my heart sinks as I realize there's far too little traffic at this time of night to slow these jerks down by much. I'm going to have to do the stupidest part of my dumb two-part plan sooner than I expected.

I race down the street against traffic, greeted by flashing lights and honking horns. Most of the scattering vehicles do the thing I really didn't want them to do—pull to the side, creating a passage down the middle.

The Mercedes has made the turn and followed my wrong-way route—evident from the still-honking horns behind me.

I drive one more block and see what I've been looking for, then hop onto the sidewalk again.

I spin the back wheel around behind me and face the direction I've just come from. I can see the two guys in the Mercedes glaring at me as they drive up onto the curb.

I don't stick around to see what they do next. I lean forward, twist the throttle, and take the moped straight up the stairway to the elevated-train platform.

As I near the top of the stairs, I hear a pop and feel concrete chips sting my leg.

One of them decided to take a shot at me.

My moped leaps over the top of the stairs, and I turn hard to race across the walkway to the other side. Going down the stairs isn't as much fun as going up them.

If my pursuers were smart, they'd stay put and try to shoot me as I come back down the open stairs on the other side.

If they're not that smart—as I suspect—they'll run to the top of the stairs and try to catch up with me.

As I bounce down the stairs, doing my best to not put myself into an uncontrollable skid or fly over the handlebars, I don't hear any gunshots.

A woman holding two grocery bags and looking like she's worked an exhausting double shift glances up from the pavement as she approaches the stairs and swears at me in Thai.

I fly past her and race down Lat Phrao in the correct direction, mentally counting the steps the men are climbing, then take a turn down another road before they can see which way I went.

I turn onto the Chalong Rat Expressway and blend into traffic, satisfied that my pursuers have lost my scent.

If they had been smart, they would have—

Wait. Is that a motorcycle following me?

I pull two lanes over as if I'm going to exit.

The motorcycle changes lanes.

Okay . . .

It keeps its distance but doesn't exit.

I merge into the center lane. The motorcycle stays put in its lane—possibly cognizant of my little feint.

I slow and make the car behind me honk their horn, then swerve around me.

The motorcycle slows as well.

Yep. I'm being followed.

I am considering another a crazy maneuver when the motorcycle accelerates and catches up with me.

The rider, masked in a helmet like mine, turns their head and faces me for a moment.

They then rev the engine on their much-faster motorcycle and shoot ahead, leaving me in their dust.

Damn. What the hell was *that*?

NIGHT MARKET

I park my moped in front of the shop where I rented it and toss the keys onto the desk, where a woman is sleeping with her head down. She barely looks up as she grabs the keys and returns to her slumber.

I have to assume whoever was on the motorcycle got the license plate of my moped and can trace it back here. They might deduce what hotel I am staying at as well. I add both to the burn list.

I take back alleys to my hotel and climb over the fence into the small yard in back where the staff hangs the laundry. Two women are listening to a radio while pinning sheets to clotheslines as I drop down onto the concrete.

I flip up my helmet's visor and smile as I keep moving. They wave and return to their work, as if a man dropping in wearing a motorcycle helmet is no big deal. They've probably seen their share of stupid tourist antics.

I use the back stairwell to get to my floor. After checking the hallway, I knock on the door next to mine. Nobody answers. I pick the lock with the key ring I keep in my pocket and enter the room.

The bed and the bathroom are empty, so nobody screams in surprise as I stroll through.

I go to the sliding glass doors, step onto the balcony, then climb over the railing and hop onto my own—landing as catlike as I am able.

Through a gap in the curtains, I see there's nobody in my room; the mirror in the bathroom reflects an empty interior.

I might be taking things a little too far, but after that face-off on the highway with the motorcycle rider, I'm afraid I'm not being cautious enough.

It takes me ten seconds to grab my stuff—I leave the fake bag and laptop on the desk in case someone decides to come snooping, and the real laptop and gadget bag I keep hidden.

I make my exit through my front door and take the back way down again and pass the same women doing laundry. This time I fully remove my helmet so they know I'm not a thief—or at least look less like a thief—and exit through a side door.

After three blocks of walking a zigzag pattern, I toss the helmet, hop into a taxi, and ask the driver to take me to the night market.

❦

Twenty minutes later we come to a stop at a roped-off street where thousands of people are wandering through brightly lit stalls filled with street food, clothing, and other goods. Because it's sticky and hot as hell during the day, Bangkok has several large night markets where you can do your shopping in slightly cooler temperatures.

I chose this one because there are a number of tourist hotels within walking distance, so one more middle-aged white guy won't get unwanted attention. I also need to update Morena and Kylie.

Once I'm anonymously enshrouded by the crowd, I call them.

"What's the yelling?" Morena asks after I connect her with Kylie.

"I think the night catch is in," I reply as I pass an assortment of fish laid out on ice.

"What have you found out?" asks Kylie, getting to the point.

"It's not good. I went to their apartment. I found three bullet holes in the floor. It looked like an execution-style hit," I explain matter-of-factly.

"My God," says Morena.

"There's more. The place is being watched. I was pursued by what I believe are local Chinese gangsters. I also think I was spotted by someone else. I don't think they were working with the gangsters, though. I'm not sure what's going on. How is it going on your end?"

"I haven't heard anything back from the government," Morena explains. "We've even reached out to contacts with the Royal Thai Police. They say that they can't speak on the matter. When we push for specifics, we get the cold shoulder. The only thing we know for sure is that there is an ongoing investigation into what happened at that address but little else."

"It wasn't even in the newspapers here. The only item said that police responded to an incident in that neighborhood," I tell them.

"If it is gang related, that makes sense. They're probably careful about leaks," says Morena.

"You're sure you saw bullet holes?" asks Kylie.

"Yes. They cleaned up the blood, but the bullet impacts were still there. It appears they were shot execution-style. *Why* is the big question. It looked like some computing equipment was stolen. Maybe something used to mine crypto, maybe what they used for ransomware attacks. I'm still trying to piece it all together. And . . ." I'm reluctant to point out the men who chased after me had no trouble pulling a trigger.

Morena catches my hesitation. "And what, Brad?"

"I got shot at by the gang guys. It may have been a warning. Maybe not, but they play rough," I tell them.

"I think we've learned enough. You need to get back here ASAP," says Morena.

"As much as I don't want to get involved in whatever bullshit is going on here, I still kind of need to figure out what happened to Vik and the others."

"That wasn't the job. We wanted you to find out what happened to the money. That's a dead end . . . I mean, horrible expression, you know what I mean," she says.

"This is more important than the money," I reply.

"And you can leave the cowboy act to the police or whoever else," Morena shoots back.

"What do you think is going on?" asks Kylie.

"I don't know. This is more complicated than we thought. And Morena, to your point, we need to know what's going on before it all points back to Kylie." I decide to use a little embellishment. "If they were involved in some kind of criminal activity that could trace back to the money Kylie invested in them, we need to be ahead of it."

"What if it's worse than we imagine? Maybe we don't want to know," says Morena.

"I'd rather we bring the bad news to US authorities than have the FBI show up with a subpoena and have to deal with all the PR bullshit," I explain.

"Goddamn it, Brad," Morena sighs.

"You don't think there's some kind of espionage angle here, do you?" asks Kylie.

"Not as far as I know. At least not internally. You still worried about the photos of the engine?" I ask.

"I don't think we leaked. I've gone over everyone who knew about the engine test. I also realized something about our methods for concealing the engine. The screens we're using are almost completely transparent to infrared.

"You realize that's how the Russians could tell what the SR-71 looked like, right? We tested them when their satellites weren't overhead and then moved them inside, but infrared film could show the *shape* of the plane where the tarmac had been cooled by its shadow. I feel kind of dumb," she confesses.

"You can never cover all the bases," I reply.

"I know," says Kylie. "Look, I want you to play it safe, but I also want to know what happened to Vik. You call your own shots."

I hear Morena take in a breath like she does before she's about to say something very declaratively, but she's silent for a moment. "Damn it," she says at last. "Be safe. The dating pool out here sucks."

"Have you ever seen anything like this?" asks Kylie.

"Not exactly. Normally the newspapers have something to say. Whoever ordered this to be kept quiet has a lot of power. It had to come from the top of the Royal Thai Police. Even then, I don't know if they have this kind of control to order it. The real power here is in the military. I don't know if that's relevant to this situation, but it makes me wonder."

"Oh great. The Thai military," says Morena.

Not to mention that motorcycle rider who knew where to catch me on the highway.

"If you get into a jam, just let us know. Brenda's champing at the bit to help out," says Kylie.

"I appreciate that, but I need her close to you."

"Well, in that case—" Morena begins but is cut off by Kylie.

"What are you going to do now?"

"Buy some new clothes, check into a new room, change, and then see if I can find out what actually happened to the kids in the apartment. I have one more place where I can look for clues."

"What can *we* do?" asks Kylie. "I know of a firm that chases down crypto scammers that flee to Southeast Asia. Maybe they could help with the xQuadrant guys?"

Having more eyes could be useful, I have to admit. "Okay. Do it."

"One more thing, Brad. Maybe it's not relevant, but you should know. I dropped by the sheriff's office to check on Josiah Levenstein's laptop. They said someone from the FBI picked it up."

"Who?" I ask.

"They didn't say, but the agent was out of DC. Their credentials checked out. I'm trying to find out more."

"Damn it. I should have taken Josiah's laptop to the LA field office. I didn't think time was on our side," I think out loud. Fortunately, I have a copy I can examine when I have the time, but that's not now. "Did Elena get a look at the laptop before they took it?"

"No. Anything that could be bad for us, you imagine?"

"Not that I can think of. I'm just wondering who decided to grab it. And how they knew it was there."

My mind has been thousands of miles away from the Josiah Levenstein situation, both figuratively and literally.

"Did we get the forensic report on him?" I ask.

"I'll forward it to you," says Morena.

"Thanks." I check my watch. "I have to run."

"Okay, Brad, just keep us in the loop. Don't just tell us about something after the fact," says Morena.

"Yeah, of course," I lie, knowing full well she would not like to be in the loop for what I'm about to do next.

COLD STORAGE

Arthit Chaiwong opens the sliding window next to the metal door and glares at me. I've been pounding on the door to the Royal Thai Police precinct morgue for the last five minutes.

"I should have known, an American," he sniffs. Arthit is in his early thirties and has what my mother would call a "bookish" face behind round glasses.

"Mr. Chaiwong, I'm Frank Lane. My office called. I'm here to identify the body on behalf of the family," I explain.

"What body? What family?" he asks.

He's wearing rubber gloves that go all the way to his elbows over a brown jumpsuit. I can't help but notice that they're wet and glistening.

"The three shooting victims? I represent the family of one of them," I tell him.

His head makes a slight nod, telling me that he understands who I'm talking about, but he pleads ignorance anyway.

"I have no idea what you're talking about. Come back during normal business hours and talk to the supervisor," he says.

"My flight leaves in two hours. I have to be back in Ohio, for court," I explain.

"Are you fucking for real?" asks Arthit.

I looked him up before knocking on the door. I was able to get a list of employees of the morgue and then figure out who was working the night shift by checking the times of their social-media posts. Arthit's quite active posting memes about movies and local politics at this time of night.

In photos, he's most frequently seen with three other people: Narongrit, Kittisak, and Kittisak's girlfriend Anong. Anong stands out in the photos because of her pixie-like face and bright-red hair.

"I'm on a tight schedule. It will only take ten minutes," I explain.

"Sorry. No can do." He begins to slide the door shut.

I grab the edge with my hand. "I can pay you."

"Fuck you," he replies. "I'm not some prostitute you can throw money at."

"But we didn't even talk about how much," I point out.

"Sorry. Bye. I'm going to call the police now."

"Don't make me show the photos to Anong," I say as he tries to force the window closed.

He freezes. "What did you say?"

"Let me in or I'll show Anong the photos," I clarify.

"I don't know what you're talking about," he says, hesitantly.

"But you know *who* I'm talking about," I respond, now having earned his undivided attention.

"Photos? What do you mean?"

I glance up at the camera above the entrance. "You have to know there are more security cameras than that, right? After that incident at the other precinct where they caught the medical examiner staff doing things with the corpses? They put hidden cameras in the other morgues too. Typical lazy government installers, they didn't bother securing the network. Let me show you."

I take my phone from my pocket and pull up a video feed and show Arthit.

He looks down at my screen and sees himself poking his head out the window looking down at my screen.

"That's you, looking at you, looking at you, looking at you, and so forth. Crazy? You should see what's on the other cameras. You should see what you've been up to."

I close the app on my phone and place it back in my pocket. "Better yet, Anong should see what you're up to." I take a wild guess. "You can even make out her red hair on your phone screen in the video."

Besides talking about movies and politics, Arthit managed to like every single photo of Anong. From the timing, it appeared that his favorite time to like her photos was when he was alone here. And like them a lot, he did.

"Who the fuck *are* you?" Arthit asks again, this time desperately.

"I'm not the bad guy. I just need to take a look at those bodies. I'm trying to figure out what's going on here. That's all."

Arthit stares at me, trying to make sense of things. His expression reminds me of Josiah when I put him in the vise.

"You'll delete everything?" Arthit asks.

"Like it never happened," I confirm.

"Fine."

It's a dirty trick—one I came up with an hour ago while walking through night market stalls and scrolling through his social-media profile.

I never hacked the cameras and have no idea if anyone at the other morgues was doing the unspeakable with the deceased. I bought a twenty-dollar Bluetooth camera the size of a pen and stuck it under the actual camera over the entrance to the morgue.

A moment later Arthit unlocks the door and lets me in, never bothering to look up at the camera just a foot over his head with my cheap gadget taped underneath.

"This way," he says, pointing me down a dimly lit hallway.

I walk down the corridor and listen closely to his steps. I expect that some part of him is contemplating murdering me to avoid whatever shame he thinks I might bring upon him.

"Once we're done," I assure him, "I'll call my friends and have them delete everything."

His footsteps stop.

"Your friends?"

I nod, friendly as all get-out. "Yeah. No worries. Nobody's seen anything. Just a precaution."

Arthit's face is completely drained of color in the pale blue light of a flickering fluorescent bulb. "Uh, actually it's this way."

He retraces his steps and takes me down another corridor.

"You weren't going to take me someplace and murder me, were you, Arthit?" I ask.

He looks back at me over his shoulder. "You'll never know."

It's worth pointing out that Arthit's favorite genre is Southeast Asian horror movies, the bloody, relentless kind. I think for a brief moment he imagined he might be role-playing in one.

He's a very troubled and conflicted young man.

While most people I know who work with the deceased have the gentle demeanor of a Presbyterian minister, every now and then you run into one who got into the business because they never grew out of their adolescent heavy metal phase.

"Here we are," says Arthit as he pushes open the door to a room with a wall full of body storage units.

He starts opening doors and sliding out drawers. The bodies are encased in plastic pouches with zippers.

I take a pair of rubber gloves from my pocket and slip them on.

"Of course you brought your own," says Arthit. "Are you going to murder me?"

"I wasn't planning on it," I reply. I unzip the first pouch and reveal an unfamiliar face. There's a nasty exit wound on the forehead where the bullet ricocheted back. "Tell me what you know."

"Well, for starters, there are these things called bullets. It looks like each of these guys came up close and personal with one. The end. Any questions?"

"I can't imagine why Anong wouldn't be attracted to a guy like you instead of Kittisak."

"Kittisak is a cheater who got hepatitis from some lady-boy," replies Arthit. "But do I say shit? Nope. Bro code. Anong doesn't know the real Kittisak."

"What about the real Arthit? Are you just some gloomy edgelord who memes in the dark while drooling over photos of his friend's girlfriend?"

"That's not all I do. Sometimes I do it during the day too," he replies.

I gesture to the first body. "Tell me what happened."

"I just clean and prep and drool over photos of Anong, man."

Okay, this kid has some serious self-esteem issues. Time to work on that.

"You're more than that. You're clever. Probably too clever. That's why they put you on the night shift. You made everyone else feel stupid," I tell him.

"You think this motivational bullshit is going to work on me?" says Arthit.

"But am I right?"

"Well, yeah. Dr. Piyarat couldn't tell a stab wound from a superficial laceration. When these bodies came in here, it was obvious they were shot with their heads to the ground. But someone said the report should say that they were seated and there were powder burns on their hands," explains Arthit.

"Implying that they fired weapons too. *Were* there powder burns?"

Arthit raises the right hand of the corpse we're standing over. "Fuck no. See the calluses on the index, first finger, and side of the thumb? This guy spent his time typing on a keyboard, not gangbanging."

He moves over to the next corpse and unzips the bag. "Take a look." He flashes his light near the nose and mouth of the victim. "See the blood vessels? He was having a seizure when he was shot. He was probably freaking the hell out and having a panic attack."

He aims his light at the side of the head and the arms, revealing bruises.

"They were tortured before they were killed. But all of it happened quickly. I've seen this before. It's what happens when they try to beat something out of you," he explains impassively.

The murderers were brutal and efficient. They clearly didn't have time to waste. They went for the most painful points they could, then killed them.

"And then there's this," says Arthit as he begins to unzip the third body.

I brace myself for the sight of Vik's face. I didn't know him, but he felt more real to me than the others.

But instead of a face I'm looking at a bloody stump of a neck. The body has been decapitated.

"Amazing, right? Now check this out," says Arthit as he raises the corpse's right arm.

The hand is missing. Same for the left.

"Eight minutes," says Arthit.

"Eight minutes for what?" I ask.

"That's how long their killers took from the moment they pulled up to when they left, according to what I heard. Eight minutes to torture, execute, and then cut off the head and hands of this poor asshole. You think I'm a gloomy, twisted freak? Look at the world we live in. I'm just coping," says Arthit. "Where do you think the head and hands will end up? My money is on his parents' doorstep."

"Why them?" I ask. "Who are they?"

"Who are any of these guys?" Arthit grabs a clipboard from the end of the slab and shows it to me. "That's Thai for 'John Doe #3.' They're all John Does. They say nobody knows who they are, but they say a lot of bullshit. Somebody doesn't want us to know who they are."

"And why is that?" I ask.

"Why do people keep buying lottery tickets when we have the worst odds and the most corrupt people running it? Just one of those mysteries we accept."

"What do you think happened to them?"

"Something bad. Something bigger than them," says Arthit.

"And who do you think is keeping this quiet?"

"I don't know and I don't care. I don't want to end up like one of these poor bastards. For all I know, you did it. Maybe you came back here for whack material," says Arthit. "Want to take some photos?"

"Actually, yes."

"Sick fuck," he sniffs.

"Not for that."

"How would *I* know? From where I'm standing there's not much difference between you and whoever did this. You come in here blackmailing me. Which, by the way, I'm thinking is bullshit. But whatever."

I take photos of the faces of the victims and get close-ups of their wounds and their hands and fingertips. I have Arthit pry open the eyelids of the two that still have heads and take photos of their eyeballs.

"What about their clothes?" I ask.

Arthit goes into the other room and returns with three paper bags. I snap photos of pants, shirts, and undergarments.

"Is this all?"

"Everything they came in with," he confirms.

"Unlock your phone and hand it to me," I tell Arthit when we're done.

"Why?"

"I'm going to put a number in it. Call me if you hear anything else."

"Why would I do that?"

"Because I'm the kind of person you want to do favors for," I tell him.

"Whatever." He hands me his phone.

I type in a number that connects to an answering service. "I was never here. Understand?"

"Sure. Yeah, I got it. So, the photos are bullshit, right?"

"Yes. But I'm going to make up for it. Bro code doesn't apply to me and Kittisak. Anong is going to get a call from a health official tracking down an outbreak of hepatitis. I don't think she'll want anything to do with Kittisak after that. What you do next is up to you. Whatever it is, lay off the edgelord-y dark vibe a bit."

By the time I make it to the front door, Arthit is asking me how long to wait before calling up Anong. I tell him she'll probably be calling him.

I'm sure he'll blow his opportunity, but that's his problem. I have more important issues to deal with right now.

Vik's head and hands weren't removed as some kind of gangland threat. It's what criminals do when they want to steal someone's biometrics.

Doing that all in eight minutes, if that's true, suggests professionals. Not merely gangsters with experience, but the kind of crew you call in when you're dealing with state-level security.

I know this because I've seen this before.

I exit the morgue and walk down the sidewalk toward the 7-Eleven where I parked my newest moped rental.

As I put on my helmet and get ready to head back to the hotel, I see the glow of a cigarette across the street under an awning. The face of the owner is in the shadows, but I can tell they're looking straight at me.

The ember flickers as they inhale, then the cigarette goes to the side of their chest, suggesting that their arms are crossed.

It all seems a bit deliberate—like they're informing me that I'm being watched.

INTERNAL AFFAIRS

The police station lobby is lined with desks and men and women in military-looking uniforms, leaning over forms or talking to people sitting across from them in office chairs. At first glance it resembles the DMV more than a classic police station with a huge duty desk.

I'm sitting here with my number, waiting for it to be called, thankful that the signage is also in English.

Walking into a Thai police station after having committed more criminal acts in the last twenty-four hours than I can recount may seem like a stupid strategy—because it probably is—but I need to at least make some official effort to learn what happened. If for no other reason than so I don't get mistaken by local police for another criminal trying to get whatever xQuadrant had.

My number gets called, and I'm motioned over to a seat in front of a police sergeant with a thick comb-over. He takes a look at me and asks, "You speak Thai?"

I place my phone on the table with the translator app. He makes a dismissive wave gesture and says harshly, "Back in line."

Okay. So much for that.

I take my seat again, pull out my phone, and start flipping through a spreadsheet of Thai words, using a mnemonics trick to memorize them.

For a word like "arrest," which translates to "cabkum" in Thai, the working part of the word is "cab," which means to hold or catch. In my spreadsheet, I put "arrest" in one column, "cạbkum" in another, "cab comb" in a third, and in the fourth an emoji of a police officer, a taxi cab, and a comb:

Arrest | Cạbkum | Cab Comb | 👮🏽 🚕 🪮

It's a new system I came up with to help me learn foreign words quickly on my phone. I find emojis or anything visual helps me visualize the words while I listen to native speakers.

Since I arrived two days ago, I've made over three hundred new entries—enough to make my way through the night market and request extra towels for my room.

Although I can use guidebooks and apps to learn the vocabulary, creating the visual chart serves as part of the learning process. I prefer to prepare this way, then use a real-time translation app as well.

Now, I'm trying to memorize the word for "criminal," which is "xāchyākr," but the pronunciation sounds nothing like the English spelling. It's more like "anchee-a-gone," which I approximate to "anchovy cheese a gone." My emoji translation is fish, pizza, cheese, and a tombstone. Like I said, it's a new system. It's a bit rough, but now I see emojis when I hear Thai phrases and can pick out certain things that I couldn't before.

"Next," says a policewoman as she points to the electronic sign with my number.

I put my phone away and take the seat opposite from her. Her hair is pulled back into a bun almost as tight as her posture. Her composure looks like that of a trained dancer. Her name tag says KHAMPHIRAPHAT, which I start breaking down mentally into syllables so I can address her by her name and rank.

"How may we assist you?" she asks.

I set my business card on the table. "My name is Bradley. I represent a company that had made an investment in a small Thai company, and I'm having trouble tracking down the owners of the company. When I went to their address, nobody answered the door. An older gentleman mentioned something about the police. I thought I should come here and ask."

"What's the business and the address?" she replies.

"The company is called xQuadrant." I pause as she writes this down.

There's no hesitation on her part, so I give her the address: "293 Lat Phrao 65."

The moment I say it, she looks up at me. She then regains her composure and writes the rest of the address.

"May I see your passport?" she asks.

I hand her my real one.

"This may take a few minutes." She grabs my business card off the desk and goes into a back room.

Since there's a phone on the other side of the small, clear plastic divider, she obviously doesn't want to have the conversation she's about to have in front of me.

I sit quietly with my hands folded and ignore the security camera that's facing in my direction.

From my Google Maps survey, I know there are three floors to this police station, and for her to get from reception to the third floor, where I presume the other party she wants to speak with works, should take about two minutes.

Add another three minutes to allow her to interrupt whatever that other person is engaged in and explain who I am and what I'm doing here. Another two for her to remember my business card in her pocket and hand it to that person.

Thirty seconds for them to type in the URL or scan the QR code with their phone. And . . . my phone vibrates as a user from a Thai internet provider visits the "Bradley Allen Trasker Consulting" profile.

Add another three minutes for them to run my passport and verify that it's real.

Two minutes after that, the back door to the reception area opens and Sergeant Khamphiraphat returns with an older man who appears to be Han Chinese and is wearing police major epaulets on his shoulders. His name tag is easier to pronounce: "Lim."

He sits down in front of me and reaches out his hand. "I'm Major Lim."

"Thank you for meeting with me," I reply.

"What is your connection to the business located at 293 Lat Phrao 65?" he asks.

I give him a thin version of the truth. "Our start-up fund invested half a million US dollars in a company that we believe is located there. We haven't heard from them in a matter of weeks. I was sent to investigate," I explain.

"And why do you think the people you were doing business with were at that location?" he asks.

An aging NSA burnout gave me the location based on a selfie. "It was an address given to me by one of our attorneys."

"And what kind of business did you invest in?"

"A technology company developing smart contracts. I really don't know the technical details."

"What hotel are you staying at?"

"The ABC Guest House," I reply.

Lim hands my passport back to me. "I'm sorry to say there's nothing we can tell you."

"What does that mean?" I ask.

"It means just that."

"Is there an investigation?"

"We have your contact information. We'll let you know if there's anything else," he replies.

Clearly, all they wanted to know was why an American was in their lobby asking questions about the case. Satisfied with my explanation, they're done with me.

"Could I speak to Inspector Srisutham?" I ask.

Lim's eyes focus on me. "Why do you want to speak to him?"

"I saw his name on the police seal at the apartment when I went there," I reply.

Lim shakes his head. "That was just a clerical detail."

"But could I speak to him?"

"About what? We've told you that there's nothing more to say."

I decide to push things a little bit more. "The seal said something about a homicide investigation."

"Mr. Trasker, we've been very patient. I think you should leave now."

I know enough not to press my luck. "Thank you for your time."

I get up and leave.

I was being given the runaround. They know it. I know it. And they know I know it.

It seems obvious that someone else is calling the shots. Khamphiraphat was simply the first person I spoke to. Lim was the person she knew to go to with this situation. I don't suspect either one of them is "in on it" as much as they are following orders from above.

Knowing who was issuing those orders would tell me a lot more, but Lim wasn't in a position to tell me anything other than to go away.

I walk back outside the station and put on my sunglasses to avoid the bright morning sun.

A man in a white short-sleeved shirt squatting by a motorcycle and smoking a cigarette flicks through his phone, then looks up at me. "You need taxi?"

An image of me holding a pen and harpoon appears in my head, and I reply, "Mị pĕnrị k̄hxbkhuṇ," hopefully declining the offer and not insulting him.

He smirks at my horrible Thai and gives me a small wave.

I continue back toward the main street, curious to know who will ping my website next.

My interaction went pretty much as I expected. But aside from formally acknowledging my presence here and trying to distance myself from any suspicion of being a criminal, the real purpose of the visit was the business card.

Whoever scans the QR code, visits the website, or dials the number on the card will leave an electronic trail. While I suspect they'll use some kind of anonymizing method to hide their locations, my website has a few tools that help triangulate where visitors come from. It's the same kind of tech used to personalize advertising on the web.

My next visitor's location should give me some idea of which parties are involved in this.

TRACKING

While I wait to see who triggers my online trip wire, I have questions that I want answered. Unfortunately, I don't have a lot of clues to go on. Other than what I've observed in the apartment and the morgue and the photos on my phone, there's not a lot to look at.

Of course, I watched Don Larian perform a miracle with a mere selfie. Maybe I need to channel my inner photo analyst and try my luck.

I buy a bowl of something noodle based and take a seat at a plastic table with my back to a giant banner advertising potato chips.

The apartment images are pretty much as I remember, the scattered mats, piles of shoes, and the chips in the concrete where the bullets hit.

I flip through the morgue images—the ones of the bodies with heads—and match the wounds to the indentations. The last one to be killed was probably Vik.

A look at their clothing and the blood spatter would probably confirm that. If only I had access to the forensic report. Who knows what else might be in there? Arthit didn't mention one, but I didn't push hard enough.

Of course, there's also Inspector Srisutham. Major Lim tried to guide me away from him, but I could simply call the man . . .

I pull up his number from my notes and dial. A moment later, a woman answers in Thai.

"Hello, do you speak English?" I ask.

"Yes. Criminal Investigations Division. How may I help you?" she replies.

"I'd like to speak to Inspector Srisutham about a case. I may have some information."

"One moment, please."

A minute later there's a click and a gruff voice says, "Yes?"

"Hello, Inspector Srisutham? My name is Bradley. I'm calling about the men who live in 293 Lat Phrao 65."

"Yes?" he says again.

"Do you speak English?" I ask, not sure if there's a language barrier.

"Yes," he responds, not exactly clearing things up for me.

"Um. Well, I was trying to find out what happened to them. My company had a business arrangement with them. I wanted to find out the status of the investigation," I explain.

"I believe you are mistaken," he replies.

"I saw your name on the police seal on the door."

"I believe you are mistaken," he says again.

"So there's no investigation at 293 Lat Phrao 65?"

There's a pause, then he replies, "I have nothing more to say."

He hangs up.

I call back again and get the same woman as before.

"Hello? I'd like to talk to Inspector Srisutham."

"He's not here," she says.

"Okay, thank you." I end the call instead of arguing over the logistics of how he could be gone so quickly.

I go back to the photos and flip through them again. Just knowing the ammo used could tell me something. Were they shot with weapons that Thai police officers use? Or something more exotic?

As I scroll through the images, I realize I've been focusing all my attention on the exit wounds on their foreheads. I've been ignoring the other trauma inflicted on their bodies.

On the second victim's temple, there's a bruise and a powder burn caused when a gun is fired next to a person's head. But there were three holes in the floor, not four.

According to my secondhand witness Tommy, there was a "pop pop pop pop" sound heard from the apartment, which reinforces the four-bullet theory.

If three bullets either disintegrated or reentered the victims' skulls, only to be collected and stashed away by the forensic team, what about the fourth slug? Could it still be in the apartment? Stuck in a wall?

It might be nothing. It might be something. There's also another bullet impact I should compare it to—back on the train platform steps, where I made my escape.

Going near the apartment again would be stupid and potentially suicidal, but it's daylight, and that has to count for something, right?

I make three laps around the block and can't spot anyone watching the premises. Either they've chosen better spots to watch from or everyone who was interested in this apartment has lost interest. But I'm still not taking any chances.

I park my rented motorcycle—no moped this time—in front of Tommy's grandfather's repair shop, close to the entrance of the apartment building.

I'm wearing a bright-pink taxi vest and have on a different helmet from before, so I should be largely unrecognizable if I'm being watched. Of course, the moment I enter or leave the third-floor apartment, all anonymity goes out the window.

I walk briskly toward the entrance, ignoring Tommy's glance as he looks up from his wash bin of soapy engine parts.

I pass the first flight and on the second landing take a quick look out onto the street to see if I'm being watched.

Not as far as I can tell.

I make it to the third floor, check the street again: still nothing. No Chinese gang members, shadowy cigarette smokers, or mysterious motorcyclists.

So far so good.

Except . . .

The door to the apartment is wide open. There's no police seal. Just the sound of some Thai radio soap opera playing.

An emoji sewing needle, a wad of paper, and a doughnut bouncing into a room come to mind. *Um, a doughnut?* Oh, a *D*.

"Šwạšdī?" I call into the apartment, awkwardly calling out, "Hello?"

An elderly woman who looks like she's just shy of her ninetieth birthday pokes her head out from the bathroom, holding a mop. The same mop that apparently just cleaned the entire floor, including the filled-in indentations in the concrete under the rug, which is now rolled up in the corner.

I flip up my visor and give her a dumb grin. Beer mugs and a musical-note emoji come to mind—the music makes them shatter, requiring them to be fixed. I point to my chest and say, "Chāng šxm."

I think I told her I'm a repairman.

She gives me a friendly smile that makes me wish she were my grandmother and returns to her mopping.

I make a show of looking at the electrical sockets and the utility closet, then go back to the living room and stand over the spot where the young men were executed. I kneel over the bullet marks. My knees immediately regret it, but I endure.

If the victim had been in this same position when the first warning shot was fired, the assailant would have been squatting in front of him with the gun beside his temple.

I touch my own and imagine a gun barrel there.

When I look behind me, I see several meters of wall covered with intricate wallpaper where a bullet could have gone. Even with a metal detector this could take a while.

I try to put my body as close to where the victim would have been before having his head shoved into the floor. I realize I have an audience and see that the old woman is watching me with interest.

I motion for her to come over. I hand her a small laser pointer and position her where the killer would have stood.

Amused by the game, she goes along with it. I place the laser next to my head so the beam hits the wall behind me.

Pebble, sandwich watch—the pebble is waiting to eat lunch. "Pæb nung," I say, asking her to wait a moment.

When I turn around, the laser is hitting the wall at a point much lower than I'd been expecting. It's only a foot above my kneeling height.

I walk over to the red spot and inspect around the paper, using my fingers to feel for any indentations. Even in a smooth wall, a bullet hole can be harder to find than you might imagine—especially if it embeds itself in the drywall.

My fingers feel a small rip in the paper. I push my index finger inside, and the tip finds a recess.

I thank the woman and take the laser pointer back. She waits to see what I do next, but I just nod.

She smiles, then returns to her mop work in the other room.

I take my pocketknife out and shove the blade into the wall. Bits of dust fall onto my palm as I hold it under the entry point and dig around inside. Suddenly an avalanche of drywall pours into my hand, followed by bullet fragments.

It's a frangible round designed for close-quarters combat. The fact that the other rounds were able to make it through the skulls of the victims and make chips in the concrete suggests that these are something special—designed specifically for bone and soft-tissue penetration but not to bounce around a concrete interior.

I place the bullet pieces in a plastic bag and slip it into my pocket. I wave to the old woman watching me from the doorway as I exit.

I can only imagine what she's going to tell her friends.

After carefully surveilling the street, I walk past Tommy and his grandfather and get on my bike.

No black Mercedes is visible. No other motorcyclists are around besides the ones going back and forth on the street. I think I'm free and clear.

As free and clear as I can be in the current situation.

I don't bother retrieving bullet fragments from the stairs where the gangster shot at me. I could tell by the sound of the ricochet he was firing run-of-the-mill lead slugs.

The one in my pocket, the type that killed Vik and the rest of xQuadrant, is a special type of ammo. So special that I'm pretty sure even Thai special forces doesn't use it.

These rounds are used by assassins. State-level killers.

I head back to the hotel, wondering what will turn up next.

HAPPENSTANCE

"Brad!" shouts a female voice as I enter the lobby of the ABC Guest House.

I look over to the small lounge and spot a flash of red hair over khaki pants and a white buttoned shirt.

"Rebecca?" I reply, genuinely caught off guard.

I look around the lobby for any other surprises. Except for the clerk minding his business behind the desk, Rebecca Gostler is the only person here aside from me.

I take a seat across from the coffee table covered in flyers for tourist attractions. I do my best to act surprised in a "what a delightful coincidence" way and not an "oh crap, my cover has been blown" manner.

"This isn't an accident, is it?" I ask the consultant.

She smiles. "Oh, no. I was asking about xQuadrant at the police station, and they mentioned you. They told me you were staying here," she explains.

"Did they tell you anything else?"

"About your criminal past? Just kidding. No. They're not very talkative," she replies.

"No, they're not. When did you get here?"

"Just a day ago. You?" she asks.

"The same."

She leans in and whispers, "What *have* you found out?"

"Not much. Like you said, the police haven't been much help."

"How did you end up in Bangkok?" she asks.

How did you end up in the same precinct where xQuadrant was located?

"We found some old paperwork with a mailing address. I decided it was worth a shot, and besides, Thailand . . ." I explain. "How about you? Crazy we both ended up here."

"Same thing. We found some filings with an address in Bangkok. It seemed like a good lead," she says.

"What address?" I ask.

"Lat Phrao something. I'll have to look it up on my phone. Speaking of looking things up. I looked you up. I had no idea you were some kind of superspy."

"That would be because I wasn't. I worked in the Marine Embassy Guards when I was younger and then did security consulting. My life is pretty boring; that's why I jumped at the chance to visit Thailand."

"I read about the shoot-out at the Mojave airport. That doesn't sound like normal security work," she responds.

"That was a very unfortunate event. We lost some really good people that day."

She picks up on the fact that this isn't a happy topic for me. "So, is this your first time here?"

"I've been a couple times before." If you only count the times I entered the country legally and was not smuggled in on a shrimp boat so I could meet with Chinese double agents.

"Well, I was hoping to find out more about what happened to Vik and the others. I haven't had much luck. The police, the consulate, nobody will say anything. Same for you, huh?"

"Just an empty apartment and the fact that I really need to learn Thai. I'm about to wrap things up and head home," I lie.

"That's too bad. I was hoping we could join forces. Maybe we could find out more if we teamed up," she offers.

I don't trust her. She obviously knows a lot more about me than I do about her. But I don't have to keep playing it quite so naively.

"Rebecca, who do you work for?"

"Theocrates. I think I told you at the conference. We do background research for investment firms," she explains.

"Knowing what you told me about xQuadrant having possible criminal connections, why would they send you here?"

"I could ask you the same thing. It's probably for the same reasons. If xQuadrant was involved in criminal activity, it could look very bad for my client."

"Because of the PR fallout?"

"Because of the security fallout. They did some contract work for a subsidiary of ours on code that they never should have had. I can't go into details, but if they inserted back doors, it could put certain financial companies at risk."

Plausible, but I don't know if I should buy it. It has just enough "we're fucked and I have to clean it all up" to make her look vulnerable and believable. But that's why I'm suspicious.

"So, what exactly were you going to do?"

"Are we in the zone of secrecy here?" she asks.

"Sure."

"Beg, threaten, or bribe whoever has their computer equipment to get at it first and clean anything that's connected to us," she tells me.

"So, tamper with evidence in a criminal proceeding."

"Whatever it takes to protect my clients."

"That's a risky undertaking."

"It pays well, and I like nice things. But since we're in the zone of secrecy here, maybe you can be a little more honest. A man like you doesn't spend two days here and come up empty-handed. Like I said, I looked you up. While I like to think I'm resourceful, you wrote the book. You know something, don't you?"

"Maybe. But I need to know if I trust you before I tell you," I say honestly.

"Look me up," says Rebecca. "Use your dark web contacts or whatever. You're not going to find out that I spent my summer breaks in

Moscow or that I was attending the Confucius Institute seminars. My dad was a police officer and my mother a paralegal. I wanted something a little more rewarding and got into finance. Theocrates hired me after I did a couple internships, and I found that I liked a job that never got boring."

"That all sounds plausible," I reply. Like it was meant to.

"It's not as exciting as being raised by a master spy and having a blue-blood father in the State Department," she fires back.

"My bedtime stories were certainly interesting. And for the record, my father wasn't really in the picture—on account of already having another wife and family."

"It seems like you turned out for the better," she says with a shrug.

"Summers in Nantucket were never my thing. Anyway, if you're serious, let me go get changed and we'll chase down a very flimsy lead."

"A flimsy lead is better than no lead. Do you want me to come up with you?" she asks, ever so slowly drawing out the words.

I've been around enough blocks to pick up on a test closing when I hear one. I also know enough that you can use it as a way to gauge someone's character.

One of my first undercover assignments as a young man was to wear tight pants and hang out in a bar a few blocks away from a foreign embassy and keep track of who tried to buy me drinks.

I learned more than I cared to know about the inner fantasy life of a sixty-five-year-old visa clerk who would buy me drink after drink and tell me all the things she would have done to me if she were ten years younger.

A lot of intelligence work is just letting people talk and show you who they really are.

If I were positive Rebecca wasn't testing me and I thought I'd get more out of her than she would out of me, I'd seriously consider accepting her offer. The thing is, I'm not paid by the government to do that kind of thing anymore, and I know a certain attorney back in California would not appreciate my dedication to my work.

"I'll only be a few minutes," I reply.

I go to my room and take a quick shower as I do a deeper background check on Rebecca Gostler and Theocrates. I wish I had the kinds of tools I had access to back when I was in the service.

I have to settle for a private firm that keeps track of social-media profiles and flags for anything that looks suspicious—like a LinkedIn account connected to a bunch of other shell profiles.

Rebecca appears to be what she says she is. There's mention of her in the Stanford student newspaper. High school volleyball photos in local news, and photos from a now deactivated Instagram account showing her from high school to soon after she started working at Theocrates.

Theocrates has a plausible footprint. It appears to be one of a thousand generic consulting firms spun out of other generic consulting firms. The CEO is a real person I was able to track down and even served on the board with a man who is a friend of my father's.

While Gostler seems to be a real person and Theocrates appears to be a legit company, it still doesn't tell me much.

There are well-established consulting groups in Washington with roots in the Eisenhower era still doing secret contract work for the Iranians and Russians. Some of it is ideological, some of it financial. Then there are myriad companies that serve as fronts for our own intelligence agencies. My own LinkedIn profile contains more than a few.

Rebecca Gostler is either an inconvenient obstacle or someone who knows more than she's letting on and a potential source of information . . . *if* I can figure out how to get her to reveal what she knows.

To do that, I'm going to have to see how far she can be pushed.

There's no hiding the fact that she knows there's more to my past than my insistence I'm just a desk-jockey consultant. Anybody smart enough and with the right contacts can read between the lines.

Since she thinks she knows Brad Trasker, we'll see how much Brad Trasker she can handle.

I finish changing and rearranging a few items in my room, then return to the lobby. Rebecca is texting when I enter in a sport coat and casual shirt. She smiles as she looks up and notices me.

"Much better. I feel a little underdressed," she says.

"You'll be fine. I don't think any of the blood will end up on you."

TRIGGER FINGER

"You ride?" I ask Rebecca as I mount the motorbike.

"Once or twice," she says, hesitantly. "Wouldn't a taxi be . . . um, more relaxed?"

I hand her the helmet. "I've found it wise to manage my own transportation and escape routes."

She nods bravely. "Well, this sounds exciting." She slides the helmet over her head.

I start the motor, and she climbs on behind me and wraps her arms around my waist. I can smell the hotel soap on her skin and conditioner in her hair. Something tells me she's been traveling for longer than a couple of days.

I pull us into the dense Bangkok traffic and start weaving through the cars, bicycles, mopeds, and motorcycles that shove their way through the streets like very urgent and (mostly) polite bees.

I have no intention of letting Rebecca know my actual plans. Right now, I want to make a good show of attempting to chase down leads, then hit a dead end and hope she either loses interest or reveals something about her true intentions.

I have a series of escalating situations I want to put her through. The point at which she decides to jump off will let me know if she's a thrill-seeking dilettante or a real player in this game.

One of the tests they do at the Summer School is to see how far you're willing to go to get a job done. While a mindless assassin who'll kill an innocent person at the drop of a hat on orders may seem like the perfect soldier, they're not. Those personalities are the most likely to run amok on you at the worst moment.

Even the ideal drone pilot who drops munitions on Middle Eastern villages while sitting in an air-conditioned trailer on a military base in Nevada has a deeply developed conscience. The best ones feel like they're making decisions that will broadly benefit humanity—whether the intel they're given is accurate, and whether they're causing more good than bad, are separate questions—but the key component is that they feel like they're doing their work for good, not that they get any kind of personal joy from it.

Some researchers have even gone as far as to hook up penile plethysmographs to remote warfighters and see how excited they get when dropping bombs. A little too much excitement and this pilot might be as apt to fire missiles at friendly targets as at the enemy.

At Summer School, you're trained to think on your feet and make snap judgments to complete your missions. The school wasn't looking for sociopaths; they were training problem-solvers. That said, our more "unconventional" training was conducted in other countries.

To "graduate" from Summer School, I had to yank a known low-level drug dealer off the street and interrogate him in the back of a van until he gave me the name of a supplier. This had nothing to do with stopping narcotrafficking. It was meant to test how far I'd go.

I heard about some recruits who went too far. They washed out of the program, but I seriously doubt they were simply cast aside.

I need to see how far Rebecca is willing to go in order to figure out who she really is.

I weave us past a bus and swing the motorcycle to a quick stop in front of the Z-Speed Internet Café, four blocks away from xQuadrant's apartment.

"An internet café? Need to check your Hotmail account?" she asks.

I don't know if she's playing ignorant or doesn't understand how widespread internet cafés are in Southeast Asia. While almost everyone you'll meet has a smartphone filled with chat apps and other programs, gaming PCs are not commonplace possessions. People come to places like Z-Speed to play video games, not check their email. A midrange gaming laptop costs several months' worth of Thai wages, far out of reach for many young people here.

"Vik and his friends were gamers. It stands to reason they may have come here," I explain to Rebecca.

"I see."

I send a text with Vik's selfie to the number Gostler gave me back when we first met. "Let's see if we can find anyone who knows him."

"You mean just ask?"

I hold the door open for her. "You have a better idea?"

Inside the café, two long workbenches with PCs and monitors line both walls. People sit in high-back gaming chairs, some leaning forward, eyes fixed on screens, others reclined, their fingers tapping keyboard buttons or custom controllers they brought with them.

In all, I see fourteen people playing games while another ten stations sit unoccupied.

Rebecca taps me on the shoulder. "We're supposed to interrupt them?"

"*You're* supposed to interrupt them while I talk to the manager and keep him distracted," I tell her.

"All right." She walks over to a young man with bleached-blond hair, busily gaming at his rented computer.

I walk past a counter covered with microwavable ramen and curry products to an office in the back.

A man who appears to be in his early twenties is tapping away on a computer keyboard, apparently playing a game himself—although I can't see the screen. He's wearing an untucked black polo shirt with the Z-Speed logo. His name tag says JAMES. From his bloodshot eyes, I'm not sure how often he leaves his screen.

He sees me, jumps to his feet. "How can I help you?"

I move to block the doorway so Rebecca's harassment of his customers can continue uninterrupted. It's also important that I make a show of bracing the manager—in case Rebecca's watching me, which I assume she is.

"I want to know if you could help find someone."

I step into his space and hold out my phone, moving it so he has to look away from the café to follow the screen. It's a simple technique I learned by watching street magicians and pickpockets.

He squints at Vik's photo.

"Have you seen him in here? He's gone missing, and his family is trying to find out where."

James leans in and studies the photo earnestly. "No. Some of my customers wear masks. But he doesn't look familiar."

"Does anybody else work here?"

"It's my parents' business. I open and close it. So it's just me. You might want to ask the zombies out there," he says, pointing to the café. "Although they don't notice anything that's not on their screen."

"Is it true some gamers will sit in place for days?"

"There's a reason why we use plastic chairs and sell adult diapers during tournaments," he tells me.

"What are you playing?" I ask, buying Rebecca more time.

James turns the monitor toward me. On-screen is a video of a slide presentation about pneumonia next to a text editor in which he has been typing notes. "It's a game I like to call 'Can James pass the medical exam while working a full-time job for his lazy family?'"

So . . . his bloodshot eyes are from studying late, not trying to slay the Elder Dog Troll or whatever.

Someone shouts what I'm pretty sure is the Thai equivalent of "fuck off."

James looks past my shoulder. "Looks like your friend met Thimor. I should have warned you."

I turn around and see a young man with a backward baseball cap glaring at Rebecca like he's about to rip her head off.

Rebecca's clearly trying to apologize, but Thimor isn't having any of it. He throws down his gaming headset and yells a string of invective at her in Thai, then English.

"I'm sorry. I didn't mean to interrupt you," she says, holding her hands up—one still clutching her phone with Vik's photo.

James whispers to me, "His uncle's in the Mafia. Not a nice guy."

I stride over and stand chin to forehead with Thimor. "I think we're done here."

Thimor's head tilts back and his cheeks sink in as he gets ready to spit on me. Spotting this was something else they taught us at Summer School.

I grab him by the throat and squeeze hard. I then pull him in so our chests touch, making it difficult for him to throw a punch with anything behind it.

"Your uncle would be very upset if he found out who you were spitting at," I whisper into his ear.

I let him go. He falls back, barely catching himself before crashing into the gaming station. His eyes bore into me, but I see fear now crowding out his rage.

"I think you should leave!" James yells loudly at Rebecca and me.

"But he—" Rebecca protests.

I take her arm and turn her toward the door. I can't explain that if James doesn't scream at us to get the hell out, he may show up at his shop tomorrow and find that it's been burned to the ground.

James follows us to the exit and raises a fist at us. "Next time you come back, I'm calling the cops!"

"This is ridiculous," says Rebecca on the sidewalk.

"I'll explain," I tell her under my breath as we reach the motorbike.

Rebecca has her hands at her sides and is furious. "I barely got a word out before he started screaming," she tells me.

"Not your fault. His family's mobbed up. He's an entitled little prick. Don't let it get to you." I wait until she nods. "Did you find anything out?"

"That gamers *really* don't like to be disturbed. He could have been stabbing me to death and no one else in there would have noticed or cared. What about you?"

If Rebecca's smart, and I have no reason to think that she's not, she's probably wondering by now whether this was a test.

"The manager didn't recognize Vik. But your run-in with that guy confirmed a suspicion."

"And what suspicion is that?"

"Everything here's connected to the local gangs. If Vik and his friends were running some kind of ransomware scam like you originally suggested, then it would be hard to believe they could pull that off without some local warlord wanting to get in on the action . . . especially if there are a lot more Thimors running around."

"Thimor?" asks Rebecca.

"The mobbed-up dickhead you started a fight with back there."

"The one whose ass I was about to kick, you mean," she tells me.

"That one. Good thing you didn't. Hopefully I didn't leave a bruise on his neck. Anyway, it stands to reason that if xQuadrant was connected to a local gang, then we should probably be looking in that direction. Especially after what we just saw."

Thimor's outburst was unexpected but a welcome addition to the drama I'm staging for Rebecca to figure out who she really is. It makes the next stop I have planned seem much less random.

I get on the motorcycle and Rebecca climbs behind me.

"Where to now?" she asks.

"If we think the local Mafia is at the center of this, then we should probably just go straight to them and ask, don't you think?"

Her response is drowned out by her helmet and the roar of the engine as I rev us into traffic.

THE FIXER

In every city there's a restaurant everyone knows is the one to go to for the best version of whatever local dish the city is known for. There's the lawyer you go to if you have a specific legal problem. The most effective emergency room to choose in a crisis. The number to call at city hall if you want to reach the person at the desk where stuff actually gets done.

Cities also have their underworld versions of these: The person you talk to if you want to find out the right or wrong massage parlor to use. Which nightclub bartender to ask about scoring narcotics. Which gym to visit if you need to hire protection for a few hours.

Bangkok is no different, and depending on what you do and who you work for, there are preferred vendors.

For Russians wanting to smuggle arms throughout Southeast Asia, there are local middlemen. The Chinese have connections to Thailand-based Chinese gangs. The US and its partners have their go-to lowlifes when they need something dirty done.

Generally speaking, the ones doing the dirty work are able to keep out of reach of the law through a combination of bribery and ensuring they don't shit in their domestic backyard.

Although I've never had to interact with George Boonma, I know his name because I saw it and the name of his company, TT&C Logistics, on a number of internal cables referencing transport contracts for agricultural equipment.

This was code for moving weapons.

Officially, TT&C was a distributor of refurbished parts for agricultural machinery. It did enough trade in that sector for it to serve as a cover for the business that Thai officials *thought* it was actually doing: selling counterfeit Adidas. But *that* was a cover for its true business: weapons dealing.

One of the best ways to hide an illegal business is to make it look like you're doing something only slightly illegal so officials don't have a problem accepting bribes. This gives you coverage and discourages them from looking too closely at the real deal.

Another alternative is to run a cover business so large and with so many partners that officials are afraid to take you down, lest they take the entire economy down with you. The skylines of Bogotá, Mexico City, and Miami are proof of how well this works.

Boonma was an asset with marginal utility and not a major player last time I checked, so I'm not terribly worried about the outcome of what happens next.

I bring the motorcycle to a stop in front of the main building in a warehouse complex near the Chao Phraya River from which Boonma runs his businesses.

To facilitate the counterfeit-sneaker trade, he runs a distribution center that imports and exports footwear. Any weapons he moves would either go straight through the port or be kept in cargo containers under rice paddies until it's time to move them.

Because Boonma is posing as a legitimate businessman doing only a slightly illicit side hustle, he has no armed guards patrolling the perimeter of the complex. I see a parking lot with only three cars and a forklift at the far end.

"What are we doing?" asks Rebecca as I park the bike around the corner from the warehouse office.

"Ever heard of George Boonma?"

"No. Who is he?"

"George Boonma is the go-to guy if you want answers about what's going on in the Bangkok underworld," I exaggerate.

Sure, Boonma knows who the key players are because he pays protection to them to leave his sweatshops alone, but he's not involved in the true Thai demimonde of sex trafficking and narcotics. I'd have better luck asking the reporter on the police beat for the *Bangkok Post*.

"He's a gangster-gangster?" asks Rebecca as she looks around the all-too-quiet shipping facility.

"Looks can be deceiving," I reply. "You can stay out here."

"No. I'm coming in," she insists. "Do you have a gun?"

"I got something better." Actually, I do have a gun, but the Thai government has strict gun laws, so the fewer people who know, the better.

I push open the door, and a petite receptionist stands up from her desk to greet us.

"Where's Boonma?" I demand.

"Do you have an appointment?" she asks politely.

"I'm making one now. Tell George that his Uncle Sam from Langley is here to speak with him."

Rebecca's eyes dart toward me at the outrageous statement.

"I'm sorry—" the receptionist starts to say, but I wave her off.

"Now, please."

She picks up her phone and dials, then says something in Thai.

Still holding the receiver in her hand, she says to me, "I'm sorry but Mr. Boonma cannot take visitors right now."

"Tell him he won't have time for visitors if the Department of Special Investigation starts digging up his rice paddies in Nakhon Pathom." I stare her down, tapping a toe.

She speaks into the phone again.

"Is this wise?" whispers Rebecca. "What if they have guns?"

"And risk killing CIA agents?" I reply under my breath.

"We're not CIA agents," she whispers back.

"They don't know that."

"I'm sorry for the confusion, Mr. Sam. Please follow me," says the receptionist.

We follow her through a side door and down a small corridor. The interior is dimly lit and has ornate wallpaper on the walls and a small fountain at the end.

She opens a door to the right of the fountain, and we enter an office crowded with filing cabinets and reeking of cigarette smoke. Boonma is standing behind his desk dressed in a white collared shirt with the sleeves rolled up to his elbows. He's in his midsixties, skinny as a rail, and has thinning gray hair.

"Thank you, Kamon," says Boonma. "Please sit down."

I make a show of leaning on the chair back and staring Boonma down before taking my seat. Rebecca perches on the edge of hers, worrying what I'll do next.

Boonma leans back and stares at us both. "I have to say, I'm very confused about why you're here."

"We're here because of three missing software developers. They went by the name xQuadrant. Now they're missing, along with nearly a million dollars of our money," I explain.

"I'm sorry to hear about that. But what does that have to do with me?"

"Because nothing happens here without you knowing about it. We suspect they were working for gangsters and crossed the wrong people. We don't care about that. We just want our money back."

"I think you have me confused for someone else," says Boonma. He looks in Rebecca's direction, hoping she can make sense of it.

"George Boonma. Import-exporter of footwear. Which is a cover for selling counterfeit goods. I think we have the right guy," I tell him.

"Clearly, you are mistaken." He begins to reach for his phone.

"You can call your contact at the RTP, but that won't help you. Right now, my asset at the *Los Angeles Times* is ready to run a story about the Thai counterfeit trade with your name on it and send the details to the attorneys at Adidas."

Boonma pulls his hand back. "I'll sue you for defamation."

"It won't be my name on the byline and lawsuits. Either way, I'll have this place crawling with government trademark-enforcement agents before your lawyer picks up the phone. The people you're paying protection money to will shut you down so fast your head will spin because they'll want to make sure that it ends here. Chances are, they'll find some narcotics and make their job easier and throw the lawyers off the scent."

"There's nothing to find here," says Boonma.

"Do you want to risk it?" I ask. "Why? When all you have to do is tell us what we want to know."

"This is absurd," he replies.

I take out my phone and dial a number, then put it on speaker. "Hello?" says a woman's voice on the other end.

"Krysta, this is Brad. You know how you've been wanting to get an interview with George Boonma for your story? I'm sitting across from him right now," I explain.

"Mr. Boonma, are you willing to go on the record?" asks the woman on the other end of the line.

Boonma shakes his head.

"He's not very talkative right now. Let me see if I can loosen him up." I click off. "I can kill the story right now."

Boonma is trying to figure out the situation. He's wondering how I know everything about him and whether I'm telling the truth about what I'm about to do. He also has the added dilemma of not knowing what the hell I'm talking about.

"I can give you the name of someone to talk to," says Boonma.

"I need more than that. I need to know who has my money and where I can find xQuadrant."

"I can't tell you what I don't know," he replies.

I get out of my chair and lean on his desk. "I can beat it out of you."

Rebecca leaps to her feet and puts a hand on my shoulder. "Brad. Let's let him talk."

"I'm sick of listening to people talk. I want my fucking money back, now!"

"Brad!" Rebecca shouts.

I take off my jacket and throw it into her arms, then start rolling up my sleeves. "Get out if you don't want to see this."

Boonma's hand starts to slide toward a drawer.

"I'll fucking break your arm off and shove it up your ass," I warn him.

"*Brad!* I'm calling the embassy!" Rebecca screams.

"I swear, I don't know anything," says Boonma calmly. "I can give you the name of a police captain who might know. He does me favors. Captain Phumisak. He might know. I swear."

Rebecca grabs my arm. I shrug it off. "Fine. If he doesn't, I'm blasting your name all across the newspapers, and then I'm coming back for *you*."

I yank my jacket from Rebecca's arms and exit the office, leaving her behind.

A minute later she meets me by the motorcycle as I get ready to leave without her. Her face is red and her fists are pale from clenching them so tightly.

"You pushed it too far!" she shouts.

"I don't think so," I reply. "You were ready for me to tear into that punk back at the internet café."

"That's different. Enough of the cowboy bullshit! You can't go around threatening gunrunners! You'll end up dead."

I can see the realization flicker across her face as she wonders if she just said too much.

She did.

"*Gunrunners?* How would a nice girl like you know that? Especially if you had no idea who George Boonma was ten minutes ago?"

You either have to work with an intelligence agency like the CIA or one of their foreign counterparts to know Boonma's real business. Rebecca just tipped her hand.

"I fucking heard it. That's all," she says.

"Right. So the big question in my mind is, Is Boonma an asset you don't want exposed, or would revealing him cause a retaliation that would affect some other asset your side wants kept hidden?"

"I'm on your side," says Rebecca.

"Bullshit. And I could tell by the way you folded your hair into the helmet and leaned into the turns that you've spent plenty of time on motorcycles. Something tells me *you* were the one following me the other night when the goon squad tried to track me down." I wait for her to respond to that.

"Brad . . ."

"Not interested." I start the bike, spin the back tire, and peel out, leaving her behind.

In my rearview mirror, her eyes bore into my back as I speed away.

QUADRANT

I'm in a seedy motel in a part of Bangkok where Western men use fake names and pay in cash to avoid awkward conversations with their wives or company accountants. On the other side of the wall, I can hear a low-life talking to two local women I saw him stumble into the lobby with.

"What's that sound?" asks Don Larian from his end of the video call.

"Some dirtbag exploiting the locals," I reply.

I sent Don a folder with all the images I'd captured on my phone. I didn't tell him much else because I needed his fresh perspective.

"The apartment was constructed in the late 1990s. They didn't have that kind of concrete until the Chinese started building plants at scale. The mats are the typical ones you'd see college-age kids sleeping on in a place like that," says Don.

"Anything else?" I ask.

"I don't know. What are you looking for?"

"I don't know either. That's why I'm asking you."

"Well, you haven't given me much to work on," he replies sharply.

"You know, that supercomputer in the basement of the NSA can't be *this* difficult to work with. Cost be damned."

"That hurts. So just so we're reasonably on the same page, you're trying to find out who killed your acquaintances and why, correct?" asks Larian.

"Basically."

"I'm looking at the photos of the bullet impacts. These appear to be the kind of slugs that fragment to limit ricochets. Even you probably noticed that."

"Even me," I reply. "I also pulled one out of the wall. It's not a standard munition."

"Which means professionals. Either for hire or some tactical unit. From the photos you took in the morgue, the victims were questioned. It looks like one of them had a gun fired near his head at close range. Probably to scare him into talking. How long you think the whole altercation took?"

"Eight minutes," I answer.

"Definitely professionals. Why not take one of the kids with them?" he asks.

"Well, they took parts of one," I reply. "My guess was they didn't want to get caught with a kidnapped victim."

"That suggests they weren't a police or military unit," says Larian. "Otherwise, they wouldn't have cared about getting caught. They could have just abducted or arrested them."

"Unless a police or military unit wanted to make it look like a professional hit," I offer.

"Fair point. Hmm. This is interesting. We're getting into 4D chess now."

"I'm hoping to simplify it to tic-tac-toe."

"Tell me more about Rebecca Gostler," says Larian.

"I was hoping you could. All I know is what I saw online. Everything she told me is suspect. Have you found out anything about Theocrates?"

"No. It has enough legitimate clients to be real. Of course, after the Office of Personnel Management data breach and SolarWinds hack, a number of agencies started creating completely off-the-books boutique groups that hire outsiders and keep their names off anything connected to the government.

"And there's the fact that the Russians, Chinese, Qataris, and Iranians have been financing legitimate-looking American consulting firms to do industrial espionage," he continues. "Most of the people working for them have no idea who their real employers are. Rebecca Gostler could think she's working for the good guys while actually working for the bad ones."

"You just called the United States the good guys," I inform him.

"I'm grading on a curve. Anyway, did you press her for more information?"

"No. I was too busy peeling out and making a dramatic exit."

"That must have shown her."

"We'll see. I need your contact for Bangkok. Who's the current station chief right now?"

"The official one? Just look at the US embassy staff list and follow the usual rotation pattern. For the unofficial one, I can tell you where to probably find him or her. But I don't have a name."

"Okay. I'll manage. So the photos? Nothing else?"

"Maybe if I have time to think about it."

"I'm probably going to get kicked out of this country sooner than later. Time is not something I have a lot of. What does your intuition say?"

"My intuition?" scoffs Larian. "Do you think this is some kind of Spidey-sense? Am I some kind of tea-party psychic to you that gets vibrations? No, Bradley. This is on you. You didn't even get photos of the bathroom!"

"What for?"

"Where do you think they sawed off the head and hands? Nobody wants to step in that much blood."

Of course. I never even thought about that.

"What would that tell you if I had photos?" I ask.

"Can you get them?"

"Not now. In fact, I think I watched all of the evidence being scrubbed away." *Damn, was that old lady playing me or was I playing her?*

"The position of the body could tell us how many people were in there. If there were more than two besides the victim, then someone else was calling the shots," says Larian.

"And that would mean it was a hired team with the person who hired them directing the action," I fill in.

"Maybe your lady friend," adds Larian.

I should have taken photos of the bathroom.

"Next time, you're coming with me," I tell him.

"Fat chance. I'm pretty sure you're going to be victim number five. I don't want to be victim number six," says Larian.

"Number four. I'd be victim number four," I point out.

"I thought number four was number four," he replies.

"What victim number four?" I'm a bit confused. "I showed you the morgue photos. Three victims."

"I thought you didn't get a chance to get a photo of the other one," says Larian.

"What other victim? We had three bullet holes."

"Plus the guy killed in the shower," Larian replies.

"I assumed they dragged his body there and sawed off the head, no?"

"Oh. That might be the case. But there are six mats total, two for sitting. Four people slept there; they used the three blue mats and the yellow one for sleeping. The yellow one looks like a sitting mat because of the color, but if you look at the thickness, you can tell."

I pinch and zoom on the photos of the mats in my album. Larian is right.

"See the concave depression in the middle? Side sleepers, all of them. The sitting mats have butt impressions. Four people were living in that apartment. I assumed you knew that. You know . . . the name and all."

"What name?" Again, I'm not following.

"xQuadrant? Get it? A quadrant has four sections. An *X* has four sections as well. It sounds like the name a group of four teenagers would give themselves. I thought you already knew that," he says again.

"Um . . . no."

"Also, did you bother taking close-up photos of the shoes?" he asks.

"No. They were in a pile in the corner," I reply.

"I can see at least eight pairs of sandals lying around. Four are the same brand."

Damn.

"Wait a second . . ."

Footwear.

I start zooming into all the corners of the apartment.

For heaven's sake, I'm an idiot.

Sneakers.

"You didn't find the Nikes from Vik's photo, did you?" asks Larian after a long silence.

"No."

"And they weren't in the morgue with the other clothing?"

"They were not," I reply.

"Then my money is that the headless victim isn't Vik. And that means . . ."

"Vik could still be alive." I feel an electric wave pass through my body at the realization.

"Exactly. And if your new lady friend is still sniffing around, that means she and whoever else she's working with thinks the same thing."

"Thanks, Don, I gotta run."

I didn't realize there was a ticking clock, but its alarm is about to go off, and I'm terribly far behind.

HEAD SHOT

I'm out of breath by the time I reach the arena. People shove past me as the sound of the announcer's voice echoes across the parking lot. Muay Thai matches are nightly events all over Bangkok, but this is one of the bigger fights with national stars. Lamborghinis and Range Rovers have parked up front with low-level henchmen watching them while their gangster bosses are inside making bets and closing deals.

Besides the criminal element, politicians, singers, actors, and a general cross-section of Thai culture come to headliner fights to socialize.

I'm here to find one man. I don't know his name or what he looks like, but it's a good bet he'll be here on a Friday night because it's the best place to meet someone out in the open and have nobody notice. It's also the perfect place to observe the country's social structure and key players.

The man I'm looking for is the CIA station chief. Not the obvious one that you can tell from looking at the embassy roster, but the shadow chief. The one who doesn't set foot inside the consulate or meet with staff.

This one has a normal spy job that allows for him to wander around and not get noticed.

Previously, the CIA liked using journalists and doctors as cover professions. But pretty soon everyone else caught on. Now the station chief is more likely to be a businessman dealing with something that explains why he spends a lot of time near the airport and ports.

He also needs to be able to meet with different contacts and hold his own version of "office hours" to get intel or give instructions to assets. While a lot of that can be done via text, it's good policy to make certain the person at the other end is actually the person you recruited.

The taxi drivers, hotel clerks, and other ordinary people he deals with don't know he's CIA. They might think he's a computer salesman who wants to know if prospective clients have checked into a hotel or a foreign attorney doing background checks. There are a thousand different covers you can use that don't spell out CIA or whatever agency you work for.

I make my way to the ticket booth and drop enough bills on the counter to give me an all-access pass.

I'm pretty sure I'll find who I'm looking for in the cheap seats, but he might have business with the sort of people you find ringside.

As I enter the arena, a modern facility lit up with LEDs and light panels splashing along the walls, I worry for a moment that I might be at the wrong place. This place feels too clean. Too corporate.

When I spot a Thai general in civilian clothes sitting next to a suited Chinese national ringside, I realize I'm in the right place.

A lithe boxer in yellow trunks throws a kick at his opponent that lands so hard I can feel my own teeth rattle.

I've had to face off against trained Muay Thai boxers, and it's not fun. My only hope was to close the gap between us as quickly as possible and use brute strength to bring them down.

I hang back in the corridor on the middle level and watch the crowd. Thirty years ago, I'd look for another white face, but chances are the CIA station chief is an ethnic Thai. He likely grew up in an American city like Fresno and was recruited out of an Ivy League college.

That's one of the recruitment advantages America has over most other countries: we have plenty of Americans who look like the nationals we spy on. The disadvantage is that our trusting nature makes it easy for first-generation spies to secretly become double agents.

The person I'm looking for is going to be seated in an aisle so he can move around. He'll probably get up several times so he can intercept people between the arena and the concession stands or the bathroom, then come back to watch the social pageantry ringside.

Besides sitting on the perimeter and always having food or a drink in hand, he probably won't be eating it. He'll sit down with a beer, pretend to take a few sips, set it under his seat, and then leave it there.

In an arena like this, which has a heavy Chinese presence as well as visitors from the Middle East and everywhere else, he won't be alone. He'll have one or more spotters keeping an eye on him and sending texts about who's here and who they're talking to.

The lookouts will be sitting in the middle of the crowd. They're the ones who're watching the audience, not the match.

Aside from the lookouts, he'll have at least two security personnel lurking around the corridors, ready to get him out of here if something goes down, but not in a position where they could get stuck in a stampede.

Some of them will probably be white. If the unit is well run, they'll all have day jobs and only see each other here and for special operations.

The security personnel should be the easiest to spot. They'll be packing about fifty pounds of muscle and dressed in loose-fitting clothes to conceal their weapons.

I make a trip around the outer area of the arena where the concession stands are and look down each tunnel until I spy a young white guy who looks almost exactly the same as when I saw him walk off the field injured at an Army-Navy football game.

He's wearing a loose windbreaker and a side bag and is holding an expensive camera with a really long lens. There's a press badge around his neck.

I take out my phone and do a search for English-language coverage of Thai kickboxing at this arena. I find photos and articles by "Doug Riggsly." There's no image of him, but the pictures look like what you'd take from his vantage point and with that camera.

I can't find any other mention of Riggsly online outside of the articles. It's a thin cover, but normally sufficient for someone whose job is snapping pics of key people.

I walk up to him and spot an AirPod in his ear. I feel a bit of envy. I used to have to hide my earpiece so far inside my ear canal I needed tweezers to pull it out.

"American?" I ask.

"Yeah," he replies, then proceeds to snap a photograph to show how busy he is.

"I heard their tibias are so full of microfractures their bone density is off the charts," I offer while pretending to watch the match.

To my immediate left I see a Thai woman in the middle section aim a camera at me and take a photo.

She could be with the station chief's team or a Chinese or Thai agency watching who's talking to the Americans. Although I doubt that. If the station chief had that much coverage on him, he wouldn't be here.

The woman texts on her phone. Probably alerting everyone else.

I triangulate where she's watching from and Mr. Riggsly's position in the tunnel and spot a crowded section almost straight ahead of me.

A short Thai man wearing a sporty-looking hoodie and holding two phones is texting on one of them.

The woman looks at hers, then covers her mouth to speak.

Mr. Riggsly is staring through his camera but aiming at a currently empty ring as he listens to what she's saying.

A moment later he speaks under his breath while still holding the camera to his eye. "There's a seat for you in section 22, seat 2."

"I guess I've been spotted," I reply.

"That's an understatement."

TRIPLE THREAT

"Mr. Trasker," the station chief says under his breath as I take the seat inside to his left.

"And who do I have the pleasure of speaking to?" I ask.

"We'll decide after you answer a few questions," he replies.

"What kind of questions?"

"The kind that can either lead to you walking out of here on your own two feet or unconscious and accompanied by my security team," he says impassively while still facing forward.

"You mean 'Doug Riggsly,' a.k.a. Parker Donaldson, the former Navy running back? Doesn't he have a bad right knee? I'd go after that first."

"I'd like to see you try. Although I wouldn't go for the knee. They patched it up well enough for him to make it through SEAL training," he tells me.

"He kind of stands out, regardless."

"When they assigned him to me, they said nobody here paid attention to American football. But none of that's relevant. Why are you here?"

"The short answer is that a company my boss invested in is located in Bangkok. I came here to find out if they embezzled money from her. Now it looks like they were killed." I pause for that to sink in. "The only thing more offensive to my boss than stealing from her is killing the people she's doing business with."

"And what would you do if you found the people who killed them?" asks the chief.

"Make sure they are brought to justice and get a fair trial," I reply.

"Right. Because that's your reputation. These dead friends of yours—are they the reason why I have more Russians and Chinese spies running around than usual?"

"Possibly. I've heard the victims were up to everything from scamming venture capitalists to running ransomware attacks. It's hard to know what they did and who they pissed off," I admit.

"So, if they're dead, why am I still seeing a lot of strange faces?" asks the chief.

I decide to let loose a detail he either already knows or is irrelevant. "That's the thing. I just found out they might not all be dead."

"Interesting twist."

"I was wondering if they might be connected to you and your friends in the Agency."

"I'd break protocol and say yes if I thought it would get you to leave the country, but I know you wouldn't believe me and just sneak back in here dressed as an old nun."

My reputation does precede me. "That was a one-time thing. Okay, tell me this." I take out my phone and show him a photo of Rebecca. "You know her?"

"She's not one of mine," he replies.

"That's not a denial."

"Let me put it this way: I never saw her face until someone who is important to our interests here sent us security footage of you and her terrifying said person," the chief explains.

"I was trying to smoke her out," I tell him.

"By ruining an asset we took years to develop?"

"He seemed generic to me."

"The world has moved on since you left. Things have changed. There are different players. Motives and methods aren't what they were when you were relevant."

"Well, you have my apologies."

"What will it take to get you out of Thailand?" he asks.

"I'm not so sure you want me out just yet. If you don't know why the Russians and Chinese are lurking around more than usual, it stands to reason that having me poke around might get you the answers you want sooner than later."

"Or cause an incident that gets me fired." He sighs. "You still haven't given me a good reason to not have you deported. There are plenty of mercenaries running around here as it is."

"Such as?"

"This is Thailand. It's a retirement village for hired sadists like you who want to spend their golden years in cheap vice. There are hundreds of you. Too many to name."

"Name a few," I request.

He shakes his head.

"Okay, name one," I ask.

"All right. He could just be here taking advantage of the local nightlife. He came in on a valid passport, so there's no reason to think he's doing anything other than taking a vacation. He's been doing legitimate private security for over a decade. But having a guy like him here makes me almost as nervous as having you here."

"Who?"

"Dustin Conover. You know him?"

"Yeah, I know of him." I make my response sound as casual and disinterested as possible—which is the exact opposite of how I feel.

I know all about Conover. He was one of the Summer School rejects who washed out and disappeared to wherever guys like him end up.

The last time I saw his name was in the Philippines, about a year before I decided to quit. I'm not saying he was the reason, but guys like that certainly weren't a reason to stick around.

I'd been working for several months in the Philippines posing as a network administrative consultant for an American shipping company in Manila. I was part of an operation that was trying to figure out how telephone communications from American businesses based there showed up in a hack of a Chinese web server.

The popular theory was that the Chinese were running an operation of listening in on cell phones and our landlines that connected the towers. We had a good idea how you could pull it off but no idea who exactly was doing it.

The operation wasn't being run out of the Chinese embassy, we knew that much. We had a pretty good idea of everything that went on inside there. Ever since Pearl Harbor, the United States has gone to great efforts to make sure they really understand the state of security in strategic Pacific territories.

The Chinese operation was sophisticated and would have required several dozen people. It had to be run from some cover company that didn't look suspicious on the surface.

The best way to hide an operation like that is to run a normal business and have your agents do day-to-day work while carrying out their espionage. One way to know if you're dealing with a real company or a fake one is to reach out to their human resources department. If they don't have one and all of their competitors of a similar size do, then it's a bit suspicious.

We concluded that an operation this sophisticated had to be run by a Chinese spymaster who came up through the Cold War studying American and Soviet methods.

Back then, the Chinese were still trying to pass themselves off as the friendly superpower that wanted to get along with everyone. Americans were still cool, and Chinese companies would hire a few token "white monkeys," Caucasian Americans, to show how diverse and hip they were. It was mostly for show but also a way to counter racism pointed in their direction.

Chinese companies would send their white monkeys to make introductions with Western firms. They usually wouldn't have any actual power, but because they were Anglo, they could get the real dealmakers into the room.

I was going to provide consulting to a Canadian firm in the Philippines while I was circulating my résumé to all the companies I could find that might be the secret Chinese operation.

This allowed me to visit the lobbies of a dozen different Chinese firms and speak to their recruiters. Most were polite when they interviewed me and didn't let on that I was out of the running the moment they met me because I was too old.

One firm was different. Anglo-East Power Supply sold transformers and generators for cellular towers. They were a division of a well-established Chinese firm that had its roots in a British utility company that existed before the Boxer Rebellion began in 1899.

When I entered AEPS, the first thing I noticed was the locks on the door. They weren't the typical kind you found in other Filipino businesses. The same for the security cameras. These were encased in metal housings and were far more numerous.

I had to go through two layers of security. There was an outer lobby with an armed guard and an inner lobby that I had to be buzzed through.

Most of the other offices were a bunch of cubicles in a barely air-conditioned warehouse.

To most visitors, this probably didn't stand out. It wasn't that different from what you'd find in an American technology company in the Philippines. But having visited so many Chinese firms, it stood out to me.

My interview was peculiar too. I spoke to a pleasant young woman named May, who was in her midtwenties and had excellent English. Accompanying her was an older woman who barely spoke English and was introduced to me as Ms. Zhang, vice president of human resources. She studied me intently throughout the interview.

What stood out the most for me, like the excessive security, was the utter contempt the older woman had for me. I've seen this before in certain Chinese people I've met. They tend to be government hard-liners who came up through schools where they teach you that the West is corrupt and Americans the most despicable of all—which, according to my late son, is not that different from what you're taught on certain American campuses.

I'm sure my Chinese government counterparts have experienced the same contempt from people not that different from me, but you won't make it far in American business with an anti-Chinese attitude so readily visible.

Now, an American-hating hard-liner in a Chinese overseas company isn't an oddity. It's basically a requirement. For a company like Anglo-East Power Supply, they're likely to have at least one or more Chinese Communist Party–affiliated members on their staff. For a telecom company, several of them would be active members of the People's Liberation Army.

But when you put all of it together, AEPS was my primary suspect. While I was answering May's questions and trying awkwardly to charm Zhang, I was looking at the items around May's office, learning more about her.

She had a Shanghai Disney picture frame with a photo of her and who I presumed was her mother on her desk. She was dressed in a 1950s-style skirt. There was also a retro record player on the filing cabinet behind her. A reprint of a Benny Goodman album was propped up against the wall.

I was pretty sure I had everything I needed to know about her.

May ended my interview politely, and Zhang gave me a forced smile that was intended to show her disdain for the useless American, and we parted ways.

I "accidentally" ran into May a week later at a swing-dancing club in Manila.

She was delighted to run into me and very happy to hear that I'd found a job at another company. She confided in me that AEPS wasn't a fun place to work.

May was delightful and filled with curiosity. She was the kind of person that made me hopeful about the future of China, before they began receding from the world.

I listened to her talk and genuinely enjoyed her company—even if it was part of the job. I filled the role she wanted me to play—the older platonic confidant she could safely flirt with.

Two weeks later, she told me that she had something important to tell me and wanted to know if I had any contacts at the American embassy.

I told her I would look into it.

Two days later she was dead.

Zhang and several other employees of AEPS had left the day before. May was seen getting into a car with two Westerners and found in a dumpster with her throat slit a day later.

In the debrief I was told there was nothing I could have done. She was killed because they knew she wouldn't go willingly back to China. To cover their tracks, they hired an outside professional to murder her.

The killing was a vindictive act of retaliation for upsetting a long-running and key intelligence-gathering operation.

All we had left was a list of potential suspects who were in Manila at that time. At the top of the list was Dustin Conover. His flight out of the Philippines departed three hours after May was murdered.

We couldn't prove anything. But I drew my own conclusions.

"Who's Conover working for?" I ask the chief while we both pretend to watch the fight.

"I didn't say he was working for anyone. I just said we spotted him at the Bangkok airport coming into the country on a travel visa."

"What were you told when you asked about the extra company in town?" I ask.

"That's confidential information," the chief replies.

"I'll take that to mean 'nothing.' Which, if you're a smart guy, you know means that there's something here but they're not telling you. Maybe they're cutting you out. Or they don't trust you. I doubt any of that would sit well with you."

"My gut tells me to sit this one out. It's probably a local matter. The Russians and Chinese could be working for the Bratva and the Triads respectively. They may not be taking orders from Moscow and Beijing. It might be industrial espionage. It might be a coincidence." He shrugs.

"And what do your Thai contacts tell you?" I ask.

"They say it's a low-level gang-related matter. Nothing that affects the interests of the United States."

"Low level?" I take from my pocket the plastic bag that contains the bullet fragments I pulled from the wall and show it to him. "How many Thai gangsters do you see running around using ammunition like this?"

The chief glances down at the bag in my palm. "Damn it."

"Do Thai special ops use these?"

"Maybe. Definitely not the Royal Thai Police tactical units. They use some Chinese shit that's got no stopping power."

"Any idea who would know?"

"Are you kidding me? The guy I'd ask? You just scared the hell out of him back at his shoe warehouse. Maybe you should have thought about asking him that instead of trying to show off for your lady friend."

"I was trying to—"

"Yeah, yeah. Find out if she's the real deal. Whatever you have to tell yourself. Anyway, I know our teams don't use anything like that, if that's what you're asking. The new rounds completely disintegrate in water or soft tissue. It makes forensics a real bitch—which is the point," says the chief.

"Yeah. Who would ever think the United States would buy the most expensive overkill ammunition possible, which probably costs a hundred bucks a round."

"You might be surprised. The Qataris and some other countries have started contracting with private militias that have gear that makes ours look positively archaic. We might spend more, but theirs is more up to date. I'm surprised a guy like you hasn't gone to work for one of them."

"Working for our side was morally ambiguous enough," I tell him.

While the domestic militaries of countries like Qatar and Saudi Arabia aren't up to the professional standards of the United States, they've found, like Russia, sometimes the best solution is to hire on the open market. It also provides plausible deniability.

Modern warfare is even more complicated than people realize. Suppose you're the president of the Central African Republic and you're facing threats from all sides, including domestic rebels. Managing a competent army and trusting it are difficult enough. You also have to pay them. While Russia might like to see you win, they're not about to send in their uniformed troops. But if someone shows up at Bangui Airport in a G5 jet wearing a $5,000 suit and hands you a contract that says if you sign over certain mineral and resource rights you can have an entire division of PMC Wagner mercenaries help keep you in power, it's hard to say no.

Ever since Wagner got caught up in the Ukraine and Putin's checks started bouncing, there's been a power vacuum for mercenary forces on the global stage. Some of the better-trained, better-disciplined, and better-equipped ones were able to step up and fill the void.

The chief's surprise that I didn't take a job with one of these groups is based in part on his perception of my complete lack of morality, plus the fact that some of those entities pay really, really well.

While there are plenty of seasoned combat fighters from special tactical units to recruit, guys like me are a little rarer. Anyone can claim they're an "intelligence analyst" who worked overseas in undercover roles. But guys who know which people *should* be bodies to be buried are hard to find.

I wouldn't call Dustin Conover a tactician like me, but his presence here right now can't be a coincidence. Odds are he's working for a mercenary unit.

The three big questions are which one, who hired him, and why.

INTERCEPTION

Although finding out why Conover is in Bangkok is critical, the more urgent need is to locate Vik before anyone else does—especially Conover.

I have to assume Vik's on the run and in hiding, unless the Royal Thai Police have him in protective custody. If that's the situation, it would explain some of the mystery about the case but not why Bangkok is still filled with people trying to find him. Being in police custody should in theory mean the game is over. But I don't even know what the game is, so who knows?

I'm back in xQuadrant's neighborhood, trying to retrace the steps that Vik might have taken if he escaped being killed like his friends. Searching over aerial maps and property records can only take you so far.

Kiet Chantapong, the owner of the honey kiosk in front of the apartment building, eyes me with suspicion the moment I pull up on my motorcycle.

I give him a friendly greeting and ask if he speaks English. He shakes his head, so I pull out my phone with the translation app.

"I'm trying to find out what happened to the people who lived there," I explain as I point to the apartment building.

He waves his hand in front of his face, indicating that he doesn't want to talk. Other than Tommy's grandfather, this man's the closest I have to an eyewitness, so I'm not ready to let him drop the matter so quickly.

"If I buy some honey, will that make a difference?"

He looks around to see if anyone is watching, then hits the off button on my screen. "How much?" he asks in English.

There are about twenty boxes on the table. "Everything." I set a wad of *baht* on the lid in front of me. "I'll need it delivered."

"Okay. One question," he agrees.

"Let's go for three."

He makes a guttural sigh.

"How many gunshots did you hear?" I ask.

"Four. Bang. Then a long pause. Then bang. Pause. Then bang-bang."

"How many men entered and how many left?"

This question makes him visibly anxious. "Four entered."

"And left?"

"I was hiding by then."

"Okay. Did you see anyone else running from the building? Like him?" I show Chantapong the photo of Vik.

"Nice boy. No."

"You knew him?"

"Yes. He bought honey and had it sent to his mother," he replies.

"His mother? She lives in Bangkok? Where?"

Chantapong waves away the question. "I don't know."

He's lying, but I decide not to push. I'll try to find that out later.

So, four men enter and who knows how many leave. Possibly without Vik, but nobody saw anything I can use to confirm that.

"Thank you. I'm going to leave my card in case there's anything else you want to tell me."

"Where send honey?" he asks.

"Oh yeah. Let me give you an address," I reply, then write the location of Boonma's warehouse complex. "Please tell him it's from Mr. Sam."

Thais aren't very big on security cameras yet, so I wasn't able to find anyone on either side of the street with footage of what happened on the day of the hit.

The only cameras I could find in that vicinity are at the 7-Eleven where I spoke to Tommy, the scooter mechanic's grandson.

Mr. Jiraprapasuk, the manager of the corner 7-Eleven, is friendly and as curious as I am about what happened.

"You weren't here that day?" I ask between bites of toasted sandwich.

"No. Manop was here. He said the police asked him what he saw, then told him not to say anything. So of course he told me," says Jiraprapasuk.

"And what did he tell you?"

"He heard four loud bangs and that was it."

"Did anyone come running here? Maybe for safety?" I ask.

"No."

I show him Vik's photo. "What about him? You ever see him in here?"

"Vik? Yes. Nice kid. They all were. Michael, Al, and Sonny," he says.

"You knew them?" This is the first time I've spoken to anyone who even knew their names.

"Yes. They'd come in here all the time to buy food. They'd read the manga and just hang out. Great customers and good kids."

"Did they talk about what they did for work?"

"Computers, I guess. Sometimes they had their laptops with them. They get a snack and sit outside typing. They spent money here, so I didn't mind."

"Can you tell me anything else about them?"

"Vik was the talkative one. Sonny likes to read. Historical novels. Old English-language books. *Wuthering Heights*, that kind of thing. He always had a paperback with him. I think he used it to talk to foreign girls."

"What about family or friends?"

"I don't remember anything. I think they all met in high school here."

"What about last names?"

"They paid in cash. Except . . . one time Sonny used a debit card. The last name was Suntorn Rattanakosin. Same last name as my brother-in-law. It was weird. Vik gave him a look when he handed me the card. I wasn't sure if it was stolen. Vik grabbed it back and handed me cash. That's when I thought maybe they were doing something a little illegal, but they always paid in cash and I never had a problem. I didn't even think about that until now," he adds.

"What about camera footage? Do you still have the security recordings from that day?"

"Yes. I looked at it after Manop told me what happened. You can only see the blur of a black car. That's it," he explains.

"I'd like to see it, if possible." There are image algorithms that can extract details from blurry footage—especially if the blurring came from a predictable cause like a moving vehicle.

"Sure. One second."

Jiraprapasuk walks into the back room and returns less than a minute later. He sets an SD card down on the table. "Here, you can have this if you just pay for a new one on the shelf over there."

"Sure. That was really quick," I reply.

"I already made this for the other American. She hasn't come back for it yet," he explains.

"The other American?"

"Yes. A very attractive woman with dark-red hair. Do you know her?"

I show him Rebecca's photo. "Is this her?"

It takes him only a moment to recognize her. "Yes. That's her."

"When did she come in here?" I ask.

"Five days ago," says Jiraprapasuk.

"Five *days* ago?" I fail to hide my surprise.

That was a day before I spoke to her at Hello World in Las Vegas, a fifteen-hour flight from here. Rebecca Gostler has been a very busy woman.

If she already knew where Vik and his friends were based, then why was she at Hello World?

I'm going to have a lot of questions for her if we meet again.

LYING LOW

I'm sitting at a noodle bar near a busy intersection close to where Vik and his friends lived. I messaged Morena and Kylie with a general update and am waiting for their call.

Kylie's idea about hiring a firm that traces crypto scammers was a solid lead. More traditional PIs wouldn't be as technically savvy.

Thailand has a large number of expats who've come here to escape the wrath of their own governments or disgruntled business partners and investors. During and after the crypto boom, this only escalated.

From crypto bros doing rug pulls to firms outright stealing from their clients, Thailand is in the top five places where these assholes end up. Number one being Dubai, but that's another story. Everything you've heard about it is true and much worse.

As I sit here eating what may be the best pad thai I've had in recent memory, I'm amazed by the fact that Vik is still alive and out of reach of the various parties trying to get him. This is a remarkable accomplishment.

I know from personal experience how hard it is to lie low—and I was trained for it.

In the months leading up to an Eastern European conflict, I was posted in a city to map out communication junctions and key telecom personnel we'd have to bring in if we needed to preempt a coup. All hell broke loose and the consulate staff departed the country, along with the team running my cover. I had to spend three weeks with no money and no passport avoiding the secret police.

Thankfully, "Thomas Dongier," New Zealand PhD student and aspiring abstract painter, was able to couch surf his way through the arts community until he could make an exit. Playing the vulnerable Dongier, I found avoiding various attempted romantic entanglements a bigger challenge than avoiding the secret police.

According to the local private investigators that Morena hired, Vik's mom and the families of the other three boys all left their homes shortly after the shooting.

We know at least two of them took taxis to the international terminal at the airport.

This suggests two things: Vik or someone else orchestrated their escape shortly after the murders went down. And if Vik orchestrated it, he must have preplanned his and their hasty exits as a contingency.

While it's possible that Vik slipped out of Thailand on a fake passport, given the dragnet that's hunting for him, that might not have been safe or feasible—especially if the Thai government is somehow involved.

My gut tells me he's still in Thailand—maybe even Bangkok. Possibly in a safe house he had previously set up.

It's quite possible that Vik had to improvise to effect the families' escape after the fact. If that's the case, then he is an incredibly resourceful and clever thinker.

Which means I also must appreciate the fact that while Vik might lack formal training, he's cleverer than I am. Cleverer than everyone else, to be honest.

So how did he pull off his vanishing act? The easiest explanation is that he wasn't in the apartment at the time of the murders—which might imply he played a part in the massacre. But then why the manhunt? And why wait to get your mother out of the country afterward? Why get everyone else's family out too?

I open up Google Street View and use my trackpad to trace the path from the front to the back of their apartment building.

Vik might have exited out the back—but that would have meant doing a three-story jump or being a sitting duck as he tried to rappel—which would have taken time he couldn't afford.

Did he slip past them? Is there a hiding space in there nobody noticed? Is he still hiding there now?

What if . . . ?

I switch to Satellite View.

The apartment building looks the same as I recall—but I wasn't paying much attention to the roof before.

A Starlink satellite dish stands in one section, and a plastic green grass mat with what I now realize are four patio chairs covers the balance of the rooftop.

They had their own little penthouse patio up there!

But how did they get access?

I scroll through my photos and videos of the apartment and stop during the video I made of the utility closet.

Both times I was in there I felt a draft I attributed to a vent. Looking at the video now with the brightness maximized, I realize there was no vent—it was a roof access point. The Starlink cable fed through it.

I'm willing to bet there's also now a ladder on the roof that Vik pulled up behind him.

But how did he escape while the others couldn't?

Maybe they thought it was a police raid and Vik's job was to remove the servers from the closet and hide them?

That sounds plausible. Vik wasn't trying to ditch his friends; he was covering their tracks. When he heard the gunshots, he understandably ran.

But ran where?

I resume Satellite View—this time in 3D and at an angle so I can see the difference in roof heights and figure out a plausible escape route for Vik.

The most probable route would take him from roof to roof and then to the end of the block. He would have climbed down on the street opposite where the attackers were parked. If he kept going in that direction, he would come to the same one-way street where I made my escape on my moped.

And then what?

Zooming in and out and all around, I notice a municipal camera under the elevated train platform. If I could get access to that—

"Brad Trasker?" says a heavily accented voice to my left.

I look over and see two uniformed police officers making their way through the tables toward me.

I put my laptop in secure mode and close the lid.

The one with sergeant stripes is looking right at me. The corporal standing behind him looks like a yak and is reaching for his handcuffs.

This is not good.

I give them a confused smile and pretend not to realize I'm about to be arrested. As I make eye contact, my right hand with my phone drops to my side and I send a preprepared recorded message to Morena.

"How can I help you"—I eyeball the name on his uniform—"Sergeant Khamvongsa?"

"Hands up. You under arrest," he says.

I get the feeling he was reading a phonetic pronunciation of that a few minutes ago.

"What am I being arrested for?" I ask loud enough for my phone to hear.

"You come now!" he yells as he pulls out a baton.

I could probably take that from his hands before he realizes it and knock both him and his pet yak unconscious—but that would earn me a ten-year jail sentence and a fatal trip down a prison stairwell.

I decide the best policy is to go quietly and hope Morena gets my message.

I tuck my phone into my thigh pocket and swap it for my burner phone as I stand.

"Can I call my lawyer?"

Khamvongsa yanks the burner from my hand and points his baton at my face. "You call later."

I hold my hands in front of my body so they won't handcuff me behind my back. I used to be flexible enough that it didn't make a difference, but not so much anymore.

Thankfully the yak follows my lead and cuffs me with my wrists in front. I can get out of this with one of the lockpicks conveniently placed around my body.

Khamvongsa grabs my bag and laptop, and I let the yak lead me to their police car parked in the back alley . . . except it's not a police car. It's an unmarked van. Another police officer is standing by the open side door.

I turn to ask Khamvongsa if this is negotiable just as he's in the process of swinging the baton at the side of my head.

It misses my skull but clips my ear—which still hurts like crazy.

"What the hell, man!" I shout at him.

I take a second glance at the uniforms to make certain they're real. They appear fitted—but they could be well-chosen replicas. Not that their being real cops makes much difference here. They can be hired for dirty work as well.

"You working for Rebecca Gostler? I can pay more," I say to Khamvongsa as he considers hitting me again.

Yak grabs me by the neck and throws me to the floor of the vehicle. He gets in behind me and pulls a hood over my head while the other police officer helps him.

"No move!" someone screams in my ear as they take a baton to my back.

I wasn't moving, but whatever . . .

I think it's time to lay a card on the table. "Sergeant Khamvongsa, I texted my friends and told them you are the one that picked me up."

Bam! A stout whack to my head.

I try to think through my next steps carefully because two things are clear to me: this isn't an official arrest, and if I want to live, I might have to kill every man in this van.

BERSERKER

Knowing when to kill is difficult enough. The kid with an AK-47 pointed at the back of your head while you're being held hostage and driven through a Latin American rainforest might just be doing a favor for his uncle, a local bandit who makes extra money by kidnapping oil workers and ransoming them back unharmed. Or the kid might be a trigger-happy sociopath who can't wait to see your brains splattered all over the muddy jungle floor.

Sometimes it's a mix of people you want to kill and some you feel sorry for but don't have much choice.

Killing people in police uniforms—especially actual police officers—brings with it a host of problems.

We had a situation in a country that neighbors Israel where the local group of Iran-backed jerk-offs found out that a Western reporter had been working with the CIA—which should only come as a shock to anyone who hasn't read a book in the last eighty years.

Word got out that they were going to retaliate by kidnapping a random American reporter because they were apparently offended by this violation of journalistic integrity—never mind the international news-agency stringers you see riding shotgun with Hamas when they launch their terror campaigns.

To keep the back channels open and not have certain large news orgs shut down the flow of information, we had to find a way to prevent this kidnapping from happening.

Somewhere in Langley, Virginia, a genius came up with the idea to let them kidnap an undercover intelligence operative instead . . .

I kid you not. That was as far as the plan went. To keep the newspaper owners in Manhattan happy, they figured the smart move was to make sure it wasn't an actual reporter that got abducted—just some poor sap working for an obscure intelligence agency.

Time was ticking so they put the plan in action, with the idea being to figure out the details as it went.

The poor sap ended up being me. So there I was, riding around on a moped taking photos of the houses of the rich backers of the local jerk-off terrorist group and making sure everyone knew "Michael Overlook" was acting a little out of bounds.

After snapping photos of a compound at the edge of the city, I got stopped by the chief of police. He asked to see my passport and papers, then made the most perfunctory examination of them while looking me over. He had the chronic bad breath of someone treating ulcers with a noxious local remedy that smelled like eucalyptus and creosote.

Fast-forward twenty-four hours and I get a call from someone named "Ali" who wants to meet me near a discotheque.

I let the support team know, stuck my earpiece in my ear, put on my bulletproof vest and stab-proof clothing, and went five blocks from my hotel to the club. The earpiece was connected to a radio in my camera battery and another sewn inside my vest—allowing me to mostly keep in contact with my handlers.

Three blocks into my walk, I'm grabbed and thrown into the back of a van by guys in hoods. I'm not terribly worried at this point because they're not going to kill me until they record me making a video; plus, I've got a tracking beacon lodged all the way up inside me, sending a signal to what I'm told is a SEAL team waiting across the border ready to fly in and rescue me.

The one hitch is that I can clearly smell eucalyptus and creosote. I whisper this under my hood to my handlers. Big mistake.

They report this back to Langley. Someone there decides that killing the chief of police would be very bad optics and lead to riots and turn the already anti-American sentiment even more anti-American.

As I'm being driven to the outskirts of nowhere to have my head chopped off, a little voice whispers in my ear that there's a new plan. Apparently, the SEAL team's helicopter is having "mechanical issues" and they're going to ransom me back.

I could spot bullshit ten thousand miles away. There was no mechanical issue, but I'm sure they got a base mechanic to sign off on that. The plan to ransom me was wishful thinking and a convenient lie they'd tell themselves while patting one another on the back for making the really tough calls.

So I had to make a tough call myself.

I'd never fully trusted the extraction part of the plan to begin with. Even though I was told I had a team, I've witnessed bureaucrats pull back and let their own people die for political reasons—followed by press releases littered with regret and plausible deniability, like mechanical issues or operator error.

The police chief and his terrorist buddies did a good job of securing me with my hands behind my back with plastic ties and weren't taking any chances—as far as they knew.

What they didn't know was that I'd been through variations of this scenario hundreds of times at Summer School. We had vans, box trucks, and other vehicles sitting in a warehouse where we practiced close-quarters combat.

We were also taught how to create and build weapons and tools that you won't see described anywhere on the internet or in movies.

One of which I had with me. On or around my person was a version of a flash grenade that sounded an awful lot like you were being fired upon from someone outside the vehicle. This was meant to distract the itchy trigger finger of whoever had their muzzle to your skull and have everyone either lying flat or looking out the windows— directing their attention away from me and my tool that could cut through plastic cuffs in a second and free my hands for the tactical blades hidden in my shoes.

I waited a full ten minutes after I was told the rescue mission was off before triggering the flash-bang.

Before the smoke cleared, I'd slit the carotid artery of the man cowering next to me and stabbed the other man through the liver. He screamed that he'd been shot, and the police chief and the driver fired their guns out the windows at an apartment complex they thought was the source of the attack.

Killing them was easy because they were facing in the wrong direction.

The flash-bang wasn't the only incendiary on me that day. I also had a directional charge that I could set off if I were lying on the deck. It could clear a room—but also knock you unconscious if you weren't positioned correctly.

The flash-bang was the right choice for that situation. After, I used the police chief's lighter to set the van ablaze and then walked back to the hotel. I called over the radio for transportation out. Nobody responded.

Later, I found out that, once they made the call to cut me loose, they shut down all communications and pulled the team relaying my radio transmissions. Which means they pulled the plug less than ten minutes after I was told about plan B.

In an interagency postmortem, I was yelled at by the person in charge of the operation and accused of fucking everything up. I told him he should apologize before I threw him out the window.

He declined.

I was halfway around the conference room table before he had a panic attack and collapsed to the floor on all fours. Pathetic. A guy like that should never have been calling the shots.

All of that leads me to my current situation. I'm trying to decide if this is the time to go berserk and use my hidden technical devices to kill everyone and make my escape. Or should I wait a little longer to make sure that's not literal overkill?

The problem is, I'm older now. I'm not the guy I was two decades ago, who could slit throats and slash vital organs with speed and ease.

I have to play dirtier now.

I have to be quicker on the draw.

The van comes to a stop, and we're here. From the speed, drive time, and number of turns made, I know we're not more than five kilometers from where we started.

We're still in Bangkok and not some rice paddy on the outskirts, which I think is a good sign.

On the other hand, it's night now, which more or less negates their need to kill me on the outskirts of the city.

I have to take this one step at a time . . . just in case, I've got a flash-bang that looks like a pen tucked into my waistband.

I feel a kick in my ribs, and a voice, not Yak's, says, "You come here do drugs and mess with girls. You sick man. You going to be very sorry."

I hear a harsh whisper in Thai. I think that's the other man being told to shut up.

If Not-Yak is trying to make threats like that, as much as he wants to make me think I'm going to be sorry, I'm suspecting that this might not end in my death. His threats sounded like an amateur attempt to scare me.

Of course, he might not be on the same page as the others, so I shouldn't be jumping for joy. He might be a useful idiot they grabbed at the last minute.

The side door opens and a baton hits me in the back.

"You get out now," says Not-Yak.

More whispers.

From the grip, I can tell Yak has grabbed my arm. We're walking across fine dirt. It feels and smells like a construction site.

I can hear cars and mopeds in the distance, but we're in a less dense area. I can also tell that we're heading toward an unfinished building because of the echoes coming from a windowless concrete structure. I can't tell how high they are. I'm sure I could spot the location on a map, but that's not terribly useful right now.

I'm pushed up a short flight of plywood steps and onto a concrete floor. I can smell engine oil and hear the sound of generators.

Normally construction sites like this have lots of cameras. Unfortunately, the kind of people who may have hired these men probably own the construction sites and control those cameras.

I'm pushed onto a metal platform and hear a gate close. I think we're in an elevator.

I see stars and I black out.

I'm being yanked to my feet. Yak is mumbling. The side of my head hurts something awful. Sergeant Khamvongsa clearly hit me with his baton again.

I stumble, but Yak's firm grip keeps me from falling.

"Money? Baht?" I offer.

"Shut up," Sergeant Khamvongsa growls.

I can feel the wind. The city sounds different. We're higher up.

Yak pushes me toward the wind and the sound. The echo changes, and I realize I'm being walked to the edge of the open floor.

His pace slows and he stops pushing me—in fact he pulls me back a step.

I've got my flash-bang in my hand, but it's kind of useless up here. The moment it makes the first pop, Yak will push me over the edge.

I didn't get a lot of thrown-off-rooftop training at Summer School. I should write a letter and express my dissatisfaction.

"Listen to me carefully, Sergeant Khamvongsa. I can show you the sent message on my phone. My friends know you took me. They're very powerful. They'll be coming for you. I can pay you. I can pay you a lot more," I tell him.

There's silence. Just the sound of Yak's heavy breathing. I hear another set of footsteps. For a moment I think it's Not-Yak, but these steps have a certain swagger to them.

Someone else is up here with us.

Behind me a voice speaks with an American accent.

BREEZE

I recognize the voice at the first syllable. I haven't heard it in decades, but I remember it clearly. Rough, precise, and very cold.

Dustin Conover.

"The first thing you should know, Bradley, is that this man's name isn't Khamvongsa. He's in the Royal Thai Police but smart enough to know not to show his actual name when he does jobs like this. The second thing you should know is that he takes this job very seriously. He finds the idea that you think he'd double-cross me very insulting."

I feel the tip of the flash-bang pen in my hand. Maybe it won't be completely useless . . .

"If I see one flinch, Mr. Sampo here is going to throw you off the roof. Don't forget, I know your stupid little tricks too, Bradley. We learned them at the same place."

"Last I checked you flunked out," I reply.

Conover laughs. "I thought you knew how it worked. The ones that have what it takes go on to the next program. The rest, like you, are taught the 'soft stuff': how to get old queers drunk enough to give up marginally useful secrets as they fondle you. That sort of thing."

"You have a very specific and vivid fantasy about the work I do."

"Did. The work you did, Bradley. I barely recognized you when I first saw you. I couldn't believe the old man I saw stumbling through the streets of Bangkok. When they told me you were here, I was sure it was for some depraved sex-tourism thing."

"Man . . . way too specific again," I fire back.

"The jokes. That was always your tell when you were nervous. I thought they were funny, I'll be honest. I'll also be honest and say that I was amazed by how long you made it in the field."

"Dumb luck."

"Indeed. I was also glad to hear that you retired. You didn't have it in you for the long haul."

"I'm touched that you cared so much."

He steps closer so that he's just off my left shoulder. "You know they don't give a damn about us. They never did. Back in Bolivia. I heard about that. And Syria, when they pulled the whole extraction team. I kept wondering how much more you were going to put up with. But you kept it up. I figured it had something to do with being a bastard and not having your dad around. You were desperate for approval."

"Your motivational podcast sucks. Can you just shove me off the fucking building already?"

"I'm not going to kill you. At least I hope I don't have to. Just tell me what you know about Vik."

"What's a Vik?"

When a guy like Conover tells you that he's not going to kill you, he most certainly is planning to do just that.

I hear the sound of a zipper, then Velcro.

"I have a syringe for you," says Conover. "While Mr. Sampo holds you down, I'm going to inject this into your neck. It's a new synthetic that even you don't know about. Targets certain parts of your brain. I'll have a conversation with your left hemisphere while the right's asleep. It will feel like a dream, and you won't remember what you told me. But you'll have told me everything."

There are two scenarios here. The first being he wants to know what I know so that he can find Vik. The second that he wants to know how much I know so he can decide if I'm a liability.

Neither one is good. While I know very little about Vik's whereabouts, it could prove useful to Conover. Also, I have many, many other secrets I've sworn to take to the grave.

"After this just go home, Bradley. Retire. Go spend that trust-fund money. Stop trying to pretend you're something you're not."

"One professional to another, nobody believes a thing that comes out of your mouth. You never had the knack for the so-called 'soft stuff' because you're just a lying sack of shit," I reply.

Yak grabs my arm even tighter and leans in, pushing my body off-balance and my toes over the edge.

Conover chuckles. "How'd your *knack* work out for that dumb little broad back in the Philippines?"

"You move another inch toward me and that will be the last thing you ever say," I growl.

I can hear Conover's breathing pause for a moment. He's thinking about what I said.

"Sergeant, would you draw your pistol and aim it at the back of Bradley's head while I administer the shot? If he even moves a centimeter, I want you to shoot him. Understand?" says Conover.

"Understand," replies the sergeant.

Conover grabs my shoulder and presses his thumb at the base of my neck.

Fuck this.

I only have one choice now.

The sole advantage I have is that Conover has no idea what makes me tick.

I do the thing he believes is unthinkable to me.

I jump.

FREEFALL

And take Yak with me . . .

That wasn't my plan. I didn't really have a plan. I also didn't plan on treating him like a 250-pound duffel bag I was clinging to as I dropped out the back of a C-130.

Apparently, my body had a plan.

As we fell over the edge, I rolled on top of him.

The wind rushes past us. Yak lets out a high-pitched scream. I flatten my body and tuck my head against his soft form.

We crash through what I think is an aluminum roof and then hit something hard. There's a cracking sound as we come to a stop.

I feel the wind knock out of me. Yak isn't moving.

The sound of a generator is loud. I think we landed on top of it.

I pull the hood off and look up through the hole in the roof and see Conover and the sergeant looking down at me.

I raise my handcuffed hands and flip them off.

Then I black out.

❦

There's a bright light in my eyes and someone slaps me. I go to raise the flash-bang pen, but it's no longer in my hand.

My vision is filled with dark blotches as I battle unconsciousness. Before I can move properly, I'm pulled to my feet and slid off Yak's motionless body. I try to jerk my arm away from the man holding on to me.

"Get up!" he yells.

I manage to stand upright and get ready to elbow him in the jaw . . . except that it's not the sergeant or the lackey from the van. This is an older man in a white shirt and dark slacks.

He has a slight build but is stronger than he looks. He pulls me out of the shed.

"Faster," he shouts.

I have no idea how long ago I jumped off the building. But if waiting around means running into Conover again, I'll take a rain check.

I follow the man and catch a glimpse back at the skyscr—three-story apartment building.

Jesus Christ. All around the building is soft dirt. I picked the exact wrong spot to land. If it hadn't been for Yak, Conover would be stuffing my broken body into a barrel.

Shadows move in the building, and I hear the whine of an elevator.

The man leads me to a late-model Toyota and sticks me in the passenger seat.

He climbs into the driver seat, turns on the engine, and peels out. Something is familiar about his face, but I can't place it through my fog of pain and disorientation.

He doesn't look like any of the men that chased after me the night before, but I know I've seen him.

He keeps the lights off as we drive down a back alley. He makes several more turns, then finally flips them on as we enter traffic.

My back hurts. My head hurts. My arms hurt. My legs are strangely fine. Nothing is broken, but everything from the pelvis up is just plain rattled.

I feel something wet and sticky on the back of my head and reach my hand behind and feel blood.

"Not yours," says the man. "No fractures."

"Well, there's that. So . . . um, not that it makes a difference right now or will change what I do next—which will be just to sit here quietly in pain—but is this a kidnapping or a rescue?"

"That depends."

"On what?" I contemplate rolling out of the moving vehicle but decide my will to survive has its limits.

"Do you like whisky?" asks the man.

"The answer is yes, even if that's code for something horrible and disgusting that goes on here."

"No jokes. Just whisky," he says.

I don't know if he's telling me to stop making jokes or that he's not joking with me. Either way, whisky sounds amazing.

"What's your name, friend?"

"Later. Whisky first."

I respect a man with priorities. I sit back and watch the lights of Bangkok go by as he calmly guides the car through manic traffic.

Eventually we reach an area near the factories where the locals go after the late shift to eat and get drunk away from the tourist zones. It looks a little rough on the surface but is really just Thai blue-collar.

The man parks the car and comes around to my side to help me get out. I don't need much assistance but realize my legs didn't hurt because I didn't have any weight on them.

I'm able to support myself outside the car. Which is good, because it's never ideal to stumble into a bar.

The bar itself is a cinder-block shack with a Japanese whisky–branded door flap.

I follow the man inside and then collapse into a booth and study the patrons while he gets us drinks from the bar.

There're only about ten other people in here. They appear to be older middle-management types with loose ties and button-up shirts. In Japan this would be a salary-man establishment. Not a high-end bar, but the kind where you go with work friends you actually like and drink whisky while facing the reality that this is as far as you got in life.

The man returns with several shots of whisky. He pushes two glasses in front of me. One is slightly more amber than the other.

He points to that one. "Good." He points to the other. "Not as good."

I get the point. I slam the not-as-good whisky first to get the buzz going, then take a small sip of the good whisky.

He gives me a nod of approval. "First question: Why did you jump off the building? Did you think you were lower?"

"I thought it was higher. They were assholes. I couldn't stand them."

He doesn't seem amused by my answer.

I feel compelled to explain a little more. "I came to Bangkok to look for some people. They were looking for them too. They were about to force me to tell them what I knew. So I jumped. But the joke's on them—I didn't know anything they didn't already know."

"You jumped to keep a secret that wasn't a secret?"

"Yep."

"That's very noble. Very stupid. Not what I'd do. But noble." He raises his glass to me.

"My turn," I reply.

"No. Still my turn. I bought. Who were they?" he asks.

"The white guy's name is Dustin Conover. He's a piece-of-shit mercenary. The other three were working for him. But I don't know them."

"Royal Thai Police," says the man.

"I know that's what their uniforms say. But I don't know if they were actual police."

"They were. Corrupt police. But police. This Conover, who is he working for?"

"I have no idea. I thought maybe a woman I know. But I'm not sure. Who do the cops work for?"

"Anyone who pays," says the man.

"That narrows it down."

I take a sip of whisky and feel a little numb where I felt pain before.

"Mind if I make a quick call? I need to call off the cavalry before my boss has this place swarming with private security," I reply.

"Sure."

I call Morena.

"Brad? I got the message. Are you okay?"

"Mostly. Long story short, I'm fine."

"I was calling all the police stations and having the PIs look for you," she tells me.

"I'm good. I'll explain later."

"One quick thing: Did you look at the copy of Josiah Levenstein's forensic report I sent?" she asks.

"No. I've been a bit occupied."

"Understood. I just wanted to know what you thought about the towel."

"Towel?"

"The police say Josiah wrapped the barrel of the gun in a towel to minimize the noise. Would that be something an assassin would do?"

"Not a good one. He might have thought it would keep the gun from making too loud of a bang. But, no. There are better ways to muffle the sound."

I put away my phone. The man looks at me. "Wife?"

"No. Just a friend."

Something about what Morena said has me thinking. A towel is a terrible silencer—but a pretty good improvised way to minimize blood spatter and hide the fact that someone was sitting next to the victim and holding their hand with the gun inside it . . .

"Just a friend?"

"Um. Yeah. Mostly. So, enough questions for me. What's your name and why did you save me? Assuming this isn't some trick by Conover, but he's not that smart."

"You can call me Simon," he replies.

"Simon? Is there more to that?"

"That's what they know me as here," he says, indicating either the bar or this part of Bangkok or maybe this continent. I'm too sore to figure it out.

"And elsewhere?" I ask.

"Simon Srisutham," he says.

My brain is foggy but something connects. "Wait . . . Inspector S. Srisutham?"

This is the homicide detective whose name was on the sticker on the door to the xQuadrant crime scene—and the very abrupt man I spoke to by phone. I also realize he was the man sitting on the ground outside the police station who offered me a ride.

Christ. What a tricky bastard.

He tilts his glass toward me and takes a sip. "Have another. I think we have a lot to talk about."

BLOCKED

Simon, a.k.a. Inspector S. Srisutham, keeps pouring the shots, and we continue drinking and talking. It's an old interrogation technique and one I've used more than once myself. I don't find it difficult to imagine him getting a gangster drunk in a police station basement, laughing, crying about women, how his boss doesn't treat him with respect, and finally where the body's buried.

I'm on guard, but I think I have a good-enough read on Simon. He's still trying to get a read on me, and I've been pretty forthcoming about who I work for and why I'm here. I know he has a lot more information about me than he's letting on, and I have to assume he's testing me a little to see if I lie, evade, or change the topic.

"This Conover. He's not working alone?" asks Simon.

"There's always a paycheck involved for him. He's not bright enough to think up anything more complex."

"You and him have history?" Simon asks with a raised eye.

"He killed someone I knew. Let's leave it at that. Your turn. Why did I see your name on the door and was then told you were off the case? And why were you such an asshole to me on the phone?"

"I didn't know who was listening. The case." He exhales and takes a drink. "The case. The case." Simon sits back in the corner of the booth, and his eyes drift to the table. "I get a call about a shooting at the apartment. I show up about a half an hour after it happens. I see the boys there. Two in the living room and what's left of one in the bathroom.

"I have my team go to work. Take photos. Get fingerprints. Start talking to the neighbors. Usual stuff. Then Colonel Thongthai arrives. I know something is odd.

"This looked like a gang killing on the surface, but I could tell something wasn't right. The men who did this were in and out in eight minutes. Very fast. Very efficient. Then Thongthai."

"What's the deal with him?" I ask.

"He's very important. He's connected to the president. He's Thailand's top cop for terrorism."

"What did he say?"

"Not much. He said he was just there to 'observe.' But Thongthai does not observe. He's very . . . what's the word? *Proactive.* Thailand has many groups. He has to stay on top of all of them. His reputation isn't to wait around and see if something happens.

"We proceeded to process the bodies and the evidence while Thongthai watched. That's when I notice certain things," says Simon.

"Like what?"

"Like what you saw at the morgue the other night," he replies.

"That was you watching me?" I can't say that I'm shocked.

"I'm everywhere," says Simon as he spreads his hands out in a dramatic gesture. "The bullets that killed the boys weren't normal loads. Not the kind gangsters use. I've also been to plenty of torture scenes. This one was more . . . efficient."

"So, what happened?" I ask.

"Thongthai. I get called into my boss's office, and I'm told that this is no longer my case. When I ask who it's being assigned to, I'm told that's not my concern. But it's clear what happened."

"Did they mention terrorism?"

"No. They took all the evidence. Then they came for the bodies the day after you went to the morgue."

"What happened to them?" I ask.

"My guess? Incinerated."

"Why are they trying to cover it up? *What* are they trying to cover up?"

"I don't know. I understand the young men were involved in cryptocurrency and bitcoin and that sort of thing. But that doesn't explain Thongthai. Why he was there or what he's doing," says Simon.

"Could he be working for the same people as Conover?"

"Thongthai isn't corrupt. He's deeply religious and committed to his job. His father and uncle were the same way. He's a man of simple means," Simon tells me.

"Sometimes those means can get complicated."

"Maybe. But this isn't just Thongthai. My boss. His boss. All the bosses. Everyone tells me it's being handled. Three dead boys and no answers. This doesn't feel like it's being handled."

"What can you tell me about the victims?" I ask.

"Vik, Michael, Al, and Sonny? They met at a technical high school in Pattaya City. They were very gifted. Everyone I spoke to knew that."

"Do the families know what happened?"

"We haven't tracked down the immediate families. They all left the country right after. In the CCTV footage from the airport, they appear to be on their own. I think they were warned. All of them had tourist visas," says Simon.

"Where were they headed?"

"Australia. But it's not uncommon to go there, then someplace else. We haven't found out what the final destination was."

"That must have taken a lot of planning. Did they know this was coming?" I ask.

"I've been wondering that too. We know the tickets were purchased last minute, but they had travel visas in place. That makes me think they may have known something like this could happen. That they might have to flee the country."

"In case the government came for them," I reply.

"Maybe. But I'm not aware of any investigation into them. And from what I've found out, they were decent kids from good families."

"What about the rumors of ransomware and online scams?" I ask.

"I don't know. I heard them. People told me about them second-hand. It all felt a little . . . planned. None of the locals I've dealt with had heard of that. If they were involved in cybercrime and connected to an organization here, it would have been at a high level."

"What about Vik? Where is he right now?"

"I don't know. He's like a ghost. There's an all-points bulletin for him, and nobody has seen him since the day of the murders. You've seen that people are after him. And they're still looking."

"I kind of wonder if the kid tripped, broke his neck, and fell into a dumpster, and everyone is running around looking for someone at the bottom of a landfill." It's a dark thought but not out of the question.

"Maybe. We had people at the trash sites, just in case his body ended up there. Last I was able to check there was nothing. It still wouldn't explain how he was able to vanish from the apartment."

I've told Simon a lot, but I have one card I haven't even hinted at, let alone put on the table. His body language, his mannerisms, and his way of talking make me think he's being sincere—at least sincerer than just about everyone else I've dealt with.

I don't have any other leads and, clearly, I need an ally.

"He didn't exactly disappear," I reply.

"What do you mean?"

"I think I know the last place he was spotted—or rather, could have been spotted. But first you have to tell me why you're here. Why are you still following this?"

"Because I'm stubborn. I didn't like being taken off the case. I don't like being kept in the dark. It's . . . insulting."

"So this is a pride thing?"

"Mostly. Also, those boys . . . that wasn't right. They were just kids. Probably never even had girlfriends. I don't want to see the people who did this get away with it," he explains.

"How far are you willing to go?" I ask.

"As far as it takes."

I take out my phone and send a text to the only person I trust with my life.

"I'm going to tell you something," I explain to Simon. "I mean this in the friendliest way possible. If I find out you're working with Conover or someone else and you stab me in the back, I have someone who will hunt you down and kill you if I can't do it. If you don't like the terms, change the topic and we'll have another drink, then go our separate ways."

"I accept your terms," says Simon. "I'll provide it in writing if it makes things simpler."

"We're good. I know how Vik got away, and I think we can find out his last steps, if you're a resourceful man."

"I'm adaptable. What do you need?"

"Do you have access to the city's CCTV footage?"

"Yes. But there are no cameras around the apartment complex. I looked for them."

"We're not looking there." I pull out my phone and show him the aerial view.

"Damn it. He climbed across the rooftops," Simon observes. "But to where?"

"Maybe the footage will tell us."

COMMAND CENTER

For a man who had multiple shots of whisky, Simon has managed to sober up quickly. That might be due to the fact he was having the bartender mix his drinks with water so he could outpace me. And for that I hold no grudge. I would have drunk double simply to mute the pain from my fall.

I took a trip to the bathroom before we left and inspected my back. It was covered with bruises, including a large rectangular one where Yak's name placard impressed itself into my scapula.

Simon observed this from the doorway and laughed. "If you fell from any higher, you might have got his name as well."

The car ride to his connection with CCTV access was slightly less painful than the ride to the bar, but the stop-and-go traffic was murder on my spine.

I've had enough bruises, breaks, lacerations, and falls to know how quickly my body is going to heal—factoring in my age. My back will be a purple collage of pain for a week, and I'll probably be sleeping on my stomach tonight, but with enough medication I should be able to pass myself off as a fully functional human in the morning.

Right now is a different matter.

As I climb out of his beat-up Toyota, the muscles in my back spasm and cry out for a hot tub.

I look around the alley where Simon parked. There's an obvious NO PARKING sign above his hood. There are also piles of garbage and a gray cat watching me from atop a tower of plastic crates.

We're in an industrial area filled with aluminum buildings interspersed with concrete apartment boxes. The layers and layers of cables strewn from the utility poles are even thicker here and completely block the view of the few windows facing the alley. Mopeds whiz past us in the street, and two young women dressed in very little watch us from under an awning as they avoid the rain.

"This is where your CCTV facility is located?" I ask, a little skeptical.

"No. This is where I go to get access to the CCTV cameras," he clarifies.

I follow him down deeper into the alley, where we have to walk atop crates to avoid stepping in dark puddles of wastewater.

It begins to get even more narrow as we squeeze through a passage barely wider than my shoulders. Rain pours down from the slanted metal roof and drenches my head and shoulders.

"This is a lot of effort if you want to kill me. You could have just strangled me in the car," I joke.

Simon keeps walking and doesn't remark.

I continue to follow him but keep my hand near one of my knives.

He steps out of the passage and into an open area filled with small metal sheds and containers. People are living in them. Electrical cables, probably plugged into the grid illegally, connect them all and lights dangle from overhead, giving the space an almost carnival feel.

The people here are clean, and their small homes are tidy if not crowded with bins and wailing children. I suspect many of them are workers employed by the surrounding factories.

"This way," says Simon as he goes up a narrow flight of stairs in back of one of the buildings that forms the secret square.

He pounds on a metal door. A moment later it opens and a small girl, maybe ten or eleven, greets us.

Simon speaks to her in Thai, and she lets him in.

The interior is a large loft above a factory floor. It's filled with metal racks containing computer components, cable, and other kinds of machinery.

The girl leads us down a hallway toward the sound of a TV playing an action movie.

A man with a beard and mustache, dressed in a bathrobe and pajamas, is asleep in an easy chair with a bottle of Japanese beer nestled in his arms.

The little girl yells at the man and kicks the chair. "Wake up!"

He swats his hand in the air like he's trying to hit a fly.

"Useless," she says. "This way."

We follow her down another passage. This one leads to a cleaner room filled with new computer components hanging from a pegboard. A large PC sits on a table with LED lights illuminating the tower.

The girl takes a seat in a gaming chair on an elevated platform in front of the keyboard. She closes the window to a video game.

"Where?" she asks.

"Lat Phrao," I tell her.

She pulls up a browser window that appears to be for a Bangkok municipal portal and enters a password. The screen changes to a search bar, and she types the address.

"When?" she asks.

"Mind if I type?" asks Simon.

"Fine," says the girl as she folds her arms and sits back.

Simon turns the screen away from her view and pulls up a video feed from the camera I had spotted on the other side of the street.

In the footage, Vik walks briskly around the corner and into view. He keeps looking over his shoulder, and his face is clearly distressed. He's wearing a backpack and has on the same fancy Nikes from the original photograph I saw of him.

Vik checks a phone in his hand and keeps looking in the direction of oncoming traffic. A motorcycle pulls up with a man in a yellow vest, and Vik hops on. A moment later he vanishes from the screen.

"Taxi?" I ask.

"Yes," says Simon.

He pulls up camera feeds for several intersections and points his finger at where Vik takes a turn. Simon doesn't need to look at Google Maps. He has the streets down cold.

He pulls up another intersection feed: Vik gets off the bike, and the rider drives away. Vik types on his phone, then calls someone and gets very animated.

A dark sedan pulls up and Vik gets inside.

Simon zooms into the image and gets the license number.

"Car service?" I ask.

"Yes," replies Simon.

He starts to type into his phone.

"You calling them to get the records?"

"No. I'm getting the address of the driver. It's cleaner that way. We'll go talk to him and look at his phone."

The driver, Norman Fong, is waiting for us in front of a minimart when we pull up. He's heavyset with thick glasses and seems nervous.

Over the phone Simon was very direct. He told Fong where and when to meet us and made it clear that not showing up wasn't an option.

Fong sees me get out of the car and points to me, then asks Simon something in Thai. I picked up a few expletives and "American."

"He's a cop from America," Simon replies in English.

Fong's face brightens. "American cop? Cool!"

I decide it's better not to correct Simon on the introduction.

"No. Not cool. He's an angry man. Watch out," Simon warns.

Fong looks at me warily.

"Let me see your phone with your driver's log," says Simon.

Fong takes a step back. "Tell me what you want to know."

"Okay: Tell the American which part of your body you want him to break first. He's not from here. Nobody will prosecute him. They'll just send him back to Los Angeles," Simon warns Fong.

I'm not well versed in Thai law, but I'm pretty sure this isn't exactly legal, even under their strict judicial system. Not that I'm about to point out Fong's civil rights.

I appreciate that Simon has been careful to not let anyone know what we know. He wiped all history of our footage search and didn't tell Fong who he was looking for or where or when.

That's all smart. He's covering our tracks and making sure we don't end up leading anyone to Vik.

Simon takes Fong's phone and starts to scroll through an app.

He finds what he's looking for and takes a photo of the screen, then asks, "Do you back this up?"

"No. Why?"

Simon uses a tool from his pocket to remove the SIM card. He hands it to Fong, then turns to me. "Give him some money to go buy a phone in the store."

"I want my phone!" says Fong.

"You'll get this one back in a few days. Trust me—you don't want it right now. If anyone finds out what's on it, you're a dead man."

Fong stares at me. "You're not a cop, are you?"

"No," Simon tells him. "He's something worse. Don't tell anyone we talked to you. Don't drive for a few days. Don't try downloading the app, because I'll know."

"What am I supposed to do?" asks Fong.

"Stay alive," replies Simon. "Now go get your temporary phone and go home."

After Fong walks into the store, Simon and I get back into his car.

"Well?" I ask, once the door closes.

"I have some so-so good news and some very, very bad news."

"Isn't that always the case?"

Simon pulls onto the street. "Sadly. Have you heard of John Pham?"

Andrew Mayne

"No. Should I have?" I ask.

"Pham is former military and now a crook. But he has enough connections that he's out of reach for a guy like me. I can nab his men when they do something stupid, but he's a different matter." Simon sighs. "Pham is . . . what's the American word? Slumlord. He owns a bunch of different apartment blocks and communities. He houses factory workers, people from villages, and others who come to Bangkok for work. A lot of people in prostitution as well. They pile up ten people in a room. Really horrible conditions.

"The politicians tolerate it because Pham keeps the people in line and off the street. But he's basically exploiting everyone," says Simon.

"What does Pham have to do with Vik?" I ask.

"Vik's last stop was one of Pham's housing complexes."

"Was that accidental?"

Simon shakes his head. "Nobody accidentally ends up there. Vik had to know where he was going."

"Why?" I reply.

"I don't know. But something else to know about Pham is that a lot of people pay him for protection. Movie stars, singers, athletes, and even politicians," Simon explains.

"Like gangster protection?" I ask.

"No. The better word is 'security.' That's how he got his start. He came out of the military and started a security service. Bodyguards, that kind of thing. People knew not to mess with anyone Pham was protecting. That led to the housing complexes and other businesses."

"So Vik may be paying Pham for security? Interesting."

"Possibly. But for Pham there's always got to be a bigger angle. If everyone is after Vik for something he has or knows, Pham wouldn't hesitate to sell him out, because Vik is a nobody."

This is kind of making sense to me. I think.

Vik knew he couldn't go to the airport because the government and those after him would look there. Instead of trying to go into hiding

Andrew Mayne

by himself, he went to Pham and offered to pay for protection . . . or presented something else.

The reason nobody has been able to find him is that they don't know where to look, and Vik has the benefit of a protector who can keep the world at arm's length.

"The men who shot at me the other night. Could they be Pham's?" I ask.

"Maybe. That would mean they were looking for someone they expected to come by the apartment. Do you have any idea who that could be?" Simon replies.

"Not a clue. I still don't know what Vik has. Maybe a lot of money from a heist. I just don't know. We'll have to ask him, I guess. Do you have any idea where Pham might be keeping him stashed?"

"None. Pham has at least a dozen complexes in Bangkok. They would also be well protected, and there's no way we could get anywhere near one without them knowing. It's why the police don't go do it. If we want to arrest someone, we ask Pham first," Simon admits, sheepishly.

"That's messed up. So how do I get to Vik?"

"First we need to talk to someone that knows where he's being hidden. Pham has a business partner, Liam Udomsakdi, who acts as his go-between. He's Western educated and very cocky. I tried to get him a while ago for the murder of a pimp. Liam had taken a liking to one of his girls, and the pimp stepped between them. Liam had the man killed without Pham's approval, but there wasn't anything Pham could do because Liam was critical to his operation," explains Simon.

"What happened on your end?" I reply.

"I was told to shelve it. 'Insufficient evidence.' Liam and Pham were more valuable in place."

"All right. How does that help us?"

"Liam is still anxious about the case. He's worried that if Pham says the word, we'll reopen it and send him away. But because of what Liam knows, Pham would just as soon have him killed the moment he set foot in a prison. So Pham uses this as leverage."

"And you want to use this as leverage too."

"We could. But first we need to get him to come to us. That's the part I haven't figured out."

"Is he afraid of showing up at the police station?"

"Not if he knows he isn't going to be arrested."

"What if he thinks he's going to be arrested for something he didn't do and has an alibi?" I ask.

"He'd show up and hold his own press conference."

"Perfect."

ACCUSED

I'm leaning against the wall as an observer when Liam Udomsakdi struts into the precinct conference room like Mick Jagger taking the stage in an arena.

Simon didn't have enough pull to arrest Liam or legally compel him to come in for questioning. He had to make Liam want to come in and talk to us. That's no small feat—fortunately I had a trick that's worked a few times in the past.

Simon explained that we'd know how seriously Liam was taking him by which attorney he brought in. If it's the old former federal prosecutor accompanying him, it's a sign that he's taking the situation seriously. If it's one of the younger, attractive, barely-out-of-law-school lawyers, then he thinks this is a frivolous matter and he wants to look good for the press conference.

Liam walks in with an attractive young woman at his side. "This is Ms. Kay, my attorney," he announces in English.

Simon gives me a wink from across the table, then graciously motions for Liam and his counselor to have a seat across from him.

"Who is he?" asks Liam, gesturing at me.

"He's an observer."

Liam makes an indifferent shrug, then nods to Kay, who unlocks her briefcase and tosses a thick folder on the table.

"I understand that you're making false and defamatory statements about my client. We're here as a courtesy but plan to take this matter up with your superiors as well as make the media aware of this," she explains.

"Fine. Fine. I'm ready to retire anyway," says Simon.

"That's going to be a lot sooner than you realize once you see what's in this file," says Liam, visibly aroused by the notion of seeing the infamous Inspector Simon Srisutham fall flat on his face and be publicly humiliated.

"One second. Mind if I record this?" says Simon as he turns on a tape recorder in the middle of the table without waiting for permission.

"As long as you provide me a copy," replies Liam.

"Of course, of course." Simon leans over a notebook and flips through the pages, then comes to a stop and silently reads. "Here we are. Where were you on the evening of August 12, 2021?"

Kay speaks up, "Mr. Udomsakdi was in Qatar, and I have the airline tickets, witness testimonies, and—"

Liam puts his hand on hers to stop her. He understood the significance of the date. She didn't. She was on autopilot the moment she heard, secondhand, why her client was being called in.

"That's not . . ." Liam begins, then falters.

"That's not what?" asks Simon. "Not the reason you thought I asked you in here?"

Last night, after Simon and I spoke, he started putting the word out that the police were looking into connecting Liam to the murder of a young woman four months ago at a reputed gangster's party.

Simon knew full well that Liam was thousands of miles away at a conference in Qatar. That's why he put out word that he was trying to pin that particular crime on Liam. He knew Liam would march right into the police station to tell Simon what an idiot he was and prove otherwise.

Simon produces a thick folder that was hidden on the chair next to him and sets it on the table. A red string keeps the flap shut, its contents ready to burst forth.

Liam is looking at the folder and seems much less jovial than a moment ago.

"I was revisiting an old case and something new came up. I wanted to speak to you about it," says Simon.

Kay speaks, "We're not prepared—"

"Shut up!" shouts Liam. "Get out!"

"As your attorney—" she pleads.

"Get out, you plastic idiot." Liam is livid.

Kay's face turns red and she starts to get up, then fumbles the briefcase and documents. Liam picks them up and throws them at her.

"Leave them. Go! Now!" he screams at her.

Liam is panicking because he doesn't want Kay to hear what he thinks Simon might say next. Besides working for Liam, Kay and her firm also represent Pham himself. Pham pays the bills, and anything said in front of Kay would surely make it back to him. The only way Liam could make a secret plea deal is if nobody answerable to Pham was in the room. It's far too late for that now.

After she leaves, Simon sits quietly, watching Liam as he starts sweating. I can see the perspiration moistening his collar as his skin turns red.

"What do you want to talk about?" Liam asks.

"There's been a development. Two new eyewitnesses on the day Kiet Vichitphan was murdered," says Simon.

"I see. Perhaps I should bring in a different lawyer."

"That's an option. But it might shut down other options for you. If you know what I mean," Simon tells him.

"Let me make it clear I'm not going to say anything to betray anyone I work with. Especially Mr. Pham. I'll take a bullet for him," says Liam in a dramatic performance.

Simon reaches over and presses "Stop" on the tape recorder. "I don't want Mr. Pham. I don't want any of your colleagues. Nasty people, to be honest. No. I just want one person. He's nothing to you. Possibly even a nuisance," Simon explains.

"Who is that?"

"Viktor Phumhiran."

Liam glances at me, then replies, "I don't know who he is."

Simon takes a photograph of Vik from his notebook and sets it in front of Liam.

Liam looks down at the image of Vik, then pushes it back to Simon. He says nothing.

"Your silence is revealing. This is what we're going to do. I'm going to put a map in front of you and give you a pen. I want you to draw an X and then write down anything else that might be important."

Simon takes a map from the seat next to him and pushes it in front of Liam.

"What about that?" Liam asks as he points to Simon's folder.

"I can forget about the eyewitnesses. Nobody's crying over the death of a pimp. This file can go back to where it was hiding."

Liam makes an X in the western section of Bangkok, then pushes the map back to Simon and fixes me with a glare. "Tell your CIA pal their bribe was an insult."

Whoa. This got even more interesting. I need to choose my words carefully.

"Sure thing. Any other messages you'd like me to pass on?" I reply.

"Yeah. She should have accepted my counteroffer. She had a nice rack. I would have shown her a good time." Liam turns back to Simon. "Are we good?"

"If this works out, we're good. Anything else I should know?"

"Fuck it. The kid is weird. The arrangement is weird. I don't know what's up. Pham won't tell me anything. I think he's got some deal he's cutting me out of," Liam complains.

"Have you seen any people from the government or any other foreigners?" asks Simon.

"No. Just Pham's own people—ones he really trusts. They've got that kid locked down tight. Nobody but a handful know he's in there."

"What's the plan?"

"I don't know. Pham asked me to get him some contact information for some Chinese and Russian spies we know about. After that he shut me out."

"Did the kid have anything with him?" I ask.

"A backpack. A laptop. That's all I saw."

"Thank you, Mr. Udomsakdi," says Simon. "You can leave now."

Liam gets up and straightens out his cuffs. "Don't burn me."

"Nobody is getting burned today," says Simon. He waits for Liam to leave, then asks me, "What about this woman he mentioned?"

"She might be CIA. Might not. I don't know."

Simon takes out his phone and flips through his photos. He slides it over to me. "One of my people has been watching the apartment and seeing who comes by. This her?"

I look down and see Rebecca's familiar face in the passenger seat of a car. The driver's face is also familiar. It belongs to "Doug Riggsly," the CIA station chief's bodyguard who was posing as a photographer at the Muay Thai fight.

"That's her. And that's definitely a CIA agent driving. If she's sniffing up Pham's contacts, we should probably move fast."

"Let me get a few things in order. Meanwhile, why don't you go talk to her," says Simon.

"Last time I saw her was in the rearview mirror as I abandoned her in the parking lot of a gunrunner's warehouse. She might not be too talkative. But I'll see."

CONFIDANT

Rebecca Gostler is sitting in a lounge chair by the pool at the Riverside Resort. She has a thin wrap draped over her bikini and a large brimmed hat shielding her from the early-afternoon sun. With two phones and a laptop, she appears to be multitasking. Based upon her furious typing, it hasn't been the best morning.

I walk over and sit on the chair next to her. She's too busy texting to look up.

"I'll take that drink later," she says tersely, then looks up and realizes she's talking to me. "And I thought the staff couldn't get more annoying." She closes her laptop. "Is there going to be an apology?"

She doesn't want to ask how I found her and look dumb. So we both play pretend that it's no big deal, and I keep my secret that I can tell which hotel you stayed in last night by the scent of the soap and conditioner you used the night before.

"Only if it's coming from you," I reply.

She sits upright and faces me knee to knee. "How do you figure?"

I take my phone from my pocket and show her the photo taken while she was in the car with the station chief's bodyguard.

"Care to talk about the company you keep?" I ask.

She glances at the photo, then thinks for a beat. "Jealous?"

"Maybe. Who is he?" I ask.

This is a test to see how honest she's going to be with me.

"If I said he was a local expat I met, would you believe me?"

"Is that what you're going to tell me?"

"What's the upside for me?"

"We get to continue the conversation."

"What reason do I have to think this will be worth my time?"

"Bye," I say as I get up.

She grabs my forearm and pulls at me. "Always ready to leave."

I stare at her. "It's served me well so far."

She sighs. "I don't know who could be listening here. Let's go up to my room."

"Same people who could be listening there. Let's just stay where we are," I tell her.

Rebecca is an expert manipulator. I don't know if she's trying to distract me, catch me in an awkward situation, buy time, or something else, but I'd rather not let her have her way.

"Who was that?" I ask again.

"I think you already know," she says.

"Maybe. But I'd like to hear you say it."

Rebecca thinks this over. I can tell she's conflicted. The easy answer is telling me to go to hell. But she isn't. She thinks I may know something that's useful—which implies I know something she and her bosses do not.

"He's CIA. Not a key guy but someone you can go to for background," says Rebecca.

"And why would the CIA give you access to him?"

"You can do the math on that one, can't you?"

"Walk me through it. The station chief didn't exactly deny knowing who you are, but I believed him when he said you weren't one of his. But how does that explain you getting the white-glove treatment from one of his underlings? My guess is that he was told to help you out. But you're not CIA. Probably some tiny little agency with connections to the intelligence community." I stop and wait.

Rebecca looks down at her phone, I assume to make sure that it's off. "Let's say you're kind of adding it up."

"Okay. My guess is that Theocrates is real. As in, it's a functioning consultancy that signs your paycheck. But you have an intelligence security clearance, and your real client is whatever agency set up Theocrates to make it easier to pass off its agents as private citizens."

"Name the agency and win a prize," she says.

"Office of Intelligence and Analysis. They work with the Treasury. They're the ones involved in foreign financial matters. They'd be the ones who'd want to hire people with backgrounds like yours but not have them look like Ivy League State Department and CIA recruits."

"Very close to accurate," she replies.

"So, it's a task force. Interagency. Probably the CIA. Maybe the NSA and DIA. I guess xQuadrant is part of something connected to you."

"That seems very plausible."

"Knock it off. I still have my security clearance. I'm the intelligence liaison between Wind Aerospace and the National Security Council. Talking to me will get you a slap on the wrist, at worst. But you already know this."

"I'm not worried about a slap on the wrist. This is a high-stakes game."

I get the sense that she's nervous not about talking to me but about the situation in general.

"They told you about me. You looked me up. Is there anything in there that makes you think you can't trust me?" I ask.

"Someone could be watching us," she replies.

"Coming out here dressed in a bikini is one way to guarantee that. Let's assume that's the case. What's more important than anything else is *time*. I need to know what the real situation is."

"Are you in a position to do something?" she asks.

"Like find Viktor Phumhiran? Quite possibly. I need to know who's after him and why first."

"Fine. Burn me and I'll haunt you to the end of your days. Have you heard of Project Grab Bag?" she asks.

"Never."

"Billions of dollars of cryptocurrency floating around out there is being used to fund terrorism operations around the globe. Buying rocket launchers for Houthis, funding Hamas and Hezbollah. Everywhere that has a conflict, there's money flowing in and out. Today, much of it flows via bitcoin and the blockchain generally.

"Grab Bag is a program intended to find those assets and seize them using gray-hat hackers. We give them targets and they find the crypto wallets and infrastructure, then find a way to take it. We pay them a bounty," she says.

"Basically, a letter of marque," I reply.

"Yes, except nobody on the task force knew what that meant. Anyway, Vik and his team were the best. We gave them targets and some tools. They got results. They were maybe a little too successful," she explains.

"How so?"

"We didn't know how much cryptocurrency was in some of the accounts we were after. Sometimes all we knew was that some member of Hamas or another organization was likely the point person, but who knew what wallet they were using? We just suspected they were involved.

"Vik and his friends were able to break open entire networks and locate funds in places we didn't know existed. We set up wallets where they were supposed to deposit the funds."

"How effective?" I ask.

"Keep in mind that some of the groups they went after were gangs that had been ripping off other exchanges. Some of that money was stolen from people that weren't involved in any criminal activity."

"Okay. How much are we talking about?"

"Nine," she replies.

"Nine million?"

"No. Nine billion. At least that's how much we know about," says Rebecca.

"Nine *billion?*" I ask, not believing the number.

"Like I said, some of that came from criminal organizations that had pulled off heists on crypto exchanges. But, yes. Vik and his buddies had managed to seize at least that much, as far as we know."

"As far as you know?" I echo.

"That's where it gets complicated. It had been speculated that they might not have been depositing all the stolen funds into the wallets they were supposed to."

"If you saw their apartment, you'd know that they weren't living the high life. What was their take supposed to be?"

"We'd offered them forty percent of the haul of anything that wasn't traceable to an exchange heist. Among other things, we're looking to return funds like those. But aside from that, Vik and his friends were sitting on top of at least a billion-dollar payday."

"All right. Then how come Vik's friends ended up with their brains splattered on the floor?"

"Because one of them screwed up. They let it get traced back to them. Someone found out. When you rip off terror groups and state-sponsored black hats, there'll be repercussions."

"Then why use a bunch of kids?" I ask.

"They came to us. Or rather, they'd contacted the CIA to let them know they'd found back doors into several dark web exchanges," she explains.

"And what did they want?"

"Jobs. American visas. A trip to Disney World."

"Seriously?"

"Yes. We helped facilitate that. We set them up as a tech company to make them look more legitimate. They wanted to call it Spy x Quadrant after a manga they liked, but we insisted they not use 'Spy' in the name. They were just kids," she says.

"Three dead kids now because of what you guys did," I tell her.

"I didn't call the shots. I came into this later. I did what I could to protect them," she says.

"Like spreading rumors that they were ransomware rip-off artists?"

"That was just—"

"Covering your ass. I know what it was. You were worried about this blowing up, and you needed a way to paint them in a bad light ahead of it all."

"I'm just trying to do my job," she says.

"Which is what, right now?"

"Recovering those funds before a terrorist organization or state actor like Russia, China, or Iran gets hold of them. Then there'll be *real* hell to pay." She looks at me in an almost pleading way. "My job's to stop that money from being converted into grenades and bullets."

"No," I say sharply. "I'm going to tell you your real job."

"Are you now?"

"Yes. Your job is to help me locate Vik and get him to safety. Then we can figure out the money. Right now, he's the priority."

"That's fine, but—"

I cut her off. "No. That's where it starts and that's where it ends. We get him, and then you get your money. No deals that might compromise him. No backstabbing. No playing with innocent lives."

"He might not be that innocent," Rebecca insists.

"He's not a killer. Are we clear?"

She nods.

"Do we have total transparency?"

"Are you going to tell me where he is?"

"I'll tell you what you need to know to get him to safety. How's that?"

"Fair enough."

"I have questions. First, why is Dustin Conover after Vik? Did he kill the others?"

"I don't know," she says.

"But you know who I'm talking about?"

"Yes. I know Conover works for Krome Global Security, a company with Qatari connections," she informs me.

I've heard a little about them. "The mercenary group?"

"Yes."

That confirms my earlier suspicion about who's paying Conover. He'd be a natural fit for a group like Krome.

"But you don't know who Krome is working for?" I ask.

"No. They have Qatari connections," she repeats.

"You said that. So does everyone. Next question: Why were Vik's friends tortured and killed?"

"Probably because the killers wanted the wallet—the hard drive they used to store the keys for the crypto they stole. Why else?"

"Okay. Then tell me who killed them."

"I don't know. I really don't," she replies.

"You sure it wasn't Conover?"

"I don't know," she insists. "If he's working for Krome, then he's probably just here to track down the money. They have a legitimate business of hunting down embezzlers for private clients."

"There's nothing legitimate about Conover," I assure her.

"Some would say the same about you."

I ignore that. "Why is the Thai government keeping this all locked down? That's a tremendous amount of cooperation."

"Because of terrorism. They take it very seriously. They have a half dozen different domestic terror groups they don't want to see get a big influx of cash. We explained it to their counterterrorism agencies, and they agreed to the blackout," says Rebecca.

"Who else is after Vik?"

"Who isn't? Thailand has everyone from Communist Chinese to ISIS-connected terrorist cells. As far as who did the killing? It might have been a tactical unit with the military who has a side deal with one of them. At least that's what I've heard," she says.

I don't know how much of what she says she knows is true. Regardless, I don't have a lot of time. If Liam cracked so quickly with Simon and me, he'll crack even faster to someone ready to do him harm.

"I can get Vik. But I need an exit plan. I need a way to get him out of the country and to the United States."

"I can do that. But you have to loop me in," she insists.

"Fine, but I'm only going to tell you what you need to know. And we're going to stay close. No offense, but you haven't earned my trust yet."

PERIMETER

Simon and I are in a delivery truck parked on a corner adjacent to Wat Village, one of the apartment complexes owned by Pham. We've already made a circuit around the block to get an idea what we're up against. Now we're trying to decide on our strategy.

Wat is a two-story complex that looks like two nested U's when you look at it from overhead. The bottom of the U is the back. An alley runs along its exterior, lined with a concrete wall on the other side.

There are one hundred units in the complex. Most of these are inhabited by young men who work in the casinos and drug operations. They're considered higher trust and earn more than street-level dealers and pimps.

I watch as a young man with a white shirt and black tie leaves an upper-level apartment, goes down the stairs, and gets on the back of a motorcycle to be whisked off to work.

An older man with a gray mustache and a leather jacket is leaning on the balcony railing smoking a cigarette. Another man on the opposite side is sitting on the stairs, filling out a puzzle in a newspaper. These are the two most obvious people assigned to watch the complex, but there are four others sitting around the stairs and back alley.

Additionally, we've seen four open doors with men inside who have a view of the streets around the apartments.

In all there are at least twenty people watching the complex that we can count.

"How many people are normally here?" I ask Simon.

"I've never been to this complex. Usually just two or three. Their job is to let the bosses know the cops are here and warn whoever needs to hide."

"Why stash him here?"

"Everyone knows where Pham's house is. The clubs and other businesses would have too many people coming and going. This is one of the cleaner properties. These casino workers are young men from out of town who just want to make some money to send home. It's young but not as rowdy as the other complexes. It makes sense. It's what I'd have done if I'd thought of it," he explains.

"How armed do you think they are?"

"Very. Pham doesn't like to be outgunned."

I look down at the printout I made from an aerial view of the complex. Little red Xs indicate lookouts and armed men we've spotted around the complex. In addition to them, there are four cars parked in the back alley facing outward, designed to block vehicle access as well as provide a quick escape route. Pham's ready to move Vik if he has to.

"Any ideas?" asks Simon.

"I was hoping you'd have some. The brute-force way would be to use snipers on the ground to take out the guards. Fly in a tactical unit with a helicopter. Use two snipers on board to provide coverage. Shoot anyone who gets in the way, grab him, and then fly him out on the helicopter. But that's not practical here."

Simon chuckles dryly. "My helicopter is being repaired. Do you have any ideas that don't involve killing?"

"You're really hampering my creativity here. Well, we'd need more people, and we'd need to get close to the compound long enough to park a vehicle."

"Vehicles. I might have something. How many people?" asks Simon.

"A team of eight people would be ideal. But I doubt we can get that in the next twelve hours."

"I can get you two, but they'll want to meet you first. Let me see if I can set something up."

Simon takes out his phone and starts speaking to someone in rapid-fire Thai.

❧

Less than an hour later, Simon pulls into a lot filled with various vehicles in different states of repair. According to him, it's an auction site run by his cousin.

As we get out of his car, a woman a bit younger than him exits her Mercedes and walks over to us.

"Brad, this is Kim. Kim, this is Brad. That's all you need to know," says Simon.

Kim starts to swear at him in Thai. Simon waves it off.

"Thank you, cousin." Simon turns to me. "Let's take a look. I'd like to have a plan before the others get here. We need to make it look like we know what we're doing."

We walk through the lot. There are dozens of cars that have been stripped, along with utility vehicles, delivery trucks with open beds, and vans—most with smashed-out windows.

I stop to examine an ambulance. It's a bit older, but not something you'd pay much attention to if you saw it driving down the street.

"What are you thinking?" asks Simon.

"It's an old trick. I mean, so old it's in old movies. And bad ones, at that. But I don't know that Pham's guys would be onto that. We could use this to get Vik out of there," I suggest.

"How do we get it close enough?"

"I'm still working that part out."

"What if Vik doesn't want to come with us? He did go to Pham for protection," says Simon.

"I think I can convince him. I suspect the plan was for Pham to smuggle him out of the country, but he decided otherwise when he realized Vik might be worth a lot more than Vik was letting on."

"Okay, but you need to figure out the other part of the plan now, because our guests are here," he tells me.

"No pressure."

He smiles. "I think that's the only way you work."

We walk to the front of the lot, where two men a little younger than Simon wait by a white Hyundai. One of them is dressed in a blue shirt and has a shiny comb-over. The other wears a white shirt and has a thin mustache and buzz cut.

"This is Gun and this is Tanin. This is the American I told you about," says Simon.

They nod but don't say anything, only study me. I get a look at them and try to do my own reading.

Tanin has a scar across his neck, and Gun has calluses on his knuckles. It's pretty obvious that Gun's done Muay Thai. I suspect Tanin has more experience in street fights.

I decide to break the ice with a direct question. "So, what's your issue with Pham?"

"Show him," says Simon.

Gun lifts his shirt and reveals a bullet scar in his side. Tanin points to the scar on his neck.

"Pham did that?"

"One of Pham's men shot Gun. Pham was able to get someone else to take the fall. Tanin got cut up by another one of Pham's men when he was trying to stop a fight," explains Simon.

"You guys are cops?"

"*Were* cops," says Gun. "Forced retirement, thanks to Pham. Then he had the balls to offer me a job."

"I take it you declined," I reply.

"Fuck him."

"What about you?" I ask Tanin.

"His English isn't the best," says Gun. "He's still working, but they put him on a shit beat."

"Okay. You hate Pham. But why do you want to help us?" I ask.

"We haven't said we are," replies Gun. "We'd like to know what your plan is."

"I can tell you it doesn't involve Pham directly. It'll just annoy the hell out of him if we pull it off."

"Annoying is good by us. So, what is it?" asks Gun.

"It's a rescue operation. He's got somebody captive we need to extract," I explain.

"That sounds fishy. Pham isn't into kidnapping," Gun tells me.

"Think of it more as a protection scheme that went wrong and within days could turn deadly."

"Kind of vague," Gun says to Simon.

"Let me put it this way: either we get this kid out soon, or Pham will either sell him to some terrorists or the terrorists will come for him and a lot of people will die," I summarize.

"Still a bit murky," replies Gun. "Simon, what's your take?"

"This will fuck with Pham and embarrass him. He doesn't come out of this looking good. Does that work for you?"

"As long as the plan doesn't suck. Let's have it," says Gun.

While I've been making the worst recruitment pitch ever, I've also been eyeing a large pickup-size vehicle with an extension arm and bucket. The sign on its side says Bangkok Municipal Electric.

"I have a plan. It shouldn't involve bloodshed. But we have to be quick."

I also need one more person to help pull this off. I'm sure she's up for it, but I still don't know whether I trust her.

LINEMAN

Simon is driving and I'm in the front passenger seat of the old ambulance. In my lap lies a computer with three video feeds. One's from a camera on the dashboard of the bucket truck being driven by Gun and Tanin. The other two feeds come from cameras I placed in boxes on the back of mopeds parked facing the alley behind the Wat complex and in front, watching the open square.

Rebecca is in a car a half kilometer away with a hired driver that Simon trusts, but she was only told enough to keep her out of trouble.

I'd rather it be someone else, but I need a pro monitoring the local police radio traffic and watching our backs.

"Any word on getting Vik out of Thailand?" I ask Rebecca over the open video call.

"Still working on it. My boss wasn't happy about me not giving him any specifics."

"And you told him nothing, correct?"

My trust for her has increased by only a fraction of a percent; my trust in her unnamed superiors remains effectively zero.

"Yes, Brad. Because you told me not to, and I don't know anything," she replies, a bit exasperated.

"Let me explain this again. Between me and whoever is setting this up on your end, we have no idea who might leak the wrong detail to someone. These things can blow up very quickly because the person making the flight plan says something they shouldn't or a name is mentioned in passing at the worst point."

"I got it," she answers.

"I need to know that. I'm trusting you."

"This is how trust feels? I'm sitting in a car with a stranger with no idea what I'm actually supposed to be looking for," she complains.

"This is what 'need to know' feels like."

Rebecca doesn't know anything about Pham as far as I know. She might be able to deduce something because of the proximity to the complex, but that's a risk I have to take.

Without Rebecca's superiors, there's no easy way to get Vik out of the country. I could call in a favor with Kylie and have her sneak him out on one of her planes, but involving my employer in human trafficking is the exact opposite of my job description. I'm supposed to keep the stupid stuff away from her.

"Gun? How are you doing?" I ask over the speakerphone on the phone dialed into him.

"We're all set," he replies.

"Simon, you good?" I ask.

"Waiting for you to make the call."

We didn't have time to rehearse this. I met my team only a few hours ago. This could be a Bay of Pigs–level fiasco. I tried to keep it as simple as possible, but even so, there're a million things that could go wrong. Our junker of an ambulance might break down. The bucket truck could—

"Brad!" says Simon as he looks up from his phone.

"What is it?"

"Liam's girlfriend just called the police and said he was taken from his home by a group of people, including a white man."

"How long ago?" I ask.

"An hour or less."

Damn it.

"Gun, you hear that?" I ask.

"Yes. I think we should get moving, don't you?"

"We could call it off," I say over the comms.

"We understand what's involved. Now or never. Your call."

"Simon?" I ask.

"Let's just get this done."

"Okay. Let's go. Gun, you and Tanin, move out."

I see their truck start to move via the dash cam. They turn down a street and head straight for the front of the Wat complex.

"Rebecca, keep an eye out for large SUVs or other vehicles. We may not have as much time as we thought," I explain over our open phone call.

I placed her near the highway off-ramp in a position where she could spot for us without knowing exactly where we were headed.

"Affirmative," she replies.

Gun's utility truck pulls up to the front of the complex and parks along the sidewalk. The yellow hazard lights start to flash, and he and Tanin get out of the vehicle and walk over to a utility pole supporting hundreds of black cables. They make a show of examining a transformer box, then confer.

The man from the steps we saw earlier gets up and walks over to them. I can't hear him, but I can make out the gist of the conversation from the dashboard camera.

"What's going on?"

"Blown transformer."

"We have power."

"Yeah, but people five blocks away don't have internet."

"How long will this take?"

"Ten minutes. Ten hours. We won't know until we fix it."

"Well, be fast, then."

The lookout takes a few steps back and folds his arms, letting them know he's going to be keeping his eyes on them.

Which is exactly what we want.

Gun walks out of view to operate the bucket arm with Tanin riding inside. A minute later I see the arm rotate into view and lift Tanin up to the transformer.

"Explain to me how we're going to find Vik in there?" asks Simon as he gestures to the apartment complex.

"The armed guys are Pham's men. There's maybe a dozen, right? When the commotion starts, we see who else pops their head out to see what's going on. Trust me," I explain.

"You sure?"

"We got Liam Udomsakdi to step forward with a similar distraction. These guys won't exactly be the best and brightest compared to him. Trust me. They'll self-identify."

The lookout watches the action as Tanin starts to unbolt the casing over the transformer.

Like a thunderclap, there's a burst of light and a shower of sparks. When the smoke clears, Tanin is slumped over the edge of the bucket.

Exactly as planned.

"Did that look too much like fireworks?" asks Simon.

The lookout's already on his phone, calling someone. He's ignoring Gun and pointing frantically at Tanin.

"It looked real enough to him," I say, then check my watch.

Gun goes out of view to pretend to work the controls but keeps Tanin suspended in the air.

"Ready to go?" asks Simon.

"Give it another beat. I don't know how long Thai ambulances take."

"I don't think Tanin could wait that long even if he wasn't faking it."

"Brad!" shouts Rebecca over the call.

I unmute my connection to her. "What is it?"

"I just saw a black SUV race past us from the highway."

"Who was in it?"

"Tinted windows. But they were driving like a bat out of hell."

Damn it!

"Let's go!"

I flip on the ambulance lights and Simon floors it.

FIRST RESPONDERS

Our ambulance turns the corner and races toward the complex with its sirens blaring. The few people in the streets scatter, and Simon swerves around those who don't.

The alley ringing the back of the complex lies a block ahead. Simon blasts through an intersection, sending a moped driver onto the sidewalk.

The last hundred meters go by in a blur. Simon brings the ambulance to a screeching halt at the mouth of the alley.

A man sitting on the hood of a car blocking our way jumps up when he sees us. He runs to Simon's door as soon as it opens.

The man screams at him in Thai that he can't park there. Simon yells back at him and races around to the back of the ambulance with me, and we open the doors to grab the stretcher.

This lookout is barely out of his teens and only knows to keep people from parking here. He starts yelling again as we unfold the gurney.

Simon screams back in English, "The boss sent us! He said a man is dying!"

This takes the lookout aback. Suddenly his whole demeanor changes. He starts to run with us as we wheel the stretcher into the breezeway to the inner area between the two rows of apartments at the bottom of the U's.

"Watch the ambulance!" Simon yells at the young man.

The kid bows, then races back to keep an eye on the vehicle—like a dog following the nearest alpha. I only hope he doesn't take a close look inside the ambulance . . .

Simon and I turn the corner and push the stretcher down the corridor, looking through open doors trying to spot the one that has Vik.

A man holding a walkie-talkie and wearing a sidearm swings open a door and screams at us in Thai. "You idiots. The man is out front!"

I wink at Simon. Armed guy with a walkie-talkie . . . looks like we found the spot. Every other guy with a gun has been standing outside watching. The only ones inside not at viewpoints would have to be the ones watching Vik.

We push the cart to the door, and Simon approaches the man.

"Show us where!" Simon shouts.

The man yells something into the room, then shuts the door behind him, turning his back to Simon—which is a huge mistake.

Simon stabs a stun gun into the man's side, and he falls to the ground unconscious.

I roll him onto his stomach and wrap his wrists in a zip tie. I'd prefer tranquilizer guns, but this was thrown together on short notice and we had to use what was in Simon's trunk.

I knock on the door to the apartment the man emerged from. A younger man with an open shirt revealing a holstered gun answers.

"What?"

Simon just stares at him.

I pop around the corner and shoot him in the face with a shotgun loaded with beanbag rounds. Blood bursts from his nose, and he falls backward like I hit him with a regular load. He might have facial fractures, and he'll definitely have a concussion, but it's better than being dead.

I toss a flash grenade inside, and Simon and I clear the doorway. It makes a loud thump and emits a blinding light.

I run into the apartment and use the shotgun on a confused man standing in front of a card table. He falls backward into a cart, and a rice cooker tips over and hits him in the head.

Another man is sitting in the corner covering his head.

"Vik?" I yell.

Simon grabs him by the arm. It's not Vik.

I shoot him in the chest, and he rolls onto his side, wheezing.

I go into the hallway and kick open the bathroom door. It hits someone in the head who has been hiding inside, and I hear a crash as he falls onto the sink.

"Vik?" I yell again as I push open the door.

Nope. Beanbag blast for you.

I kick open the door to the last room and find a bare room with a floor mat, bucket, and one very dirty and frightened Viktor Phumhiran crouched in the corner.

"Get up. You're coming with us," I tell him.

"Who are you?" he asks.

"Kylie Connor sent me," I reply.

"Kylie Connor?" Vik's eyes light up like I just told him Gal Gadot was asking him to prom.

"The only one." I reach down and help him up.

We make it to the doorway, and Vik sees the men lying on the floor. "Are they dead?"

"No."

Simon is watching the living room, where he's dragged the gurney inside.

"Get on," I tell Vik.

He looks at me strangely, then seems to get it. I help him onto the stretcher, then put an oxygen mask on his face and slide a huge bandage over his head to keep him from being identified. I then spray a bottle of fake blood over the bandage and his clothes.

Simon peers outside the apartment, then grabs the other end of the stretcher and rolls it out.

We race back to our ambulance the way we came. I catch a glimpse over my shoulder of Tanin and Gun's ongoing pantomime.

Their lookout is yelling into his phone, trying to find out why the ambulance kept driving past. Gun has lowered the arm and laid Tanin in the grass, where he's performing fake CPR. The last thing I see before entering the alley is him looking right at me, then slapping Tanin.

Our lookout is still waiting by the ambulance.

"Open the doors!" Simon shouts at him.

"What was all that noise?" he asks.

"I don't know," Simon tells him as we load Vik and his gurney into the back.

The young man sees the shotgun in my hand. "What's that for?"

"This," I reply as I fire a beanbag into his chest.

While that may seem cruel, I probably saved his life. He doesn't want to be the only one left unscathed when Pham finds out how Vik was stolen away.

I take out my knife and jab it into the tires of the cars blocking the exits so they won't be chasing after us.

Bang! Bang!

"I think your friends are here," says Simon.

I see a group of armed men dressed in tactical armor and wearing face shields shoot the lookout watching Tanin and Gun.

Thankfully, our men are nowhere to be seen. Hopefully they made it to the moped we parked across the street.

I throw a tear-gas grenade into the alley, race back to the ambulance, and shove Simon out of the driver's seat.

"I know these streets!" he shouts.

"But I know how to keep us alive."

WHIPLASH

I trust Simon's knowledge of the area, but I trust my evasive-driving skills more—that and the fact that I've memorized five different escape routes from Wat.

We only had a few hours to prepare, but I spent part of that time looking at the map of the Wat complex and breaking the vicinity into sections. I traced all the ways we could reach side roads, highways, and any other routes that might work, depending on who was chasing us and from where.

In the first scenario, it was Pham's men. If we didn't make an exit quickly enough and they got to their cars, we would have them hot on our tail. Although the ambulance is fast, it's not as fast as some of the cars I saw parked in the alley. Thankfully, with their tires slashed, they won't be going anywhere.

The second scenario was a police chase. There was a high probability that our actions would draw the interest of the Royal Thai Police—who may have been keeping a watch on Pham as well.

In that situation, our best bet was to take the ambulance onto back roads and ditch it as quickly as possible. They'd be looking for an ambulance and have the advantage of being able to rally every other RTP officer into looking for us with a single radio call.

The third scenario and most dangerous is the one we're in now, in which one of the unknown actors hunting Vik decides to pursue us.

I take a left and bring the ambulance onto a side street that runs at an angle away from the complex. I also switch off the siren and lights.

"Is that wise?" asks Simon.

"I don't think broadcasting our position is any wiser," I reply.

I slow down a little for intersections, but not much. The hit team has probably already made it to the alley and are getting the details of who took Vik from the confused young lookout.

"Tanin and Gun made it out," Simon tells me.

"Okay. Tell them to keep moving until they get to the safe house. We don't know if the police have been called or who else is looking for them. It's better to stay out of sight."

I make a right onto another street and slow down.

"Brad, are you headed toward Phimai Village?" asks Rebecca on my phone.

I unmute my microphone. "Maybe, why?"

"Because the SUV just made a sharp turn down Sombat Road."

"What the . . . ?"

I should have lost them by now. I roll down the window and look up.

Damn it.

I spot a helicopter in the distance.

"They have a chopper. Do you know how to get their tail number and find out who it belongs to? I need that helicopter taken out, one way or another."

Simon cranes his neck to look out the window.

"Who are these people?" he asks.

"You have any idea about that, Vik?" I ask our passenger lying in back.

"I'm very confused about all of this," he says faintly.

"Any idea how to stop a helicopter?" asks Simon.

"If I had enough laser pointers, the answer is yes," I reply. "We either need to head for a dense-enough area where we can lose them or to a military base where they can't come close."

Our exit plan was to park and switch vehicles on a side street up ahead—but that plan didn't include a helicopter hovering overhead that would spot the switch and report it back to our pursuers on the ground.

I run through the map in my head, scanning each sector. We'll have to improvise.

"Rebecca, where are you?"

"Following the SUV," she replies.

I want to yell at her for doing that, but I do need eyes on them right now.

"Where, exactly?"

"Half a kilometer down Sombat Road from the turn," she responds.

I check my rearview mirror. There's a tiny black dot getting larger as it races toward us, weaving through slower cars.

My only option is to confuse the helicopter and make them second-guess where we're heading.

I spot a tall building on the left next to a row of blue canvas structures covering an open-air market.

"Simon, we're going to pull in here, and I want you to hop out," I explain.

"Why?"

"Because they'll do one of three things: Keep following me. Follow you. Or drop off a couple people here to look for Vik. And two of those options are better than what we have going on right now. Call the police now and tell them there's been a shooting at this market. Just in case. Text me with what you see."

"This is a horrible plan."

I slam on the brakes and pull into the side road that leads to the parking lot in back of the market. While the helicopter is out of sight behind the building, Simon gets out and heads into the stalls.

I do a sharp right turn and take us out onto another road leading away from the market.

"Vik, you okay back there?" I call out to my passenger.

"This is a very surreal experience," he replies.

No kidding.

We're on a more remote road now, with overhanging trees. I floor the gas and hope nobody decides to cross without looking. This is my chance to get some distance on our pursuers. And right now, distance equals time.

I have an exit strategy of sorts. But it won't be ideal with the helicopter overhead. It's something we were planning to do in a denser area.

Sat Sawaka Village is two kilometers ahead. It's a cluster of small homes where the streets are barely wider than my shoulders at some points. The main entrance is approximately the width of this ambulance—perfect.

My phone buzzes with a text from Simon:

nobody got out of the SUV. just kept going.

So that didn't work.

"Rebecca, where are you?"

"Heading down a road with trees. Sorry, I didn't get a look. I'm trying to get their FAA to call back the helicopter," she explains.

"Keep on that. Tell your driver to turn back around now. It's going to get a little hairy. I don't want you guys near here, okay?"

"Affirmative. How is Vik? Is he okay?"

"He's fine."

"Are we set for the rendezvous point?" she asks.

"There's been a change of plans," I respond, then cut the call.

It's actually not a change of plans. I just didn't tell her I never intended to bring Vik to her until it was clear how she was going to get him out of Thailand.

"Was that Rebecca Gostler?" asks Vik.

"Yeah. I want to talk to you about her later, when we're a little less preoccupied."

I see the SUV gaining ground on us in the distance.

We reach the entrance to Sat Sawaka and I turn the ambulance around, putting the front end toward the road, then back up until it seals the entrance to the community like a cork in a bottle.

"All right, Vik. Time to change our mode of transportation." I climb through the small space into the rear of the ambulance.

Vik is sitting on the stretcher, which we had to cram into one side of the interior to make room for a moped. I squeeze past and open up the back doors.

"Grab the helmets and my black duffel bag by the front," I tell Vik.

As he gets those, I set a board on the bumper to use as a ramp and roll the moped out of the back of the ambulance.

"Got them," says Vik as he climbs out onto the street.

A man comes out of a small home and starts yelling at us for blocking the street.

I ignore him and toss Vik the shotgun while I search the duffel bag.

"Do I shoot him?" Vik asks incredulously.

"No! Tell him to get the hell out of here."

Vik shouts something at the man. He comes across quite forcefully with the gun in his hands.

I pull out my knife and jab it into the sidewalls of the rear tires to make pushing the ambulance out of the way a little more difficult.

By my mental count, we have only a few more seconds.

I grab a tear-gas grenade, pull the pin, and toss it into the street.

White smoke begins to spew out, covering the road in a cloud.

I toss another in the back of the ambulance, and smoke begins to billow out.

"Hop on!" I tell Vik as I straddle the moped and slide my duffel bag around to the front. "And give me that." I take the shotgun and shove it between the bag and my chest. "Here." I hand him a belt with three smoke grenades instead. "When I say so, pull the pin and drop it. Got it?"

"Yes," Vik says hesitantly.

"Hold on!"

I hear the roar of the SUV's engine as it echoes off the aluminum-sided buildings that make up the street-facing side of Sat Sawaka.

I aim the moped down the path and take us to the first T junction. "Smoke!" I shout.

Vik drops the smoke bomb and obscures the route we took.

Overhead I can hear the sound of the helicopter as it descends in search of a better vantage point.

If I'd planned this better, I would have brought along a drone to fly at the helicopter and convince the pilot to turn around. If I'd planned this better, we wouldn't even be in this situation.

I turn the moped down another alley, this one even narrower than the last.

"Smoke?" asks Vik.

"No. We want to hide our position now, not tell them where we are."

I bring the moped to a stop and listen for a moment.

I can hear men shouting from the entrance where we parked the ambulance. If they're smart, they'll look at a map and figure out where we'll be trying to exit from.

There are four streets that form the perimeter. There's the one where we entered and the other three. Though the street that's farthest from them might seem like the best choice, the helicopter is going to take up a vantage point soon to keep an eye on that position.

Right now, my biggest concern isn't being spotted by the helicopter. It's having the men in the SUV catch up with us.

I twist the throttle and take us down a slender alleyway toward the back exit of Sat Sawaka, near the Chalerm Expressway.

"Smoke?" asks Vik.

"No. No more smoke!"

We reach the end of the alley, and the expressway's visible ahead as vehicles whip by.

I take us onto the frontage road and head away from the village.

I can't hear the helicopter over the roar of our tiny little engine, but I can see its shadow as it crosses the sun.

It's a few hundred meters above us.

"They're still following us!" Vik shouts.

As long as they don't start shooting, I think we'll be okay. The SUV remains far behind us.

I see the signs for the Chalerm and feel the tiniest bit of relief.

I ignore a red light and make a right turn and take us to the route I've been trying to get to all along—the road *underneath* the expressway, where the helicopter can't follow or see us.

One problem solved. One more to go. I need to figure out where to hide Vik while we wait for Rebecca's superiors to come through with his exit plan.

SPACESHIP EARTH

Vik doesn't trust me. I don't blame him. I wouldn't trust anyone after what he's been through.

He hasn't said much since we reached the Airbnb rental I booked through a corporate account registered in the Netherlands. I'm pretty sure nobody can connect it to me, but I made four other reservations to be safe.

We haven't had a lot of time to talk. I've been smashing all the phones I used to talk to Rebecca and Simon and making sure nobody can trace us to where we are now. Not even Morena or Kylie.

I knew we were dealing with professional killers the moment I saw the murder scene back at Vik's apartment. But the helicopter and tactical team make it clear these are extremely well-equipped and well-funded killers.

While I have questions for Vik, I'm using a cheap laptop, probably filled with Chinese spyware, that I bought at an electronics store around the corner to check the registration of the helicopter.

It belongs to a charter service located at Bangkok Heliport. If I had the time and resources, I could probably find out who rented it, but I don't. I just have to assume it was someone with a lot of money.

Vik is sitting on a mat, eating a sandwich and some chips from a 7-Eleven. He looks shell-shocked. Besides the events of the last hour, he wasn't in such great shape when I found him. I should probably take him to a doctor, but we'll have to settle for some comfort food and an open window with a gentle breeze.

I pull up a website for Krome Global Security and find photos of them training for tactical missions. One of their services is K&R—kidnapping and rescue. Which is kind of amusing, because in Vik's case they were only trying to pull off the kidnapping part. Do they get paid less for only doing half?

The images show men dressed much like the ones I saw back at Wat Village. The brands of bulletproof vests and masks are a perfect match. The one difference was the men I saw were wearing jeans and light khaki pants, suggesting that they were in civilian clothes before they were called in to grab Vik.

This tells me a bit more than they might realize. This wasn't a military team waiting at a barracks. These were men who came into the country on tourist visas and were probably waiting at some motel for a call.

I pull up the Bangkok heliport on a map and search the vicinity. I count three hotels nearby.

At least one of our pursuers was staying near the heliport, ready to hop onto a chartered helicopter at a moment's notice. I don't know how useful that knowledge is right now, but it's a detail nonetheless.

A company like Krome doesn't charge a flat fee. They bill their clients down to the bullet. In most cases, they demand payment up front.

If the men chasing us are the ones who killed Vik's friends, that means they're racking up bill after bill. For each operation, there must have been a payment. Which suggests that there's been a steady back-and-forth between whoever hired Krome and the entity coordinating their actions.

This is something else to think about. But for now, I need to direct my attention at Vik and find out what he knows.

I close my laptop and focus on the terrified young man huddled on the mat.

"How are you doing?" I ask.

"When can I talk to my family?" he asks.

"Are they on WhatsApp?" I reply.

"Yes."

I take a burner phone from the table and hand it to him. "You can call them now."

He looks at the phone like it might explode in his hands. "Is this a trick?"

"No. You can walk out the door anytime you want. You're not a prisoner. Although I can't guarantee how long you'll live if you do that. Rather than call them, I suggest you send a voice message. We don't want anything to trace back to here. But you probably know more about that than I do," I admit.

If I were dealing with anyone else, I'd have to give them a lengthy lecture about how easy it can be to trace a location . . . how something as innocuous as a photo can carry metadata with precise location information.

Vik puts the phone down by his side.

"What about Michael, Al, and Sonny? Can I talk to them?" he asks.

"They're dead," I tell him.

"I know. I was just seeing if you were going to lie to me like Pham did."

"I don't plan on lying to you. And understand, you don't have to lie to me. You can just tell me something is none of my business." I point to the door. "Like I said, you're not a prisoner."

"You said you work for Kylie," he notes.

"Would you like to talk to her?"

Vik looks down at his dirty clothes. "Maybe when I've had a shower and I'm not as anxious."

"I'll get you something to wear in a little while. You can hide out in the bathroom with the shotgun."

"I've never shot anyone," he replies, looking at the weapon sitting in front of me.

"It shoots beanbag rounds. It generally won't kill someone unless you aim for the eyes. Generally. Just don't shoot the cleaning lady."

"You're not leaving, are you?" asks Vik.

"No. I want you to tell me what you can. What was the situation with Pham?"

"That was a mistake," he replies. "We'd planned out all kinds of contingencies in case someone came for us. A plan for the police. A plan for gangsters. A plan for the Russians. It was kind of a game. I'm the only one who took it seriously. Well, me and Harry."

"Harry? Who is he?" This is the first I've heard of another person.

"Harry was new. Good at security stuff. All five of us were in the apartment when Sonny saw the black SUV pull up from the balcony. We thought it was no big deal, but we still treated it like a drill. Harry and I grabbed some stuff and climbed onto the roof to wait. That's when I heard the shooting and knew it was real," says Vik.

"What happened next?"

"Harry and I went our separate ways."

"What about the crypto wallet?" I ask.

"You know about that?"

"Who doesn't know about that? It's why your friends are dead and everyone is out to get you," I tell him. "Explain Pham's involvement."

"I offered him money for protection. I had a friend who knew his son. I knew I probably wouldn't be able to make it to the airport to leave with my family," he explains.

"What about them? How did you know to get them out?"

This has been a burning mystery for me.

"We'd been planning on taking our families on a vacation to the US. We were going to go to a conference and then to see Walt Disney World. Everything was already in the works. I called everyone and told them we had to leave two days early," says Vik.

"From the roof?" I ask.

"Yeah. Mom thought something was up. Sonny's family too. But they left. Thank God," he says.

"And Harry's family?"

"He made their arrangements. He's very secretive."

"Do you trust him?" I ask.

"Absolutely."

"Okay. Back to Pham. What happened?"

"I told him that a crypto gang was out to get me. I offered to pay him to get me out of the country," says Vik.

"How much?"

"In US dollars? About half a million," he replies.

"And you don't think a guy like Pham would find that suspicious?"

"I didn't have a lot of options."

"Well, for future reference, once you tell a guy like that a number that high, he's going to be very curious. You should have lowballed him with something like $38,000 so he thinks it's your life savings. When he hears half a million, he immediately wonders, 'Why not a full million?'"

"I learned that fast. I tried to tell him that Harry controlled the money. But Pham didn't understand. Someone told him about the crypto wallet, and that's when he went kind of crazy," says Vik.

"How come you're still alive and Pham doesn't have the wallet?" I ask.

"Me and the guys tried to think of a way to communicate in a situation like this. We were always thinking about weird stuff. We'd watch a spy anime and try to think of a smarter solution. One of the situations is where the bad guys know you have something but can only grab one of you. But the others have it. How do you keep them from torturing the guy they grabbed?

"We thought it through and decided that you have to make it so the only way to talk to the other guys is a way to make sure the first guy is safe," says Vik.

"I'm not sure I follow."

"Okay. You know what proof of life is?" asks Vik.

The kid has no idea how well I know. "Yes. It's how you prove the kidnapped person is alive. Like having them hold up a current newspaper."

"Right. So we started thinking about this like security protocols. How could you ensure the safety of a member of the group and prevent the channel of communication from being exploited?

"The problem with proof of life is, it opens up another vector for the bad guys. They can use it as proof of torture. Like if someone wants something from the free parties, they can keep sending them photos of the person losing body parts and being tortured," says Vik.

"So you solved this?" I ask.

"Clearly, no. But we did come up with a kind of half solution. Let's say we all went into hiding but wanted to send the all clear. How do we know that the person sending the all clear isn't compromised? How do you keep someone holding a compromised person from sending proof of torture through the communications channel?"

"You mean a dedicated communications channel that can only be used by someone if they're not being held captive or tortured?" I ask.

"Exactly. That means the people who didn't get kidnapped have to promise not to check any other channel. Which is hard, but it's the only way the other person is safe. You understand?"

"Mostly. So you figured this out?" I reply.

"Yes. I explained it to Pham. The only way to get access to the wallet was through Harry. And right now, Harry isn't accepting any email or texts. They all bounce back. I gave him Harry's info to try it himself."

"Okay. Then how *do* you communicate with Harry?" I ask.

"Spaceship Earth," says Vik. "We were watching YouTube videos about Walt Disney World and saw that you can send a video email from the Spaceship Earth ride."

"Yeah. Since before you were born. I'm not sure I follow."

"Harry has only one email account. It only accepts messages sent from Spaceship Earth. It's also got an image-detection filter so it will only accept a video showing one of us. Anything else is ignored," Vik explains.

"So you told a Thai gangster that he had to send you to Disneyland to get paid?" I ask.

"Disney World," says Vik.

"And how did that work out?"

Vik stares at his sandwich. "He locked me in that room and told me he'd start beating the shit out of me if I didn't tell him where the money was."

"I see. You don't look too beat up."

"He tried giving me some drug. I kept mumbling about celebrities. He gave up. He could tell I had a very low tolerance for pain. That's when he asked me for a list of who might be after me. I realized he was going to try to sell me off to one of them."

"Explain how you know Rebecca Gostler," I ask, changing the topic slightly.

"We met her after Mr. Raden."

"Who is Raden?" I ask.

"We'd reached out to different US government agencies about vulnerabilities in networks and crypto wallets," says Vik.

"Why the US?"

"I don't know if you follow Thai politics, but it's not exactly the most stable government. We wanted to fight terrorists and stop the Chinese from taking over Asia. Also, we were teenagers and read a lot of manga.

"Anyway, a man named Raden said he was from the CIA and wanted to talk to us. He told us about a special team the government was putting together with the most elite hackers from around the world. He'd give us accounts to go after, and we'd drain the funds. He also gave us some special tools," says Vik.

"Tools? What kind?" I ask.

"I don't know if I should tell you."

"The door is right there, Vik. I'm not stopping you," I remind him.

"How much do you know about blockchain and cryptography?" asks Vik.

"Enough to probably understand what you're talking about—but barely."

"There's a very popular encryption protocol being used right now that's supposed to take a quantum computer a million years or so to solve. The problem is, the way the algorithm is written, a step is missed. While it looks complex, you can crack it in a couple hours with just a pair of A100s. Raden said the NSA used a supercomputer to crack it and build the software tool he gave us. We had to sign letters saying that we understood even mentioning it could mean the death penalty or getting assassinated," says Vik.

"That's not how the CIA or any other agency works," I assure him.

Raden, who I suspect is Rebecca's boss, was feeding these kids a line of fantasy bullshit designed to get their comic-book-shaped minds racing with excitement.

"It sounded cool to us. Plus, we were told we could keep five percent. We called it our 'letter of marque,' but neither Raden or Rebecca knew what that meant."

"How did you meet her?"

"Raden sent her to help us create our corporation and start-up. Which we were actually really excited about. She arranged it and helped get us into the incubator where we met Kylie."

"How much did she know about the crypto-jacking?"

"We didn't talk to her about it. Raden said to only tell her we were doing penetration testing. We kept our mouths shut because we thought it might be a test."

"What about the money? I saw your apartment. You weren't living a lavish lifestyle."

"We were afraid to. Sonny's dad knew a guy that won the lottery, and gangsters bashed his head in until he gave them the ticket. We only told our family we were doing consulting. We asked Raden about moving to the United States, where it might be a little safer. He said that would be hard but he'd look into it," Vik explains.

Someone in Raden's position should have been able to get them into the US, complete with visas, with just one phone call. Something's fishy there.

"We were paranoid about someone coming after us or a double cross," says Vik.

"From Raden?"

"Sure. Anyone. So we set something up he didn't know about. Basically, a dead-man switch. When I heard the first gunshot, I pressed a button that moved the money and locked the wallet so nobody could get to it."

"What about Harry?" I ask.

"Yes. Other than Harry, I mean."

I know Vik is lying to me. I just don't know about which parts and why. He's painting a picture of himself as the innocent whiz kid caught in something he doesn't understand. I suspect Vik is also improvising the details a bit here to protect himself. But I do believe that he moved the money out of reach of Raden and everyone else.

"Did your team do anything else besides moving money?" I ask.

Vik thinks this over for a moment. I sense he's trying to decide how much to say. "We built some things."

"What kind of things?"

"Little stuff. Websites. Some blockchain network stuff. Raden paid us extra. We worked fast. He liked that."

"Could you show me some of it?"

"It was white-label stuff. We'd make it with a generic name and details. He said he'd have other developers do the rest," Vik replies.

"I'm going to want you to sit down at some point and make a note of all of that." It sounds like this Raden person was using Vik and his friends as an informal dev team for other projects. "Right now, I need you to hide in the bathroom and sit tight until I get back."

"Can I use the laptop?" asks Vik.

"I'm taking that with me. But you can use that phone. Which is pretty much the same thing to you. Just be smart about it. You know all the scenarios. The bad guys could be sitting in the living room with your families right now. Who knows? The best thing to do is not talk to anyone. It's your call. Just don't get me killed," I tell him.

Not giving him access would have only led to him straying from the hotel room and creating more problems.

"Where are you going?" asks Vik.

"I need to find out about your escape plan."

I also need to learn what else Rebecca hasn't been telling me.

"What's going on?" asks Morena after she picks up.

"Some things happened. The less I tell you the better until I'm out of the country," I reply.

"I need more than that."

"I got Vik. I have him in a safe place right now. I'm trying to figure out an exit plan," I explain.

"I see. That's complicated. Do you need anything from me?" she asks.

It's very complicated. Getting Vik out of Thailand is easy enough physically but fraught with legal complications. If I trusted the shadow CIA station chief, I'd ask him, but considering the fact that he was less than direct with me about the connection to Rebecca and I have no idea who she's really working for . . . the US government won't overtly be Vik's ticket out of Thailand.

Morena can't outright offer me the use of Wind Aerospace resources for what at this point amounts to a human-trafficking operation in slipping Vik out of the country. Given enough time, we could probably find a way to smooth that over, but time isn't an option with Conover and the Krome team hunting for Vik.

"I just want to see if you can find a way to get him out legally," I say. "But, you know, don't give specifics."

"Understood. If you need me to get *you* out in a hurry, just let me know. I've made arrangements."

"What kind of arrangements?"

"You do your job, I'll do mine," Morena replies cryptically.

I don't have time to argue with her. I need to save my strength for my coming confrontation with Rebecca.

ESCAPE ROUTE

I pound on the door to the hotel room where Rebecca and I planned to meet after grabbing Vik. I chose this location because it was close to several highways and the airport, with a clear view of vehicles entering and leaving the area.

I see a flicker of light behind the peephole, then the door opens. Rebecca looks into the hallway. "Where is Vik?"

"Safe," I reply.

I spoke to Simon in the parking lot, where he and Gun and Tanin are keeping an eye on the hotel.

In the room, Rebecca has set up her laptop on a table by the window so she can watch the parking lot.

I take a seat in the chair where she was sitting. Partially to keep my eye on the screen and partially to see what she was doing.

Unfortunately, she already signed out of her account. She's not stupid.

Ross Ulbricht, the mastermind behind the Silk Road dark-web marketplace, made it easy for prosecutors to prove their case because he was still signed into all his accounts when he was arrested at a San Francisco public library with his laptop.

Authorities first suspected him because a Google search of the first account to ever mention Silk Road was tied to his real name. He made serious mistakes on his way up and serious ones on his way out. It's kind of amazing he stayed out of reach of law enforcement for so long.

But then again, many of the "experts" chasing him were still using passwords with the word "password" in them.

Vik, xQuadrant, and Rebecca are of a different caliber. All capable of making mistakes, but less likely to do so.

"I really need to talk to Vik," says Rebecca.

"In time," I tell her.

"You don't understand. There's a lot at stake here."

"I'm sure. Why don't you sit down and enlighten me."

Rebecca takes a seat in the angriest way possible. "We don't have a lot of time, Brad. You did your part. You rescued the kid. Now let us take over from here."

"Who is *us*? Who's Raden?"

"So you've been talking to Vik. Do I need to point out that this is all confidential? You're basically interfering with an investigation," she warns me.

"'Basically' . . . odd choice of wording. The smart choice would be for me to contact the FBI office in Bangkok and let them settle this," I counter.

"And they'll turn Vik over to local authorities until they figure out what to do next, and inside prison he'll get killed or worse. You know that's a stupid idea."

She's not wrong. "Help me out. I don't trust the kid. I don't trust you."

"I haven't lied to you since we spoke, have I?" asks Rebecca.

"You haven't exactly told me the whole truth—or at least the important, relevant parts. Let's start with Raden. I assume that's a fake name. Is he your boss?"

"Sort of. He's the one running the task force."

"How many people are on this task force? I'm guessing it's you, Raden, and a couple other people performing perfunctory roles while they zone out during conference calls. When did you get involved in all this?"

"Eighteen months ago. I was doing research at Theocrates for the Office of Intelligence and Analysis, as I told you before. I was looking at blockchain transactions and tracing them to patterns," she says.

"What kind of patterns?"

"Looking for relationships between financial transactions and terrorist activities. It's not a new field. But I was able to use a new artificial-intelligence system that was originally designed by a black-box hedge fund. We increased the data and compute and starting seeing patterns."

"Who are *we*?" I ask.

"Me and two data scientists at Theocrates. I wrote some reports about it. We'd spotted what looked like a single actor who was moving money before events and then moving it shortly after," she said.

"I work better with specifics."

"There was an outbreak of attempted attacks on oil tankers three years ago. Oil prices spiked. It turned out later that someone had paid a group connected to the Houthis to target specific tankers. About $600,000 was transferred to a crypto wallet linked to the rebels. Meanwhile, after the spike in attacks, the same account that paid them collected on positions tied to oil-market speculation. They made about $60 million," she explains.

"A hundred times return. Not bad. So this is some kind of moneymaking scheme?"

"I don't know. The money keeps moving. Someone is either trying to use terror to get very rich or getting very rich to fund terrorism," Rebecca replies.

"Why not both?"

"Maybe. I realized that these funds kept growing. This person was amassing more money than the defense budgets of many countries. He's already hiring private armies, by the looks of it."

"Krome . . . You think they're working for this person? How is xQuadrant connected?"

"I don't know. They didn't touch anything attached to him, as far as we know. I'm just speculating. I don't know who else would be throwing these kinds of resources at this," she says.

"Besides the Russian, Chinese, Iranians, and North Koreans, not to mention some Qatar-based assholes," I suggest.

"I guess I mean this technically savvy."

"So, you see this pattern. Then what?"

"I send my reports to the Office of Intelligence and Analysis, CIA, DIA, and elsewhere. And not much happens. Finally I got contacted by a group that's been trying to track down someone they call 'Aetheon.' Who sounds a lot like the entity I've been tracking," she explains.

I don't know if Aetheon is some boogeyman they concocted for more funding or someone real. I know I'm starting to draw connections between things I wouldn't have a week ago.

"Did they have anything to add?"

"Quite a lot. Their working theory is that Aetheon is someone active in technology and possibly a known person. Someone in the start-up and venture-capital scene," she says.

"And not some loser in a basement?"

"To pull off what he . . . or she did, they'd have to have a kind of understanding of geopolitics and other matters that doesn't come from playing video games all day. The other assumption is that this person may have ties to the intelligence community. They might own or control a company that's involved in signal communications. We have reason to believe that Aetheon was able to get access to extremely confidential data. This is part of why I've been so hesitant with you. We don't know who he has access to or how he gets his information," she explains.

"And what changed your mind?"

"Watching you go through the effort to save Vik," she says.

"I could be working for Aetheon."

"That had been considered."

"Seriously?"

"Your boss, Kylie Connor . . . she'd be in the position to pull something like this off. Also, the fact that she'd reached out to xQuadrant. That seemed like an off-brand investment for her," says Rebecca.

"She also invested in a toy company that makes vinyl Godzilla dolls. What does that tell you?" If Kylie is one of their suspects, I have very little confidence in this task force.

"We have to consider everything. You showing up here doesn't exactly make her seem less suspicious."

"And now?"

"I vouched for you," says Rebecca.

"And how far did that go?"

"If we can get Vik to safety and keep the wallet out of the hands of Aetheon, then it'll go far."

"What would this wallet look like?" I ask.

"A thumb drive. A portable hard disk. Something that can store a master key that controls the accounts," she says.

"Why not a simple password?"

"This would be a private key that controls the address where the money was moved to. It has to be sixty-four characters long. Normally people store them on a local device with a simpler passcode that can't be entered in via a network," she explains. "It might require biometric data like an eye scan or fingerprint."

That confirms my suspicion about the missing hands in the morgue.

"It looks like Pham searched Vik pretty thoroughly," I tell her.

"Then he might be storing it in an online account like a Google Drive document. Did you give him access to the internet?"

"A phone."

"You shouldn't have done that. He could have moved the money or done who knows what with it."

"Move it where? And as far as I know, it's his money. Either way, you can sort that out with him. How is your end going?" I ask.

"We have a plane. I'll send you the location of the hangar."

"The sooner, the better. One more thing. Did Vik or any of the others ever mention someone named Harry?"

"No. Who is that?"

"Nobody," I reply.

FLAK

I'm sitting on the floor watching while Simon and Gun strap Vik into body armor. Tanin kneels next to me, adding metal plates to our motorcycle helmets.

None of them needed to keep helping us like this. Their pledge was fulfilled the moment we embarrassed Pham, but they eagerly offered to help when I explained that I needed to get Vik to the airport and onto a plane to America.

When I told Vik that these cops and ex-cops had volunteered to save his life, he bowed and hugged them. He's been through a lot and isn't sure who's being authentic with him and who isn't.

He clearly still doesn't trust me. Some part of him still fears that this is an elaborate long con to get him to talk. I don't blame him. I've played almost this same exact role in situations like this that *were* long cons.

"You check in with your family?" I ask Vik.

"Yes. They're okay. Scared. I haven't told the others what happened to Sonny, Al, and Michael yet. I don't know how to," he admits.

"Don't worry about that now," says Simon as he pats Vik on the shoulder. "Let's focus on keeping you alive."

"Rebecca and Raden are going to ask you about the wallet. They're going to want to know how to get access to it," I explain to Vik.

"I know. That's up to Harry. If he sees me waving from Disney World, then he'll send the key. They understand that, right?" asks Vik.

"I figured I'd let you explain it."

I don't know how much I believe what Vik's telling me. It's not my place to challenge him, but I also don't have to hawk what he's selling to Gostler's task force.

"Let's go over the plan. Gun will drive the van. It'll look like something we'd hide you inside of. But you'll actually be on the motorcycle with me, and Simon will be right behind us with Tanin on the back of his," I explain.

"Why not in the van?" asks Vik.

"Because the people we want to avoid will be looking for something like that. And in Bangkok traffic, would you rather be in a big van or something that can go around everything else?"

"I understand," he says.

"Well, there's more. We're heading to an airport. And the bad guys will probably be keeping an eye out. Thankfully, there are several airports. That said, we have to be careful and ready to run if something goes bad."

"I looked up the Krome group while you were gone," says Vik.

"Their website or the forums where people talk about what they really do?"

"All of it. I found their public key too," says Vik.

"For bitcoin?" I ask.

"Yes. They have a public key on their website, but they use another one connected to a tumbler."

"What's a tumbler?" asks Simon.

"It's a way to launder bitcoin transactions. Let's say I want to pay you one thousand dollars but I don't want it to connect to me. I put the thousand into the tumbler and give you another key, kind of an IOU that lets you remove one thousand from the tumbler. But the thousand won't come specifically from *my* bitcoins, see?"

"That's legal?" asks Simon.

"That's bitcoin," Vik replies.

Simon gives me a shrug. "All the criminals I know are working too hard."

"Can you spot transactions as they go to Krome?" I ask.

"Yeah. The tumbler they're using has some vulnerabilities. But I'd really need to use a laptop to explore more."

"Do yourself a favor: don't freely offer this to Rebecca or Raden. You might need to use it to bargain with," I explain.

"Are you saying I shouldn't trust them?"

"Is that a joke? Don't trust anyone. Even well-intentioned people. They'll make you a lot of promises, but they might not be able to follow through. So don't give them everything just yet," I advise him.

Simon hands Vik a zippered jacket to put over the body armor. I put on my own tactical vest and a loose-fitting coat over it. Tanin hands us our helmets.

"Ready to saddle up?" I ask.

PINPOINT

I keep a safe distance from Gun as he drives the van. Simon and Tanin in turn follow behind Vik and me far enough back that it doesn't appear we're riding together.

My head is on a swivel as I keep a lookout for the black SUV and the Krome team.

While I never saw Conover get out of the SUV, I'm pretty sure he was one of the men who raided Pham's complex. I'm also sure he was there when Vik's friends were killed. Right now, he's searching for me and Vik. Although I had on a mask and was wearing a hat, Conover is smart enough to figure this was the kind of operation I'd pull off.

I don't see any helicopters or cars following us. We planned a route that would use side streets and straightaways to help us detect tails. The biggest risk comes when we get closer to the airport. That's where we're most likely to run into people on the lookout for us.

Besides Krome, we had the other groups on the hunt for Vik. If Conover was able to eventually figure out where Pham was keeping Vik hidden, chances are others could as well.

The airfield is close to the ocean. It's a small airport with only a few hangars and no fence. At the far end is a flying club that's still active. The main hangars look like they are used to store construction machinery now.

As we get closer, I hang back and let Gun drive the van down the main road, listening for updates over my AirPods.

"I don't see any cars here," says Gun. "I'm going to drive around the hangars just to make sure."

I bring the motorcycle to a stop to wait for his report.

Thick green bushes line the road and feel like they're about to overtake the pavement. Thailand is a lush country, and even in industrialized areas, nature likes to remind you that the land could revert back to jungle at any moment.

"What are we waiting for?" asks Vik.

"Just making sure there isn't an ambush heading our way," I reply.

"There's nobody here. Just a bunch of stray cats," Gun's voice says in my ear.

I wave to Simon behind me and we drive down the road, keeping our eyes on the surrounding foliage. It would be very easy to hide a hundred men in there a few meters back.

As I reach the tarmac, I see the hangars I spotted on Google Maps. One of them has blue tarps hanging over the entrance. To my right, the fuselages of two Cessnas are obscured by tall grass.

On my left is the runway that looks like it's in good condition. At the far end is a modern building that belonged to a now out-of-business tourist charter.

While this location is perfect for clandestine trafficking operations, it makes me a little uneasy.

Rebecca said that the CIA station chief told her it was "ideal" for our needs. I'm not sure if he understood I wasn't trying to smuggle arms into Burma away from the prying eyes of the cops. We're trying to avoid the kind of people who'd feel at home here.

Simon pulls up next to me with Tanin.

"What do you think?" asks Simon.

"It makes me feel nervous."

"Me too," he replies.

"Do you know how to pick a lock?" I ask.

"More or less."

"You see that building down there? I want you to take the kid and wait inside there. Bring the bike inside too. I'll hang back here near the hangar with Tanin. We'll also have Gun park the van in the middle of the tarmac out here, then stay close to Tanin and me. Good?"

"Cautious. Cautious is good."

We switch riders, and Simon takes Vik to the other building. He'll have a good vantage of what's going on and be able to keep the kid safe in case everything goes to hell.

While there's only one road into here, on the western side across a narrow field there's a golf course that runs all the way to another road I can use as an exit point if necessary.

After making sure Vik and Simon are inside the other building, I pull my bike into the open hangar with the blue tarps hanging over the entrance.

The interior is filled with more fuselages and wings. There are no tools or anything of value, unless you really need a picked-apart Cessna airframe that last saw service when I was a teenager.

I swing a wing around in its cradle and create a kind of barricade that I can use to look out on the tarmac from behind. Gun and Tanin join me and take up strategic positions behind engine blocks, and we wait.

I call Rebecca.

"What's the update on the airplane?"

"Working on it," she says.

"What does that mean?"

"The plane encountered some weather and is running a little behind," she replies.

I don't like the sound of that. "How late?"

"I'm asking. All of this is last minute. You know how these things are."

"Can you at least give me the tail number so I can confirm?" I ask.

"They haven't given it to me yet."

I'm getting anxious. This could just be another CIA fuckup—or not. Gun snaps his fingers and points upward.

"Rebecca, you better not be fucking with me," I say before hanging up.

I listen. It's not an airplane that Gun heard. It's the high-pitched sound of a drone.

Krome has found us, and the fuckers are using a drone to scope out the airfield.

I hear the drone fly around the back of the hangar. The sound fades, then picks up again as it moves down the tarmac toward our van.

"Should we make a run for it?" asks Simon over my AirPods.

"No. They're probably parked at the front ready to shoot anyone who comes running. Just stay put. If I have to draw them away from you and Vik, I will. What you *can* do is call the Royal Thai Police. See if we can get them to show up."

I aim my shotgun, still loaded with beanbag rounds, over the edge of the wing and wait for the drone to fly closer to the entrance of the hangar.

The blue tarp ripples in the wind, and I catch a glimpse of the UAV as it flies past a tear in the fabric. The shadow of the drone moves along the thin material, and it comes into view again at a large gap.

The drone could be for surveillance only, or it could have a grenade strapped to it. While shooting it will reveal our position, it's not like Krome doesn't know we're here.

I fire a round at the drone, and the propellers shatter into hundreds of pieces. It falls to the ground, dead and disintegrated.

"Well, they know we're here now," I mutter under my breath.

"I can't get through to the dispatcher," says Simon.

"What do you mean?" I ask.

"I keep trying to call the emergency number. It's busy. Vik says they might be doing a denial-of-service thing. He says there are websites where you can pay to have all the cell towers jammed."

Tanin makes a gesture and points toward the back wall of the hangar. Boots are scuffing against the ground. It sounds like they're getting ready to make an assault.

Gun and Tanin already have on their goggles and N95 masks. They're experienced police officers and understand that the logical next step will be to try to gas us out of here and take us down when we make a run for it.

What they want to avoid is having to come in here and risk getting shot. These men are mercenaries with a number in their head indicating how much it's worth to risk their life.

I'm tempted to have Gun shoot a few rounds into the aluminum wall to let them know we're playing for keeps. I hesitate because that might just get their adrenaline flowing and make them charge in regardless of the price they've put on their lives.

"We'll keep this simple, Bradley," Conover says over a megaphone. "Send the kid out and everyone goes home alive. Including the kid."

I wasn't expecting that tactic. He really doesn't want a fight, or else his mercenaries don't.

I motion for Gun and Tanin to stay put. They get it.

Our best strategy is to stay inside and wait them out. Conover has no idea how many people I have in here unless Rebecca is connected to this.

"Brad, come on. This is stupid. You're not even getting paid for this," says Conover.

He makes a fair point. But I'm kind of committed right now.

A tall, very muscular man covered in tactical armor and wearing a face shield strides across the tarmac and over to our van.

He uses a knife to slash our tires, then looks back in our direction, challenging us to do something. I have my muzzle aimed at his head but don't want to be the one to take the first shot.

"There goes your ride out of here," says Conover through his megaphone.

He knows we have a plane coming, right? I mean, we *do*, don't we?

Mr. Bowie Knife stands in the middle of the tarmac, facing us.

I know the type. He's the kind you send in first because he thinks he's invincible. He's also the kind you want to make sure you have some spares of, because he's not.

We sit and wait. We know what we're facing. Conover and his men don't.

Bowie Knife looks in the direction of Conover's amplified voice and walks out of view.

Bootsteps retreat from the back of the hangar. A moment later, there's the sound of doors closing and truck tires on gravel as it turns around.

"Simon, what do you see?"

"They've left," he replies.

"Why?" I wonder aloud.

I call Rebecca.

"Where the hell is the plane?"

"Ten minutes out! I swear. I'm coming to you," she says.

"Convenient. Conover and his men were just here," I reply.

"What?" She sounds genuinely surprised.

"How the hell did they know to come here?"

"There was a fuckup. Someone filed a public flight plan to this airport using a plane registered to a known CIA front company," she explains.

Plausible . . . but suspicious.

"If this plane actually lands and I can't trace its tail number back to the US government, I'm blowing it up on the runway with a rocket launcher."

I hang up and let her wonder if I actually have a rocket launcher.

I get a call from Simon. "Vik wants to talk to you."

"Mr. Brad?" asks Vik.

"Yeah?"

"I know why the men left. I'm pretty sure, at least."

"And why is that?"

"Remember how I was telling you that Krome was using a tumbler to accept crypto payments—you know, to make them untraceable?"

"Yeah?"

"I also said there was a vulnerability. You can forge a withdrawal from the same receiving account. When they showed up, I looked for any recent transactions from an address into the tumbler that could match with a Krome withdrawal. I found one for two hours ago."

That wouldn't have been long after the flight plan was filed . . . about when this airport's location became knowable.

"All right. So why did they leave?"

"Because I reversed the transaction. I basically canceled the IOU."

"You mean you stopped Krome from getting paid? But they moved out of here so quickly."

"I sent a message to an email address connected to the account and said we had to cancel the operation right now," Vik explains.

That probably went to Krome's field supervisor. The moment he realized they weren't getting paid for this job, they pulled back.

"That's smart thinking, Vik. How long before they sort it out?"

"Right now, I'm using my server network to keep pinging the tumbler. I'm blocking every other transaction too, so I'm sure the people running it will shut me out sooner than later."

"Okay. You bought us some time. Krome will probably be demanding some other method of payment. They also have to be worried that their transactions aren't invisible anymore. Were you able to track any other payments, by chance?"

"Hundreds. I had to sort through them to find the one for today," says Vik.

"Send that list to anyone you trust. Not just Harry. That could be very valuable information."

And dangerous, I think to myself.

But it could also be a way to shut down Krome entirely.

DEPARTURE

A taxi pulls onto the tarmac and comes to a stop near the bumper of our flat-tired van. I watch from inside the hangar as Rebecca gets out carrying a backpack and a small travel bag.

The driver turns around and drives off.

"Are we clear?" asks Simon over the phone.

"Not yet. Let me go talk to her."

I get up from where I've been hiding behind a wing and walk out of the hangar.

"Are you okay?" asks Rebecca.

I look down the road where the taxi is departing and scan for any sign of Conover and his team.

"That depends," I reply.

She glances into the hangar behind me. "Where's Vik?"

"He'll be here when I think it's safe. Is it safe, Rebecca?"

I'm not comfortable trusting her. Unfortunately, I have zero other options at the moment. I could try to get Vik into the US embassy or that of another friendly country right now, based on what he has on Krome. But that would require getting past Conover, whose team must be anticipating such a move, among others. Getting to an embassy could well be impossible.

Rebecca checks her phone. "The plane should be here in ten minutes. I promise."

I see a twinkling light on the horizon beyond the edge of the runway.

"If Conover shows up, I'm shooting you first," I reply.

"Brad . . ."

"I'm serious. I'm in a no-fuckups-or-coincidences mood. Too much has gone wrong already."

"You still don't trust me?" Rebecca makes her voice sound hurt. "In nine minutes, you'll see that I kept my part of the bargain. We'll get Vik to US territory and make sure he's well taken care of."

"Where?" I ask.

"Our first stopover will be at Kadena Air Base in Japan to refuel. Then Hawaii to change crews, then Los Angeles."

"I'll text my people to make arrangements for Vik in Los Angeles," I reply.

"We have that taken care of. Don't worry," she says.

"Um, no. I'm getting this kid a lawyer and making sure my people stick by him."

"Brad, that's not going to be necessary. And there're also the security implications. He can't tell a lawyer what he knows."

"There are DC lawyers with security clearances he can talk to. We employ them all the time to handle our government contracts. I know you know this, so right now, that trust you want me to have in you? Isn't there."

"I know. I know. I'll sort it out on our end. They won't be happy, I can tell you that."

"My job's to keep Vik alive. As far as Kylie is concerned, he's a member of the Wind Aerospace corporate family."

Kylie didn't exactly put it that way, but she'd back up my claim, given the situation.

The lights of the jet grow brighter and the sound of the turbines gets louder. I can tell by the noise this is a G650. It's the same kind of jet Jeff Bezos uses to get around. Rebecca's people certainly came through on that end.

The jet touches down at the end of the runway, and the pilot brings it to a stop with plenty of room to spare. These jets are designed to use small, local airfields like this one, but it's still impressive to see someone make a landing with that much precision on a strip they've never seen before.

The copilot opens up the door and lowers the stairs to the plane.

Rebecca turns to me. "Good enough?"

I could point out that Kylie is currently testing a G800.

I walk over to the tail section and take a photo of the numbers and text them to Morena and Kylie.

Rebecca introduces herself to the copilot. "I'm Rebecca Gostler. This is Brad."

I give the pilot a nod, then text his name, Fraundler, to Morena and Kylie.

He couldn't be more nonchalant about the fact that I'm wearing body armor and have a shotgun slung over my shoulder.

"Can we bring Vik out now?" asks Rebecca.

"I want to take a look inside."

"Feel free," says Fraundler.

I step inside the plane and glance around the interior. It's nice but not lavish. It's more corporate than decadent. I poke my head into the cockpit and nod to the captain.

I text his name, Williams, to Morena and Kylie as well.

Just to make sure Conover isn't hiding inside the bathrooms, I check both the forward and aft washrooms. They're empty.

It's just the two pilots.

I thank the captain, then step outside.

"Are we good?" asks Rebecca.

"One second."

I check a text message from Morena.

Plane belongs to Infinity Flight Services. Privately held, but lots of departures and arrivals from an airfield in Virginia with support aircraft for intelligence agencies. Used a lot for summits. Kylie says she knows pilots who fly for Infinity. They're ex-military. Looks to be legitimate. No connection to Krome we can find. We'll keep looking.

Then:

Fraundler did flight school with George Benford—one of our test pilots.

"I think we're good," I tell Rebecca.

I call Simon and tell him to bring Vik.

We watch as he drives Vik on the back of his motorcycle from the building at the far end of the runway up to the jet.

Vik hops off the back of the bike and marvels at the plane.

"Wow! G650," he says excitedly.

It is the first happy expression I've seen on his face since I found him curled up in Pham's apartment complex.

"Hey, Vik," says Rebecca.

He turns to her and his eyes light up even more. "Ms. Rebecca! So Brad was telling the truth."

"Most of the time," she replies.

"You ready?" I ask him.

The smile on Vik's face fades as he looks at the copilot and then the plane again. Captain Williams is standing just inside the entrance.

"Where are we going?" he asks.

"A quick stopover in Japan, then Hawaii, and then Los Angeles," Rebecca explains.

"When can I see my family?" asks Vik.

"Soon. We'll arrange for that," says Rebecca. "We just need to get you out of here. The sooner the better."

"Do you have any bags?" asks Fraundler.

"Just this," says Vik as he holds up the phone I gave him. He looks to me. "Is this safe?"

"It's the only option right now." I point to the copilot. "Captain Fraundler went to flight school with a friend of mine, George Benford."

"You know George?" replies Fraundler.

"He's one of our test pilots at Wind Aerospace," I respond, pretending I've said more than three words to Benford.

My real goal is to let Fraundler know that my colleagues and I know who he is—to discourage any screwups.

I hand Simon my duffel bag and shotgun. "Take the others out on the bikes. Drive like hell. I'll arrange for someone to pick up the van. I suggest you all take a vacation and get out of town. It would make me feel better if you let me send you all something as a thank-you."

"We'd be insulted if you did that," he replies.

"I can live with that. We'll connect and talk about next steps regarding our mutual enemy," I reply, not wanting to say "Pham" in front of the pilot.

I gesture for Vik to take the stairs.

"You first," he says to me.

Fraundler puts a hand out to stop me. "I'm sorry, but we're only authorized to take Ms. Gostler and Viktor."

"Rebecca?" I don't hide my frustration.

"I'm sorry. Let me check."

Rebecca walks away to talk on her phone. In the distance I can hear the sound of terse words being exchanged.

She walks back over to us with the phone's microphone pressed against her stomach.

"I'm sorry. They're adamant. Trying to get Vik out involved a lot of paperwork. Having you leave too on this plane is a bureaucratic nightmare. They said they can arrange for the next flight out of Bangkok on a commercial plane. You should arrive in Los Angeles at the same time. Maybe a bit before because of our layovers," she explains.

I look at Vik. He's staring at me.

"They can't make you get on this plane, Vik," I tell him.

"What about the men who are after me? Will they come back?" he asks.

"Probably. But I can get you out of here and make other arrangements. It's your call."

Vik turns to Rebecca. "No Brad, no Vik."

"We went through a lot of expense to bring this jet here, Vik . . ." she begins.

"Stop fucking with the kid's head," I tell her. "Explain the situation to your bosses. It's that simple."

Rebecca storms off in frustration. We can hear her arguing with whoever is on the other line from where we're standing.

It sounds like she's pleading our case and not explaining how she's going to talk us out of it. I sense that she's very much stuck between a rock and a hard place.

She's dealing with the same people that told the families of fallen soldiers after the disastrous Afghanistan pullout that they had to pay for the bodies to be flown home. Still, the person at the other end of the call will have the authority to allow me on the plane.

Rebecca walks back to us. She seems slightly more relaxed.

"Brad can come with," she explains to Fraundler and Williams. "They'll send you a text to confirm."

"All right," replies Williams. "Let's get moving."

"You ready, Vik?"

Vik looks at me for reassurance.

I fake it. "Now comes the easy part. Although I noticed there's no flight attendant, so you'll have to pour your own drinks."

DESTINATION

The plane takes to the air, and I finally relax. I'm exhausted. Every bone in my body still feels rattled from my fall from the building, and I have bruises that may live longer than I do.

Vik is sleeping in the recliner next to me, curled up in a ball.

Rebecca sits across from us, her seat facing our direction as she types into her keyboard. She looks over at Vik. "Hey, buddy, I hate to bother you, but I need to send a report before we lose signal. You have the key for the wallet, correct?"

Vik can barely open his eyes. "When I'm safe, Harry will give you the keys."

"Right. It's just that nobody knows who this Harry is. We never authorized him to be part of this." She glances over at me. "I'm sorry, Brad, but could you give Vik and me a moment to talk?"

"No Brad, no Vik," Vik says again.

"Okay. One second, Vik. Brad, may I speak with you?"

I follow Rebecca to the tiny galley at the front of the plane.

"Listen, what you've done is great. I can't tell you how grateful we are," she begins.

"So grateful you wanted to leave me back in Bangkok with Conover and his men running around?"

"That's a fuckup. I'm sorry. They didn't understand the situation. But we're in the air, and everything is fine now. You did your part. I need to be able to talk to Vik about important and sensitive matters."

"I think you should let the kid sleep. But he's his own boss," I tell her.

"Well, right now, he's looking to you for permission to do anything. You saved him, and now he's got some kind of . . . Stockholm syndrome . . . um, bad choice of words," she says, correcting herself.

"I'd say. The kid doesn't trust anyone. That includes me. He only slightly trusts me because I'm the only one with any skin in the game."

"I get that. But I'd like you to tell him he can trust us," she says.

"You mean lie?"

"Brad. What have I not come through on?"

"There's always been a catch. Either way, Vik can do whatever he wants to do."

"Right now, I need to talk to him and you're in the way."

"He shouldn't say another word to you without a lawyer present," I say with zero sympathy.

"This isn't a legal issue. It's a national security matter."

"I don't think the distinction is as clear as you think it is. Governments will use either one to get what they want."

"Correct. And right now, there are nine billion dollars floating around out there we need to make sure don't fall into the wrong hands. Do you get that?"

"I understand. But given the fact that he and his friends are the ones who figured out how to take that money away from the wrong hands and have so far kept it away, I think it's probably safe right now."

"And what if you're wrong?"

"Would you like me to pin his arm behind his back and dunk his head into the toilet until he talks?"

"Don't be stupid. That's not what we're asking. I just need him to cooperate."

"And I know your superiors are yelling at you to get answers. Look, you need to stand up for yourself and do what *you* think is right."

"Is that what you always did?"

"No, Rebecca. I didn't do it nearly enough. All I can say is that the few times I did stand up and do what I thought was right, I never regretted it. There were repercussions, but no regrets."

Her arms are folded across her body in a defensive posture. "I wish it was just that simple. All I want to do is get Aetheon."

"Who may or may not exist and have no connection to Vik. Let the kid relax. He'll be more helpful if he doesn't think he's one step away from some black-box interrogation site."

Rebecca lets out a long exhale, then walks back to her seat. I take mine across from Vik.

"Everything okay?" he asks.

"It's all fine. Get some sleep."

Vik covers the side of his face so Rebecca can't see and mouths, "I think she digs you."

I shrug and look out the window at the fading sun.

I feel like I've aged five years over the past five days. The aspirin and booze are taking longer to kill the pain, and I'm afraid no amount of sleep is going to make me feel less exhausted.

We hit a bit of turbulence and I wake up. I was more tired than I realized. It's pitch-black outside, and I can see stars glittering in the distance.

I check my watch. Only forty minutes have gone by.

Vik is asleep, and Rebecca has finally closed her laptop and is trying to get some rest herself.

Only forty minutes?

That's a bit odd.

I get up and walk toward the front of the plane and knock on the cockpit door.

Fraundler unlocks it and slides it open.

"What's up?" he asks.

"I noticed that it's a bit dark for this time. Are we still headed to Japan? This seems like we're taking a more eastern route."

"I can tell you're a frequent flier. Yeah. There was a change of plans. We're actually headed to Guam."

"Andersen or Won Pat International?" I reply, asking if we're landing at the air force base or the civilian airport.

"Won Pat," he replies. "Less red tape."

"I need to tell my boss there's been a change of plans. Is the satellite still working?"

"Not right now. We get blackouts over this part of the ocean," says Fraundler.

"Can I give you a message to relay over the radio?"

"Sure thing."

I look him in the eyes. "Captain, we *are* going to Guam, right?"

"Yes. Of course."

I want to tell him that if I find out that's not the case, he's going to have a very unruly passenger on board, but decide it's best not to forewarn him.

I walk back to the rear of the plane and kick Rebecca's seat. Her body shakes and she wakes, looking confused.

"Are we there?"

"Where, Rebecca? Where do you think we're going?"

"Oh, that. Guam. I forgot to tell you. We're stopping there, then Hawaii, then Los Angeles. It'll be easier to process you and Vik there."

"Are you positive?" I ask.

"Yes. I swear. Would it have made a difference if we knew before we left?"

"I just want to keep my employer updated."

"I'm sure they can relay a message. Not that it makes a difference. We're still headed to the same final destination," she assures me. She reaches up and touches my arm. "You can relax now. You don't always have to be on guard."

I glance over at Vik, who is sound asleep. I remember when I'd walk into Jason's room after I returned from a long trip, sometimes with flecks of blood still on my shoes, and I'd see him all balled up as he slept.

Whatever worldly fears he had while he was awake—trigonometry exams, asking Caitlin Singh on a date—faded to mist while he slept.

I sit back down and take another drink and hope my own anxieties fade away.

MOST WANTED

Captain Williams's voice wakes me up as he announces over the intercom that we're about to make our descent into Won Pat Airport.

I look out the window just to be sure and spot sunlight reflecting off the large solar array located at the eastern end of the island.

Rebecca is already on her computer, and Vik is yawning.

I check my phone and see a text from Morena:

Noticed the flight change. We're monitoring the situation. Found a lawyer for Vik.

I'm glad things didn't stop moving on our end while I was asleep.

"Where are we?" asks Vik.

"Guam. We have to refuel and change crews. It will be a few hours. We'll need to let them clean the plane," says Rebecca.

"What about immigration?" I ask.

We just flew in from a foreign country. It's not like we get to hop out and have the run of the island.

"Someone is meeting us at the airport," she replies.

Well, that's good. I'd be worried if the plan was to throw a hood over Vik's head and shove him into the back of a van.

Williams and Fraundler bring the jet to a smooth touchdown, and we taxi to the end of the runway to a section with private hangars. Two police cars and an SUV are waiting next to the tarmac near there.

Rebecca is staring at her phone and glances over at me, then back, and texts something.

"Everything okay?" I ask.

She points out the window. "Satisfied this isn't all one big psyop?"

"I didn't get to be this old in this line of work without a high degree of paranoia," I reply.

She nods. "Once we get Vik settled, we should grab dinner and you can tell me all about it."

The plane comes to a stop, and Fraundler walks over to the hatch and undoes the latch. Warm tropical air blows into the cabin, and the temperature immediately climbs by a few degrees.

"Let's go stretch our legs," I say to Vik.

"Thanks, gentlemen," I call to Williams in the cockpit and Fraundler by the exit.

"Have a safe journey," Fraundler replies as we walk down the short flight of steps.

"Who are these guys?" asks Vik as two men get out of the SUV.

Both are wearing suits. One has a badge clipped to his breast pocket. The other is holding a sheaf of papers and is striding toward us with a neutral expression on his face.

The man holding the papers shouts over the sound of the turbines. "Viktor Phumhiran, a.k.a. Steven Blacknight, a.k.a. Thail Mikat, we have a warrant for your arrest."

Vik freezes in his tracks and turns to me, confused. I glance over at Rebecca, who is already reaching for the papers.

"What's going on?" I ask.

"Thank you for bringing Mr. Phumhiran to justice. He's been implicated in several hacks of government servers and ransomware attacks, including a recent one involving the Atlanta Children's Hospital," says the man.

"What's your name? Who are you with?" I ask.

"This is Agent Nunez." He indicates the FBI agent next to him. "I'm Cartwright. Agent Nunez, would you place Mr. Phumhiran in custody? Ms. Gostler, your superiors request your presence stateside, immediately. One of these police officers will escort you to your departure gate."

Rebecca hands me the papers. "I don't understand. It sounds like the FBI saw our flight plan and Viktor's name."

And here I was worried about Krome or the Russians tracking us.

"Let me help you with your bags," says a police officer to Rebecca as she holds open the passenger door to her cruiser.

"Brad?" pleads Vik as he's being placed into handcuffs.

"We appreciate your help, Mr. Trasker," says Cartwright. "We've made arrangements for you as well."

Nunez is putting Vik into the back of the SUV.

I ignore Cartwright and walk up to Nunez.

"What's going on?"

"Looks like you helped catch one of our most wanted," he replies.

Vik looks at me from inside the SUV. "I don't know what they're talking about. I didn't do anything."

Well, other than rip off a bunch of crypto exchanges and who knows what else . . .

"Mr. Trasker, considering the national security concerns, it's advisable that you not discuss this with anyone," says Cartwright.

"Who do I follow up with?" I ask.

"You can contact the FBI, but rest assured we'll be reaching out to you."

Nunez shuts the door on Vik's confused face and gets into the driver's seat. Cartwright gets into the passenger side and everyone drives away, leaving me on the tarmac alone.

PASTEUP

I'm sitting at the Burger King inside the airport terminal trying to understand what just happened. I've sat in this very booth a number of times, either on my way to or coming back from a mission in the Pacific.

Sometimes I sit here and reflect on what I should have done differently. Other times I think about what I should do next.

I've eaten Whoppers here while staring at photos of Jason and my ex-wife on my phone, wondering what life would have been like if I'd taken a normal job and not simply pretended to be like everyone else.

While things didn't turn out so well between my wife and me, Jason made it to college without feeling too much resentment for me. And then he died.

I'd tell myself at least I was there for him more than my own father was around for me—but Dad was never there at all, so it's not a great comparison.

My biggest fear is letting people down. I have two modes: overcompensating or cutting them off entirely.

I'm trying to find reasons to cut Vik off now as I read through the indictment.

There are a lot of damning accusations that paint a different picture of him than I had formed. There's nothing in here like going on a strangling spree, but the alleged ransomware attacks and probes of government security are clear felonies.

I also have to admit that these are entirely plausible things that Vik would be capable of doing. The kid managed to hack an illicit crypto server on a throwaway phone I gave him.

My phone buzzes as Morena calls me back.

"What's new?" I ask.

"The ransomware attacks check out. I'm still looking into the hacking of federal agencies. It doesn't look good," she says.

"How come we didn't know this sooner?" I ask.

"You didn't find out his last name until two days ago. You'd think your friend Ms. Gostler would have said something . . ."

"That's a whole different situation. She seemed caught off guard. But who knows."

"Lucky break for the FBI watching the flight logs," says Morena.

"Indeed. It smells funny, but I can't figure it out. They could have extradited him."

"They didn't know who he was until a few days ago," she points out.

"But it doesn't do Rebecca and her superiors any good to have Vik in FBI custody."

"They might be cooperating with them on a larger operation."

I didn't tell Morena everything Rebecca told me, out of respect for it being told to me in confidence. For instance, I never mentioned the agency Rebecca works for or anything about Aetheon.

"We can make arrangements to fly you back," says Morena.

"I'll let you know. I'm still trying to figure it all out."

"We could also give you some support there. Send Brenda and a few others over," offers Morena.

Morena and Kylie have suggested this multiple times. "No. I'd like to contain this mess to just me," I reply.

"I know. But help is just a call away," she says.

I could have used it back at the airport in Bangkok, but the last thing I need on my conscience is more dead people—at another airport, no less.

"Thanks, Morena. Let's catch up on that Netflix show when I get back."

"Which one?"

"Any of them."

I stare at the papers in front of me, aware that I haven't ordered anything and that I'm not really hungry.

I never stop to "process" my feelings. I simply keep moving forward, trying to put as much distance as I can between them and me.

Right now, I'm aware that I'm angry. I'm angry at Rebecca. I'm angry at Vik for bullshitting me. And I'm angry at myself for being such a goddamn fool.

I missed the field, true. Being a man of action, I had zero hesitation bringing Inspector Simon and his cop buddies into harm's way because I wanted to prove to myself that I was still relevant and not a broken-down wreck with an ass so bruised I could pass for a baboon from behind.

I wanted things to be black and white. Sure, there were the usual gray people like Rebecca. But Vik was the innocent and Conover the villain.

Looking at the charges against Vik, I'm wondering how much of his story I need to rethink. I knew he was withholding from me. I assumed it was because he didn't know who to trust.

But should I trust Viktor Phumhiran, a.k.a. Steven Blacknight, a.k.a. Thail Mikat? Maybe Viktor would never sell out his friends, but what about "Steven Blacknight" or "Thail Mikat"?

People can get caught up in spy role-play. I saw Rebecca getting lost in it with her little flirtations. I myself did it by putting other people into dangerous situations as if they were my own tac-ops team.

Vik the mastermind . . . In a way, I can see that. He's clearly the smartest person in this whole affair. His sole weakness is a lack of experience.

I pick up the document and shake my head. Who's the real Vik?

I put on my reading glasses and look closer at the aliases.

I get that electric feeling on the back of my neck when I realize something is off.

Something is really, really off here.

I send a hurried text to Morena, then find the nearest exit so I can get a cab and find Vik.

HABEAS CORPUS

The Guam FBI office is in the same building as the Immigration and Customs Enforcement, across the street from a Home Depot—where I once had to buy parts for improvised explosives on my way to another small Pacific island where the Chinese were building listening posts.

I press the buzzer and the door unlocks. Agent Nunez gets up from a desk behind a glass window and meets me at the counter.

I'm relieved to see that Nunez is real and the whole airport interception wasn't an elaborate ruse.

"Can I help you, Mr. Trasker?"

"Is Viktor still here?" I ask.

"He's in a conference room with the other gentleman," replies Nunez.

I lay out the paperwork Agent Cartwright gave me. "Take a look."

"What am I looking at?"

"The font used for Viktor's name. It's different from the aliases' font. His name's not even aligned with the other text."

"I'm not sure I follow."

"This was forged. The kid in there, he's not Steven Blacknight or the other alias. Look up the original wanted notice: Viktor's name isn't in there."

"This one was just updated and issued," Nunez says.

"Issued by who? A ten-year-old with a bottle of Wite-Out and his dad's typewriter?" I ask, exasperated.

"I'm just the facilitator here. This case doesn't belong to this office. This is the other gentleman's case," Nunez explains.

"What FBI office is Agent Cartwright out of?" I ask.

"Mr. Cartwright's not an FBI agent," says Nunez.

"I'm sorry, what?"

"He's acting on behalf of the State Department."

"'On behalf of'? Is he outside counsel?"

"That's not for me to speculate."

I get the sense that there's some kind of tension here. Not between Nunez and me, but between Nunez and Cartwright. There might have been some interagency shoving going on.

"Has Viktor been arrested?" I ask.

"No. We're still waiting on paperwork."

"Can I speak with him?"

"He's in with Mr. Cartwright at the moment," Nunez says, impotently.

"Listen to me: The kid has no representation. He has no idea what's about to happen to him." I point to the papers. "We both know this looks suspicious and rushed. Let me talk to Vik."

I expect pushback, but instead Nunez nods and shrugs. "Why not. Nothing's been normal today. This way."

I follow him down a short hall to another room with a glass wall. On the other side sits Vik at one end of a table and Cartwright at the other.

I notice that Vik's hands are no longer handcuffed. In front of him is a blank yellow legal pad and a pen.

"What's he doing here?" asks Cartwright as he sees me.

"He wants to speak to Mr. Phumhiran," says Nunez.

"Well, he can't. Please escort him out of here," Cartwright responds.

I want to wince at how bad of a move that was, but I don't because it's about to play out in my favor.

"I'm sorry," says Nunez. "Did you not see the large, bold letters outside that said FBI? Did you not see my badge that also says FBI? Did you forget where you are?"

"You're in fucking Guam, Agent. Think about that one," replies Cartwright.

"I like Guam," I say as I take a seat between Vik and Cartwright.

Vik looks over at me, but with more of a glare than relief. He's back to not trusting anyone.

"This is ridiculous. He can't be in here while I talk to the suspect," says Cartwright.

"Then you're free to leave," replies Nunez.

I throw the papers in front of Cartwright. "Maybe you can go talk to whoever did this horrible paste-up job while you're at it."

"It would be best if you leave, Mr. Trasker," says Cartwright as icily as he's able.

"Maybe. Could you show me some ID so I know who the hell you are?"

"How about I just tell you to go fuck yourself. You'll find out later what kind of a mistake you're making," he growls at me.

"I'm going to get back to work," says Nunez, leaving the three of us alone.

"Don't tell this man anything, Vik. We're still trying to get it all sorted out. We have a lawyer for you. You can talk to him," I say past Cartwright.

"I wouldn't put too much stock in what this man says. He's a hired mercenary," counters Cartwright. "He killed three men in cold blood last year and shot another unarmed man in the kneecap because he was angry at him."

I think Cartwright just made the least persuasive argument he could have.

"The men were armed and trying to kill Kylie, my boss. The guy missing the kneecap, I don't know anything about. I heard it was an accident. But he also betrayed Kylie." I look at Cartwright. "Bad things happen to people who try to hurt my friends."

I notice the pad in front of Vik. "Is he asking for the private key?" Vik nods.

"Did you tell him that Harry is the only one that has it?"

"Yes. He thinks there's no Harry. But he says he can help my family and get the people who killed my friends. I don't know who to believe," Vik admits.

I think I know the truth about Harry, but I can't come out and say it in front of Cartwright. That could put Vik in even more jeopardy. I need to be oblique.

"You have to go with your gut, Vik. I know trusting me is the reason you ended up here. But I didn't know what we were getting into. And as far as Harry is concerned, I'm pretty sure I met him before," I say.

"Sure. We all have," says Cartwright.

I ignore him. "You and I talked about security protocols. One of the things we didn't discuss is what happens if Harry is compromised. Doesn't it make sense for Harry to have his own backup? Basically, a way to transfer what he knows to a secure party?"

Cartwright is listening and trying to figure out what I'm talking about. I can see the gears turning in Vik's head.

"You met Harry?" he asks.

I nod. "Pretty sure he's the same Harry you know."

"Can you prove that?"

"Try me."

"Did he ever ask you to imagine a mansion in your head?" asks Vik.

"A version of that."

"How many rooms could you imagine?"

"Hundreds," I reply.

"And you could remember your path through there?"

"Absolutely. Backward and forward."

A tiny grin forms at the corner of Vik's mouth as he confirms what I'm telling him.

"I know Harry too," says Cartwright. "I can imagine thousands of mansions."

Vik makes a small snort. Cartwright thinks this is some kind of secret code phrase.

If only.

"Anyway, I'm glad to hear that," I say to Vik. "I don't know what's next for you. Probably a lot of rooms like this and long flights. My son Jason and I used to play a game where we tried to think up as many absurd things as possible and say them out loud. You ever do that?"

"Like what?" asks Vik.

"Yeah, like what, Brad?" replies Cartwright, mocking me.

"Like . . . Marilyn Monroe swinging a lightsaber," I reply.

Vik's eyes widen.

He knows.

I know.

Cartwright doesn't have a fucking clue.

"Let me try," says Vik.

"Go ahead."

"Well, I like to think of real and fantasy creatures. Like an arachnid weaving a web or an orc swinging an axe. And then I mix them up," says Vik. "You understand?"

"Yes. This is a little different than what Harry taught me, but I know the gist."

Cartwright realizes something is up but can't figure out what.

"This sounds like a fun game. You mind if I record it?" he says as he places his phone on the counter.

Vik looks to me.

I nod back at him.

"How about, Frankenstein leaping out of a trash can?"

"Okay," I reply.

"Hmm, a serpent sniffing a newspaper?"

"Good one."

Cartwright is getting nervous. He can't figure out what the hell's going on. He hurries out of the room, and I hear him talking to Nunez. There's a bit of an argument.

Vik keeps naming absurd things.

Nunez finally relents and enters the room. "I'm sorry, Mr. Trasker, I'm going to have to ask you to leave."

"But we're still playing the game," Vik objects.

"The game is over," says Cartwright.

"It's fine, Vik. Another time. I'll be there in Los Angeles when you get there," I say to reassure him.

But I know full well that if I don't get out of here fast, Vik might never make it there.

SUPER STUDENT

I'm sitting on the edge of the sidewalk in front of the FBI office, trying to slow my breathing. My hands are still sweaty, and I feel a pit in my stomach. Morena texted me several times while I was inside, but I ignored them to keep my mind focused.

I close the lid to my laptop and take out my phone and text her back:

Still here. Working on it.

She replies:

Let me know if I need to send in reinforcements.

Morena, Kylie, and Brenda are all good people, but I don't think they understand the stakes here.

The door opens behind me, and Cartwright emerges with Vik in handcuffs, followed by Nunez.

"What's going on?" I ask.

"You were right," says Nunez. "Somebody made an error. There's no warrant for Viktor."

"That's great! Then he can come with me."

"No. He can't," Cartwright responds. "He's here illegally and is wanted back in Thailand for questioning. We're taking him back now."

"Brad?" says Vik.

"Hold on. Now?"

"Conveniently, there's a government-chartered plane arriving now doing a stopover before heading to Bangkok," says Cartwright.

"Conveniently," I echo.

"Maybe you can get him a good attorney in Thailand," says Nunez.

"He's not going to Thailand. This is one more dumb trick by Cartwright and whoever's pulling his strings," I explain.

"Not my circus. Not my monkey," says Nunez.

"Why don't I come along too?"

Cartwright lets out a laugh. "You're lucky Agent Nunez doesn't arrest you on the spot."

"For what?"

"Entering the country illegally, for starters. You're supposed to self-report to Immigration and Customs if they don't meet you at the plane."

"He has a point," says Nunez.

I point to the Immigration and Customs sign at the far end of the building. "You mean right here, where I'm standing?"

"He also has a point," Nunez replies.

"Sorry, Brad," says Cartwright as he pulls Vik toward an SUV parked in front of the office.

"How about if I pay my own way?" I call out.

"You don't have that kind of money," he replies as he walks away.

"How about one seat next to Vik for . . . I don't know . . . eight billion dollars?"

Cartwright stops. He lets go of Vik's arm and turns around. "What are you saying?"

Vik is watching me carefully. I give him a nod.

"Why don't you check yourself. See if I'm good for it."

"What's going on here?" asks Nunez as he stands at the door watching.

"I'd tell you, but I don't want to implicate myself. But don't worry, it'll all come out in the wash."

Cartwright checks his phone and starts frantically typing. He stares at a screen for a moment, then types again. His arms go slack, and he lowers the phone and glares at me.

His composure then comes back and he shrugs. "Fine, you can come too."

"What the hell just happened?" asks Nunez.

"This is better if it's kept between Trasker and me," says Cartwright.

He's trying to do damage control and figure out his next steps. I just fucked everything up for him. Well, Vik, Harry, and I did . . .

Neither Vik nor I actually know Harry. When Vik first mentioned him, I thought he was a fabrication. But the more he spoke about Harry, the closer I came to realizing that Vik was talking about a concept.

A concept based on a real Harry—Harry Lorayne, author of the book about memory I saw on Vik's shelf. I read his books long ago, and I've been using Lorayne's methods my whole life.

Once that dawned on me, I also realized that there *was* no physical wallet. No hard drive. Vik and his friends knew networked devices couldn't be trusted, and even something as simple as a thumb drive could be infected with malware.

They saw the tools that Raden had given them and understood the only way to keep things safe was *not* to write them down.

The sad irony is that Vik's friends were tortured and killed because Conover was too stupid to realize there was no physical key. He never imagined they could hold a sixty-four-character cryptographic key in their heads.

But that's exactly what they did, using memorization techniques.

They employed what's called a "person action object system"—but used creatures instead of people for the letters and numbers. Using a method like this, you can memorize a sixty-four-character string with just twelve silly examples. "Frankenstein leaping out of a trash can" equals 5TR (private keys all start with a five in the wallet import format). That's how I knew Vik was giving me the master key.

He recited the entire private key in front of Cartwright. I left in a hurry before I forgot anything.

It took me twenty minutes to get all of his encoding. I had to figure out that he considered Godzilla a normal animal and not a fantasy animal. I also had to guess at two others, but it wasn't difficult to get all of it with a little trial and error. Unlike some security systems, the blockchain doesn't stop you from making infinite guesses. Your biggest limiting factor is the heat death of the universe. A good sixty-four-character key will take trillions and trillions of years to crack. Every particle in existence will have decayed before then.

"Hop in," says Cartwright. "You can escort Vik all the way back to Thailand if you like."

"I don't know what you all are playing at, but the sooner you're off my island, the better," says Nunez before going back into his office.

I climb into the back seat with Vik and realize that while I may have put Cartwright into check, this isn't checkmate.

I moved the eight billion dollars, but I haven't saved Vik yet. I need to think of something before the plane takes off, because I'm fairly certain our next stop won't be Thailand.

FRIEND REQUEST

The SUV pulls up next to a G700 jet at the most remote part of the airport. I can see another jet parked a few hundred meters away, but its lights are out and almost invisible in the moonless night.

Cartwright gets out of the passenger seat and opens Vik's door. I get out and look at the jet and the tail number, then text it to Morena.

Cartwright sees my hesitation. "You don't have to come if you don't want to."

"I could just knock you on your ass and take the kid with me," I reply.

"And then what? Get charged with assault and human trafficking? You won't get off the island. If you do, it won't be without committing several felonies," says Cartwright.

I close the door to the SUV and Cartwright taps the hood, telling the driver to leave. It pulls away, leaving Cartwright, me, and Vik on the tarmac.

"Do you feel like you just outmaneuvered yourself, Trasker?" says Cartwright as he walks toward the steps leading up to the jet.

"Fuck this." I walk over and grab Vik by the arm. "We're going to walk over to the airport police and have them call Immigration, and I'll call DC and try to arrange a deal."

"You're not in as strong of a position as you think you are," says Cartwright.

"From where I'm looking, I am. I've got eight billion dollars and am one phone call away from you being out of our lives forever," I explain.

"Get onto the plane and we can make a deal," Cartwright tells me.

"Can we just walk away?" asks Vik.

"Sort of," I say. "They'll want to detain you until they figure out what to do with you."

"You could be detained for a very long time," says Cartwright. "Hop on the plane and that won't happen. But Mr. Trasker has to come with us."

"I'm good here," says Vik.

"You heard the kid." I take out my phone to dial 911.

"You stupid man," says Cartwright.

My phone buzzes. There's a message from Morena:

DONT GET ON JET

No kidding.

Cartwright waves to someone inside the plane, and three men in full body armor holding tactical submachine guns step onto the tarmac and point their muzzles at my head. "Would you please escort Mr. Trasker and his friend onto the plane?" he tells them.

"Put the phone away," says Cartwright in a calm voice.

I try to decide the odds on whether they'll actually shoot me right here in the middle of an American airport. I notice they have noise suppressors on their weapons and realize the chances of that might have risen from a moment ago.

"Put the fucking phone away, Bradley," says Conover's raspy voice from behind an armored mask.

Goddamn it. This is worse than I realized. So much worse.

Conover and Krome are working for Rebecca's boss. I don't have the full picture, but what I see is not good.

"You!" Vik screams at Conover. He turns to me. "I know his voice! He killed my friends!"

"Settle down," I say to Vik. "He's a clumsy shot. Not to mention a dumbass."

"Just get him," says Cartwright.

"Wait," I say, trying to buy time. "I didn't tell you everything."

"Tell me on the plane."

"I didn't just take the eight billion. I moved it. I split the private key into three parts. One to the CIA, one to the FBI, and the other to my boss," I explain.

"You pulled a Voldemort," says Vik.

"Um, yeah. Basically."

"I don't fucking care!" shouts Cartwright. "Maybe you did. Maybe you didn't. We can figure all that out. Mr. Conover, will you please escort them onto the plane."

Vik looks at me as one of Conover's goons grabs him by the neck.

Another one keeps his gun aimed at me as Conover walks over to where I'm standing.

"Are you going to come along nicely, or are we going to have to take out a knee?"

"How'd it work out the last time you tried to threaten me? Did all of your guys go home safely?" I ask him.

Conover laughs. "That was very fucking amusing. I can't wait to see the highest place we can drop you from in Guam."

I'm out of quips. My best bet is to run like hell, hope they miss, and get air traffic control to keep the jet from taking off. Even then, my odds of making it more than ten feet are effectively zero.

I sure wish I'd—

"What the fuck?" says Conover as a green dot paints the right eyehole of his mask.

"You want me to waste this asshole?" shouts Brenda Antolí from somewhere in the darkness behind me.

Jesus Christ.

Apparently Morena decided to let Brenda off her leash. Thank God for that. Now I know who was in the other jet on the tarmac.

I ignore Conover and speak to Cartwright. "I suggest you and your men go inside your plane and leave."

Conover leans in and growls in my ear, "You sure you want to put your mall cops against my trained soldiers?"

"Do you want to take that chance?"

"I hope you don't get this one killed, Bradley," he replies.

"Let's go," says Cartwright, realizing he's done here. "Mr. Trasker and his friend have no idea what they're dealing with."

Conover makes a hand gesture, and his men follow Cartwright back into the plane.

Vik looks at me, confused. "Is it over?"

"Not quite, kid. Not quite."

PIT STOP

Our plane takes off from the runway and begins a wide turn to begin the long flight to the Wind Aerospace airfield at Mojave. I have Vik covered with a blanket and Brenda's stern orders to get some sleep myself.

Instead, I take out the receiver for the satellite phone and call Morena.

"Thanks for sending reinforcements," I say as soon as she picks up. "I guess I finally understand your cryptic comments about help being nearby."

Brenda turns in her chair and gives me a wink.

"So, what's our strategy to avoid human trafficking allegations?" I ask.

"Already have it taken care of. Since he was processed into custody by the local FBI in Guam, we're now merely aiding and abetting an escape from justice," she explains.

"Cool. Cool. That will just be two to three years in federal prison. I can do that standing on my head."

"Relax. We're already talking to Broadhurst at the FBI, and I have a judge calling me back. If we can't sort it out before you land, we'll just reroute to Costa Rica and you guys can wait it out on the beach."

"Did you work for Pablo Escobar in a previous life?" I ask.

"No. But I did a stint with the US Attorney's Office, in case you forgot. I know all the tricks."

"Those tricks might still come in handy."

"Did you talk to Kylie yet?" asks Morena.

"No. I was going to call her next."

"I'll give you a heads-up. I thought she was getting paranoid, but now I'm thinking she's onto something regarding Josiah Levenstein and the photos.

"She's convinced someone at the Department of Defense has been leaking our testing schedule for the engine. Better let her explain it. You've clearly rubbed off on her."

"Is Vik safe?" Kylie asks a few minutes later.

"He's sleeping safely ten feet away from me. Thanks to you," I tell her.

"Or his friends are dead thanks to me," she responds.

"Don't look at it that way."

"I have to. Did Morena tell you I've gone nuts?" she asks.

"Not quite."

"All of this has been bothering me. So I decided to be proactive," she explains.

"How proactive?" I ask hesitantly. In our last lengthy conversation, she was contemplating creating her own spy force.

"I wanted to see if someone was leaking details about our testing schedule on the DoD end. So I sent a message to the Pentagon project supervisor, Major Cardiff, with a link to a design change. It was opened eight minutes later. But not by him and not at the Pentagon. It was a residential address in Virginia. Just to be sure it wasn't him, I called him up and asked if he'd had a look. He said he hadn't checked his email yet," Kylie explains.

"Was he hacked?" I ask.

"Not quite. I asked him who else could look at his email. He said just his assistant, someone named Lieutenant Ari Ridgely. I've spoken to Ridgely before. Kind of odd. Very quiet.

"Anyway, I looked him up. This is where it gets interesting. Ridgely worked for Colonel Melchor *before* Cardiff."

"These people move around a lot. Especially the ones we talk to. But I get what you're saying. I'm not surprised Ridgely was reading the email for his boss," I reply.

"Brad, let me finish. The address where it was opened wasn't Ridgely's. It was *Melchor's*. Ridgely forwarded it to him. Melchor opened the link," says Kylie.

"I understand. That's not too unusual for the military. Especially for a project they're all involved in."

"I'd like to think that only the person I'm sending a message to is the one reading it. But we know that there are others in that loop. Isn't that useful?" she asks in a leading tone.

Kylie's obviously stressed by all that's been going on. I need to carefully listen to her, then gently explain how you can't start making too many causal connections—otherwise you see conspiracies everywhere.

"Then there's the other thing. Before working with Melchor, Ridgely did a rotation with the Office of Intelligence and Counterintelligence. That's a Department of Energy intelligence agency," says Kylie.

Interesting. Ridgely is looking less like an innocent ladder climber and more like a go-between for corrupt officials.

"I'm familiar with them." *Very familiar.* That's who Rebecca says recruited her. Vik mentioned someone named "Raden," but I assume that's an alias.

"And here's another thing," Kylie continues. "I looked back at the list of people on an email chain when I was invited to the Hello World start-up program, and Ridgely was on it. He was working for Melchor then."

"Damn." This connects Ridgely to Melchor *and* her boss.

"It gets worse," she says.

"Let's get Morena on the call," I say quickly. "Something really weird is going on. I think I might have an idea what."

I bring Morena into the call and quickly recap what Kylie told me and all the players.

"So we have Raden and Melchor connected by Lieutenant Ridgely in some kind of spy ring?" asks Morena.

"Yes," I reply. "I think Ridgely is a plant in Cardiff's office and feeding details to someone else—most likely Raden and/or Melchor. The Melchor connection I hadn't even considered. But now we know Ridgely was sending him information too."

"Melchor was the one who sent you after Josiah Levenstein in the first place," Morena notes.

I nod. "He seemed pissed when he thought I'd killed Josiah, but that could have been a performance. He also told me not to tell you. Plus, there's the fact that someone picked up Josiah's laptop. Well, that and the fact that someone may have killed Josiah in the first place."

"You said Josiah alluded to there being bad things on the laptop," says Morena.

"Yes. I assumed it was child pornography or the like. That's one of the reasons I dropped it off with the sheriff's department. I didn't want that in our possession. Now I'm thinking it might've been something else."

"More corporate espionage?" asks Morena.

"Possibly. Ridgely would have access to a lot of information coming through Cardiff's office and God knows where else he's worked. Instead of leaking documents directly, he could act indirectly, like using our schedule info to dispatch a guy like Josiah to take photos."

"Okay. But what's the connection with xQuadrant and Josiah?" asks Morena. "Besides Ridgely?"

"I think there are two connections. The first being that Vik and his friends are useful hackers. Raden had them doing side projects, creating small things like the website Josiah was posting on. Could be that Vik and his friends were being used to leak and hack without knowing it," I explain.

That's the sad tragedy of it all. Vik and the others wanted to fight the bad guys. Instead, the bad guys used them.

"What's the second connection?" asks Morena.

"Us. We have money. We have secrets. And we're naive about all of this. Someone saw an opportunity. Use Kylie to legitimize xQuadrant—maybe for some bigger purpose. Sell our secrets to the Chinese. Bleed us through a thousand cuts.

"We sat down at the defense contractor poker table and didn't realize we were the sucker," I explain.

"Why kill Josiah?" asks Morena.

"He was the weakest of the weak links. I think Melchor was hoping *I* would kill him. I think he looked at my history and thought I was some kind of assassin for hire. But in the end, he had to do it himself."

"Okay, but why you? Why tell us?" asks Kylie.

"Raden was paranoid enough to have Vik's friends killed. He probably feared an active investigation—which the FBI would never tell us about, if that's the case. Same for Melchor. He was spooked and wanted his connection killed before he could talk. As it turns out, he even had a backup plan to that effect.

"If it looks like I killed him, all the attention is on us if there's some kind of FBI probe. The xQuadrant murders wouldn't be connected to any of this. Melchor never gave me Josiah's information. I found that out. He never did anything that could directly implicate himself. He just steered me in that direction."

"Okay. We need to take this to Broadhurst ASAP," says Morena.

"Yes, but we need more. Right now, it's a bunch of connected dots. And I'm still not clear on the timing. Why did all of this go down now?"

"So, what do we do?"

"I land at Mojave. We refuel. I try to beat the last piece of the puzzle back to DC before they go missing."

Something strikes me. I ask Brenda in front of me, "Hey, did you get the tail number for the plane Conover and his men were using?"

"Sure did."

"Morena, I want you to check its flight records. I'll bet dinner at your favorite restaurant it was in LA the same night Josiah was killed."

A depressing thought hits me. It may even have been at the same airport I was at—arriving as I was leaving. Making sure that the Josiah situation was cleaned up one way or another.

SPOTLIGHT

Rebecca Gostler steps into her town house in Tysons Corner, Virginia, pulling the same small suitcase she was hauling when she left Guam. She's wearing the same clothes as well. It doesn't look like she's had a chance to shower in the last sixteen hours.

I, on the other hand, was able to get a full four hours of sleep on Kylie's G800 after dropping Brenda and Vik off in Mojave.

I wanted to beat Rebecca back here, not just for a fuck-you dramatic effect but because there's a ticking clock.

Vik's now at the Los Angeles FBI office explaining his experience to Special Agent Shirley Broadhurst under the watchful eye of an attorney Kylie hired for him.

As compelling as his story may be, it's only part of the picture. There is a small window of opportunity before Raden, Ridgely, and Melchor close ranks. If they convince the right people, Vik could get pulled from FBI custody and sent somewhere we'll never find him. Meanwhile, something incriminating about me could magically appear and connect me to Josiah Levenstein's death.

"Long flight?" I say from the living room couch.

"Jesus Christ! Brad," says Rebecca as she drops her bag. "How the fuck? What the fuck?"

"The last person to betray me and the people I cared about had his knee splattered over the booth of a diner. People forget my reputation isn't an anecdote. It's a living, breathing thing that only gets meaner as I get older and have less fucks to give," I explain.

"I'm just as in the dark as you are," she pleads.

"That's bullshit. You have no idea how angry I am right now. I was *this* close to getting hauled off by your people to some Krome black site in the middle of nowhere and getting tortured to death."

"Can I sit down?" asks Rebecca.

"I don't care what you do."

"Well, I don't see a gun, so that's a start."

"Now is not the time to be cute."

Rebecca sits down in the chair opposite from me. "What do you want to know?"

"The man at the airport who said his name was Cartwright. That was Raden? Your boss?"

"Yes. He has a few different aliases. They're all bona fide. They're for conferences and the like," she explains.

"Are they traceable to him? Is someone at the FBI going to be able to connect him to that name?"

"Probably not. These are meant to be very deep cover. State level," she tells me.

"And the name Raden?"

"Not his name. Not how I know him. He's Joseph Calumet at the Office of Intelligence and Counterintelligence. The OICI is a weird little intelligence agency that's under the Department of Energy but has wide-reaching powers. That's who I came to work with," she responds.

"What about Aetheon? Is he real?"

"I think so," she replies.

I don't want to let on what I know and what I suspect. I need to see how much she'll tell me.

"Do you think Calumet and Aetheon are the same person?"

"No. Calumet isn't that technical. I've had to explain things to him," says Rebecca.

"What about the other people on the task force? How involved are they?"

"Minimally. This program was basically a Microsoft Word document with a budget. When I started writing about Aetheon and explaining how he could be moving money, Calumet was the only one paying attention."

"So he calls you in and you explain it all to him? And then he suggests Project Grab Bag?"

"Yes. Basically."

"What kind of oversight?"

"We got a budget and an okay. That was it. He wasn't asking for much. Just some travel documents and accounts."

"I talked to Vik about the wallets. We went through the email and the instructions he was given. You know there was more than one wallet he and xQuadrant were supposed to place funds into?"

"I know they were supposed to move funds from time to time," she replies.

"Vik says there was one set aside they never moved money out of. It would go in and then someone else would move the money out." I wait for her reply.

"What are you saying?"

"About four hundred million dollars. It's gone. Vik was able to show me every penny of what he moved and what he spent. Down to the money he and his friends used to buy plane tickets to send their families here. This other wallet, he has no idea where it went."

"What are you trying to say, Brad?"

"I think your boss was using Grab Bag to steal. He exploited Vik and his friends for his own gain. He exploited you. Unless . . ."

"Unless what?"

"Unless you're in on it. Are you?"

"No. No." She balls her hand up into a fist and bites the knuckle. "I have to think about this."

"You don't have time. I'll explain how I think it went down. You present him with this Aetheon theory. He sees dollar signs. He comes across Vik and his friends, who have earnestly been offering their services as white-hat hackers to anyone in the US government.

"Calumet sends you to Bangkok to set the kids up. Meanwhile he gives them a different set of instructions regarding the wallets. Things are good, but he's getting paranoid. This is a lot of money. He doesn't have any oversight . . . but if someone looked closely at Vik and his friends, or if they got caught, he'd have problems.

"His biggest fear is someone at the CIA or FBI noticing. When he hears that Vik and his friends are coming to the United States, he really freaks out. He hires Krome to kill them. But he knows he also needs the crypto wallets. He also lets others he's working with know that things might be going south."

Which is why Melchor freaks the hell out and worries his dim-witted spy Josiah Levenstein might be a little too exposed.

"Meanwhile, he sends you in right after to start telling people these kids were involved in ransomware and ripping off the wrong people. First, you're in Bangkok. Then you're in Las Vegas. Who told the Thai government that this was a terrorism issue?" I ask.

"I swear to God, Brad, that wasn't me. Calumet told me that one of the kids had fucked up and leaked an address that connected them to the thefts, and we had to keep the operation a secret so the Russians and Chinese didn't find out."

"How much of that did you believe?"

"I don't know. All of it? Some? I don't know. Things were moving fast. When I had questions, he had answers."

"What about in Guam? You were face-to-face with him. You didn't say anything or tell me."

Rebecca is hunched over as she tries to process all this. "He texted me. He told me not to acknowledge him. He had the FBI with him, Brad. Why wouldn't you believe that? It starts to look like a crazy conspiracy theory if you assume they're all in on it."

"It only takes two or three people for a conspiracy. What do you know about Colonel Melchor?"

"Melchor? How do you know him?"

"That was my question to you."

"He and Calumet are friends. I think they worked on some projects together," Rebecca tells me. "We had xQuadrant make some websites and stuff for Melchor."

"Like anonymous forums? Maybe aviation related?" I ask.

"Something like that, I think. I didn't handle that. Calumet dealt with Vik and them directly—as Raden."

"Okay. Did you see anyone else copied in on the communications surrounding this?"

Rebecca looks to the ceiling, searching her memory. "I saw one other person on a few email exchanges," she says at last.

"Who was that?"

"A lieutenant. Ari Ridgely. He didn't work for Melchor directly, but they had history. He moved around a lot with different air force–connected projects."

This makes me wonder, Is Calumet calling the shots or Lieutenant Ridgely?

"What about the name Josiah Levenstein?"

She shakes her head. "No. Who is that?"

"Another piece they wanted to clear off the board. Either way, here's the situation: As far as I know, there was no investigation into Calumet. He panicked, and then Melchor and Ridgely panicked. They tried to clean things up. But they're not too good at it. Or rather, they're very messy at it. I have a fair sense of what was going on, Rebecca, but you're the one person who can help tie this all together. We nail Calumet, we get Melchor," I explain.

"I don't know, Brad . . ."

"Rebecca, you're screwed either way. What you really are is a loose end. One that Calumet needs dead. Vik's friends aren't the only ones they've killed. They can reach you anywhere."

"What do I do?" she asks.

"We go over to the FBI building right now. You make a statement. You tell them everything. I've got people there I trust," I tell her.

"And if Calumet says I made it up or I'm in on this?"

"Are you?"

"No! I feel so stupid, though. I don't know what I should do," she says, clearly beyond exhausted.

"What was your last contact with Calumet?"

"He called me at the airport as soon as I landed. He said you may have been compromised and I should not talk to you."

"Anything else?"

"Yeah. Fuck it." She lets out an exhausted sigh. "He says there's a person in Colombia, another hacker, I need to go speak to. This person might be able to help us get the other wallets."

"When?"

"Now. I was supposed to hop on another plane at the airport. But I had to come here and get clean clothes," she replies.

"Does Calumet know you came here?"

"Yes. He's been texting me telling me there's only so much time to talk to this person. Like I said, I told him I'd catch the next flight."

"Anything else?" I ask.

"Typical Joseph bullshit. I'm supposed to tell my family it's a vacation. Like I'd want to go to one more fucking place after all the travel I've been doing."

"Let me remind you, Rebecca: Aside from Vik and me, you're the biggest loose end. You have the other parts of the puzzle. You're a liability to him."

"You mean he's going to have me killed on this trip? Like, now?"

She seems genuinely baffled by the concept.

"Why don't you ask Vik if I'm kidding. There's also the parents of the young man who was taking photos of our base. They'd like to know why their son ended up dead in a parking lot. Calumet wants you in

Colombia, ASAP, right after all of this falls to pieces? Let me show you something."

I reach into my pocket and take out my phone. I hand it to her with a screenshot open.

"What's this?"

"It's a copy of a spreadsheet. It shows the logs of an airplane. See the date next to 'Bangkok'?"

"Yeah. That was just over a week ago. What about it?" she asks.

"That was two days before Vik's friends were killed. Now see the date and location next to that?"

"Burbank?"

"That was a few hours before the young man I mentioned died by 'suicide' a few miles away. See the next date?"

"Guam? Yesterday?"

"Yes. Calumet got onto that plane with Conover and his men. The plane belongs to a company owned by Krome."

"Okay? I'm not sure I understand."

"Wherever that plane goes, death follows."

"That's fucked up."

"Yes, Rebecca. It is. Look at the flight plan they filed an hour ago."

Rebecca reads the line on the spreadsheet.

Bogotá, Colombia

"Fuck."

"Coincidence? Who do you suppose they're going to kill there?"

Rebecca stops gnawing on her knuckle, and her face goes pale. "What do I do?"

I can tell the shock is setting in. I explain it to her again. "I told you before: we race to FBI headquarters and explain everything to a roomful of people."

"And that's it?" she asks.

"Mostly. If we move fast, we can catch Calumet and Melchor off guard."

"Will that be enough?"

"Probably not. But I'll do what I can."

Meaning, I'll need to do a little board clearing myself and take certain people out of the equation.

AFTER-PARTY

Lieutenant Ari Ridgely pulls into the parking space in the carport under his apartment complex and gets out of his BMW dressed in his civilian clothes.

It's after midnight, and I've been standing in a shaded corner, waiting for him.

"Ridgely," I call from the shadows.

Startled, he drops his phone. "What the fuck! Jeff, is that you?"

I step into the light. "No."

Ridgely's eyes focus on me. Recognition sets in.

I'm dressed in dark coveralls. I'm holding a toolbox in my left hand.

"Oh shit." He thinks fast, kneels down to grab his phone, and starts to walk away.

"Keep walking and you're a dead man," I call out to him.

A green dot from a laser sight paints his chest; it emanates from a car parked across the street.

He turns around to face me, unsure what to do next.

"You can try to outrun a bullet, but I've broken a key off in your lock. You're not getting inside. Call for help and we'll drop you right here."

He takes a few breaths and looks around to see if anyone else is watching.

"I don't know who you are or what you want," Ridgely lies.

"Just shut the fuck up and listen."

"I'll go to the cops," he says.

"I hope you do. You can tell them verbatim what I'm about to tell you."

The green dot disappears, but Ridgely doesn't move.

"You have a choice. You get into your car and drive to the FBI office and tell them everything," I explain.

"I have no idea what the hell you're talking about," Ridgely says again, without much conviction.

"I said shut up and listen. Talk to them or I have you killed. It's that simple. I don't know if you're the one pulling the strings or if it's Calumet or Melchor or someone else. Right now, I don't care. Cooperate or die," I reply.

"This is extortion."

"No. This is premeditated murder," I respond. "Maybe you think you can wait it out and see what happens next. I wouldn't if I were you."

"Because you'll kill me?" says Ridgely.

"Because I already delivered the same message to Calumet and Melchor. They know what I am. You know what I am. Now we find out how smart you are."

"You'll let me get back into my car?" asks Ridgely.

"Yes. And if you're not at the FBI offices in a half hour, I'll know your answer."

I snap my fingers, and the green dot alights on his chest again.

"And no matter where you hide, one day, this will be the last thing you see."

Ridgely climbs back into his BMW and pulls out of the carport, his eyes on me, the road, and the black SUV across the street.

I watch him leave the complex, then walk over to the SUV and get into the driver's seat.

Over my shoulder sits a figure under a black blanket who aimed the sniper rifle out the window.

"You hear all that?"

"Every word. Will he talk?" she asks.

"I think he'll run. That's fine. It'll make Calumet and Melchor more eager to talk. All we need is one."

I start driving and take us on a zigzag pattern, avoiding the municipal CCTV cameras. I don't care if I'm caught on video. I just don't want my companion recognized.

"Is this what you do?" she asks.

"Not often. But this is what it means to be truly proactive. Are you okay with this?"

"Yes," she replies.

I pull onto the freeway and take us toward rural Virginia, where we landed at a private airfield.

"You understand the others can't know. It's for their protection," I say.

"Understood."

"Not Morena," I explain.

She nods.

"Not even Brenda."

"I understand," says Kylie.

"It's safe to come out now."

She shrugs off the blanket and climbs over the center console into the passenger seat next to me. "Was the blanket necessary?"

"Last thing I need is America's richest female CEO caught on video holding a sniper rifle. This is the last time I let you do something like this. I just want you to understand what it takes," I explain.

"I get it. What now?" she asks.

"You go back to Mojave. I have one more errand to run. It's something personal."

MOONGLOW

Captain Alonso looked past the rain at the crime-scene tape stretched across the alley and knew he wouldn't be making it back in time to the restaurant to finish dinner with his wife, his brother-in-law, and his wife's sister. Alonso liked spending time with them. Jorge told sidesplitting stories that could make Alonso cry. He had been looking forward to the dinner all week.

Lieutenant Castaño greeted her captain holding an umbrella as he exited the vehicle. "I'm so sorry, boss. I only called you because it was important."

"It's fine, Amelia. Let me have it," he replied as he followed her into the crime scene.

"The body was found just an hour ago. The grocer was emptying out his waste bin. He said he'd been here no more than thirty minutes before," she explained.

"What do we know about the victim?"

"American."

"Oh Christ. Drug related?"

"I don't know. Their throat was slit. We think that's what killed them," she explained.

"You think?" Alonso laughed. "No. You're right. Never assume." He walked over to a yellow plastic sheet on the ground. "Did we find a weapon?"

"Not yet. We're looking in the sewer drains," she said.

Drains that had been flooded for the past several days because of the heavy rains.

"That will be useless."

Alonso slipped on a pair of latex gloves and knelt to look under the sheet.

The cut was deep and efficient. The victim probably had only a second to realize what was happening before they lost consciousness and died.

There were worse ways to die. But being thrown aside in a dumpster like human garbage wouldn't be his choice.

"For the love of Jesus," Alonso murmured to himself. "What kind of monster does this to another person?"

"I don't know," said Amelia. "We just got an ID over the radio. The corpse matches a passport photo."

"And what was this poor soul's name?" asked Alonso.

"Conover. His name was Dustin Conover."

Two thousand miles away in a private jet flying over the Atlantic Ocean, a man reclined in a cushioned seat, looking out the window and trying to understand what drove him.

He'd once thought it was loyalty.

Before that, a sense of duty.

And now?

Now it was anger that motivated him.

He noticed something on his shoe and wet a paper napkin.

The pain in his body made him groan as he leaned down to wipe away the flecks of blood.

About the Author

Andrew Mayne is the *Wall Street Journal* bestselling author of *Night Owl* in his Trasker series; *The Girl Beneath the Sea, Black Coral, Sea Storm, Sea Castle,* and *Dark Dive* in his Underwater Investigation Unit series; *Angel Killer, Fire in the Sky, Name of the Devil,* and the Edgar Award–nominated *Black Fall* in his Jessica Blackwood series; and *The Naturalist, Looking Glass, Murder Theory,* and *Dark Pattern* in his Naturalist series. The star of Discovery Channel's Shark Week special *Andrew Mayne: Ghost Diver* and A&E's *Don't Trust Andrew Mayne,* he is also a magician who toured as an illusionist when he was a teenager and went on to work for Penn & Teller, David Blaine, and David Copperfield. Ranked as the fifth bestselling independent author of the year by Amazon UK, Andrew currently hosts the *Weird Things* podcast and works on creative applications for artificial intelligence. He was also the first prompt engineer and served as science communicator for OpenAI, the creators of ChatGPT. For more information, visit www.andrewmayne.com.